STOIC REVENGE

DOUGLAS THOMAS

Copyright © 2024 Douglas Thomas
All rights reserved
First Edition

PAGE PUBLISHING
Conneaut Lake, PA

First originally published by Page Publishing 2024

ISBN 979-8-89315-916-5 (pbk)
ISBN 979-8-89315-935-6 (digital)

Printed in the United States of America

Another day to find meaning, foundation, and most of all, to survive. He endured the blistering heat that found its way through the soles of his boots. The unit had been marching for two days to reach the foothills where the enemy was entrenched. As he slowly kept pace with his comrades, he could feel his skin sticking to his body armor. He longed for the sun to set in the west so he could enjoy the evening breezes that would follow.

No one had seen the enemy since the unit left the base back in Mosul. His orders were to search and destroy a rogue sect of the radical Islamic Hezbollah tribe. In this area, tribal disputes were prevalent, as were their sporadic attacks on the common people trying to survive another day in hell. Hezbollah took advantage of this tribal unrest to exploit the difficulties these local disruptions created for the American and Iraqi forces.

Captain Brady was embedded with a special unit of the Iraqi army for the purpose of directing sneak attacks upon the rebels and flushing out their leaders for interrogation or execution. The local population consisted of a few vendors, refugees that had been divorced from their homes and family. A few young boys tagged along behind the unit, hoping to provide some usefulness to the soldiers in exchange for tidbits of food and water.

Brady ordered the unit to prepare a campsite for the night. They could use the rest. With the setting of the sun, Brady knew they would be more vulnerable to snipers and suicidal attacks from the rebels. Soldiers formed a perimeter around the camp, and tents were erected. Fires were forbidden for obvious reasons, and conversations kept to a minimum. Radio communication with headquarters was monitored, and superior officers were periodically briefed on the unit's location and situation.

During the night, Brady was awakened twice to the sound of sniper fire. The first was followed by the blood-curdling dying gasp of the perimeter soldier who had just been shot. The second time was the hail of bullets that ensued following the first. It was the retaliatory fire that eliminated the sniper. Upon being assured the area was cleared, Brady went back to sleep.

The world in which Brady now found himself consisted of vast desert wastelands, surrounding foothills, dismantled vehicles, and carcasses of buildings, most of which were once homes and sanctuaries for families from the outside world. Hunger was rampant; simple everyday necessities like clothing, food, water, and safety were at a premium. Brady's new comrades were members of a makeshift combat unit, and Brady was given orders to assist and advise them in special operations such as the one he had just begun.

The easy part of his assignment was the advice and training he provided; the difficult part was enduring the one-hundred-degree-plus heat each day, the snipers and suicide bombers scattered among the innocent, and the IEDs implanted beneath the highways and rural routes. Brady was the only American in this ragtag combat group, and the Iraqi soldiers never let him forget that important aspect as he instructed, advised, and in some instances, derided, shamed, and appealed to their national and religious heritage. This was done to prod them into combat action that might free them and their countrymen from the terror that had infected their country and its armed forces.

Brady, at thirty-five years old, was a typical American, six feet tall with light brown hair, patriotic to a fault perhaps, a lover of sports, having played quarterback in high school and college, and well-read in philosophy and politics. He was raised in a strict Catholic family, and his father was an alderman back in Chicago, Illinois. Brady missed his family, Lois his wife of fifteen years, and their two children, Michael, fifteen, and Sarah, thirteen.

Brady entered the Army his second year after college graduation. Unable to find anything other than menial, non-challenging jobs, he decided to enlist as an officer and chose the Rangers for his branch of the Army. After boot camp at Fort Jackson, South Carolina, Brady was assigned to the Army Intelligence School at Fort Holabird, in Baltimore, Maryland. This training would become useful throughout his life. After seven years, Brady was considered an extraordinary soldier proficient in every facet of specialized warfare, particularly in intelligence gathering and analysis as well as interrogations.

His training in guerilla warfare and terrorist tactics had served him well in his three tours of duty in Afghanistan. He had endured knife fights, hand-to-hand combat, survived suicide bombings, and captured several hundred terrorists, usually those who had endeared themselves to the locals or in some instances were members of the local communities.

Brady longed to return home to the United States and to reconcile with his family. The only thing that remained before his discharge in thirty days was this last mission. He had an abundance of incentive to keep his fellow soldiers and himself alive on this final operation. But Brady had little inkling of what the immediate future was about to bring and the challenges to his deepest beliefs and inner convictions.

Dawn came with a flurry of activity. Major Isaac Khouri awakened him. The Hezbollah had apparently been alerted to the imminent attack by Brady's unit and had decided to strike first. There was bedlam all about as he rose from his cot. He heard yelling and Sergeant Khalid barking orders to the troops to form a perimeter while sending his second platoon forward to meet the insurgents head-on.

Both Major Khouri and Sergeant Khalid were veteran combat fighters, and this was not their first encounter with insurgents. Brady had found Major Khouri to be well-trained in tactical warfare and commanding respect and discipline from his men. Sergeant Khalid was big for an Afghan, about six feet and about two hundred and twenty pounds. Sergeant Khalid also commanded respect from the soldiers under him, having survived several battles, including those involving hand-to-hand combat.

Major Khouri discussed their options while Captain Brady threw on his shirt and body armor. In rapid-fire, Brady asked how many were attacking, their equipment, and whether they were breaking through the posted guards. Major Khouri estimated there were fifty to sixty in number, they had rocket launchers, rifle grenades, and automatic weapons and appeared to be well organized.

As Major Khouri and Captain Brady emerged from the officer's tent, Sergeant Khalid had already positioned their two tanks on the left and right flanks. Troops fell in behind the tanks while A platoon led a counterattack straight at the oncoming insurgents. The yelling and sounds of rifle fire combined with the exploding grenades and rockets were deafening. The smell of gunfire and grenades permeated the area.

The insurgents were close enough for Captain Brady to see their faces. They were dressed in Arabic robes and covers with no apparent military designation. This was obviously a rogue outfit from one of the extremist groups. Captain Brady had seen more and more of these combatants, and he attributed this to the schism between the fundamentalists and the radical elements of the Islamic religion.

The battle was tense, the insurgents seemingly ignoring the fact they were outnumbered five to one. One by one, the screaming fanatics rushed forward only to be neutralized by the automatic weapons that had been posted around the perimeter the night before. Some screamed, "Allahu Akbar!" as they rushed into the gunfire and fell to their demise. However, there was a contingent of what appeared to be officers that had remained outside the perimeter and out of the conflict.

Those few, realizing the battle was futile for the insurgents, turned their vehicles around and headed for the foothills some five miles away. Captain Brady and Major Khouri saw this and ordered the armored vehicles to pursue. The insurgents left behind were encircled and their ranks decimated by the time they threw up their hands and surrendered.

Captain Brady shouted to Major Khouri to see to the completion of the taking of prisoners while he, Major Khouri, and their soldiers in armored vehicles chased the insurgents' leaders that were heading for the foothills. Captain Brady called in the Blackhawk helicopters that had been put on standby. The copters were there in about three minutes, firing rockets at several enemy vehicles that were racing for the foothills. Of the four vehicles, two were immediately hit by the rocket fire. One veered off towards the south, while the other headed straight into the foothills. The vehicle heading south was tracked by the one helicopter, and the chase only lasted a minute or two before the copter zeroed in and eliminated their target. All occupants had been killed.

The one vehicle contained two occupants, and one passenger kept pointing in the direction he wanted the driver to follow. Just as the second helicopter was about to fire its rocket, the vehicle seemed to disappear into the background. In fact, the vehicle had driven into an entrance to an underground tunnel, which led to a network of tunnels considered safe havens by the insurgent leaders. These tunnels were prevalent throughout eastern Afghanistan.

The Blackhawk fired its rockets into the entrance, but it was too late, and the vehicle had disappeared from sight. Captain Brady was in radio contact with the copter pilot and instructed him to return to base. He then selected a four-man contingent from his unit, including Sergeant Khalid. Brady ordered the rest to return to their base under Major Khouri's command.

Captain Brady picked Khalid and three privates he had personally trained in guerilla warfare and tactics. Sergeant Khalid also had training as a Ranger and was proud of his green beret. Brady trusted him with his life. They thought alike in tight situations.

Sergeant Khalid slipped into the driver's seat of the Hummer, with the three privates crowded into the back. The Hummer had a fifty-millimeter machine gun mounted on the roof. Sergeant Khalid instructed Private Ali to mount the top of the Hummer to man the gun. Brady, sitting next to the sergeant, instructed him to get them close to the cave entrance to the first of the foothills. The sergeant did so by zigzagging to avoid the rifle fire they were receiving from inside the cave.

Ali had trouble keeping a target in his scope, but he managed to get off about fifty rounds directly into the cave entrance. One of the snipers staggered out of the entrance and slumped to the ground. Just as he did so, Ali took a hit from another sniper from within the cave. Captain Brady reached up and pulled Private Ali into the Hummer. He was bleeding badly from his left shoulder. Within seconds, Brady applied a compress to his wound and applied pressure.

Meantime, Sergeant Khalid was doing his best to keep the Hummer upright. One bullet had already pierced the windshield, and another cracked the side mirror. Khalid drove straight at the cave entrance, and just before he reached it, he swerved to the left side and applied the brakes. Khalid reached for a grenade to toss into the cave entrance, but Brady grabbed his arm and ordered everyone out of the Hummer except Ali. Each dove to the ground amid rapid fire now coming from just inside the cave entrance.

Brady, realizing Ali would not last long without medical attention, ordered one of the remaining privates to drive him back to safety while Brady raised Major Khouri on the field phone. He asked Major Khouri to provide cover fire so the soldier could get Ali back to safety. Brady also told Khouri to send in air strikes on the backside of the foothill opposite the cave entrance. Brady's theory was that the insurgents who had disappeared into the cave entrance were probably moving as quickly as possible to some exit located on the backside of the foothill.

Within minutes, the Blackhawk copter appeared on the horizon and fired two rockets into the foothill. The explosion not only created a small crater but dust gushing from the cave validated Brady's theory. The tunnel had been blocked by the rockets, and Brady knew what he had to do next: enter the cave to capture and/or terminate the enemy.

Ali and his driver arrived a few minutes later at a fallback position that Major Khouri had ordered. Fortunately, the bullet had pierced the fleshy part of his shoulder and went all the way through. The medics patched him up and applied fresh bandages. Ali said he felt fine and wanted to go back to help Captain Brady, who had just saved his life by stemming the flow of blood from his wound.

Khouri ordered Ali to take a back position and rest up while Major Khouri attended to Captain Brady's situation. Brady, Sergeant

Khalid, and Private Samu were now taking cover among the large boulders that provided ample protection from the intermittent rifle fire emanating from the cave entrance.

The trio was only fifty yards now from the cave. Brady assumed that the remaining insurgents who had retreated into the cave were either dead or trapped inside. Brady called Major Khouri and asked him to send the first platoon to the other side of the hill, where the Blackhawk airstrikes had unloaded an assortment of air missiles into the areas where the tunnels exited.

Within minutes, the platoon was deployed and surrounded the various exits to the tunnels. The rifle fire from the cave had ended suddenly. Brady ordered Sergeant Khalid and Private Samu to work their way around to the right of the entrance while Brady covered the left side. Slowly and deftly, Sergeant Khalid and Samu worked their way in and out of the rocks and boulders until they reached a protected area about ten yards from the cave.

Brady had jumped into the driver's seat of the Hummer and quickly maneuvered them to a spot just in front of the cave. Brady dove to the ground, taking cover behind the Hummer. Rifle fire had ceased, and there was no movement near the cave entrance. Brady motioned for Sergeant Khalid and Samu to move up to a position just a few feet to the right of the cave while Brady provided cover with a burst from his M16.

The cave was dark inside. Brady had studied these caves and tunnels several times on previous occasions and encountered enemy fire coming from various outlets and exits. The insurgents built supports that allowed men to half stand and half crawl through them. The tunnels, which were no more than forty yards long, usually had pumps to circulate fresh air and small generators to provide light to dimly lit sections.

There was no indication of this tunnel being air-conditioned or illuminated. In fact, the expulsion of smoke and dust from the cave entrance after the airstrikes indicated the tunnel in this cave was not more than about forty to fifty yards long.

Brady motioned to Sergeant Khalid to toss a hand grenade into the entrance. Simultaneously, Brady rushed to a position immediately aside the entrance. The grenade exploded. Brady, after the dust settled, was the first inside the entrance. There was no movement from within, and Brady waved Sergeant Khalid and Samu to move in.

With Sergeant Khalid and Samu on one side, Brady slowly edged into the small opening. About ten feet in, the tunnel narrowed so that only one person at a time could slouch and move through. Brady went first, pushing his M16 in such a way that he would be able to return fire if needed. After a few yards, Brady stopped. He had not detected any sign of the insurgents, and no bodies save the one that Ali had shot prior to his being wounded.

Rather than risk any further the safety of Sergeant Khalid, Samu, the private, and himself, Brady told them to fall back behind the Hummer. Brady was not satisfied that all the insurgents had been killed by the airstrikes. This particular contingent of insurgents had been a thorn in his side for some time now, and now appeared the time to erase them as a threat.

Brady now had a dilemma: Should the three of them storm into the cave, which was just short of suicide if there were insurgents in close proximity, or simply detonate some C-5 at the entrance and seal the cave? The latter option was not only less risky but it also allowed them time to search for other exits to the tunnels.

Sergeant Khalid pulled a packet of specially sealed C-5 and, with Brady and the others providing cover, strategically placed it near the cave entrance. Once Khalid had finished and returned to the protection of the Hummer, Brady took aim with his M16 and exploded the C-5. There was a loud boom that could be heard back at the base. Major Khouri took notice and immediately contacted Brady on the field phone. The cave entrance had been permanently closed with large boulders and earth pouring down from above.

Major Khouri was briefed on the situation and that Brady and the balance of his trio would begin scouring the foothills for signs of possible escape routes for the insurgents. Major Khouri insisted Brady await reinforcements he was dispatching to assist them, but Brady proffered that he, Sergeant Khalid, and Samu could travel much faster through the rocks using the rocky and undulating hills for cover. However, Brady surmised that there was wisdom in having a contingent of reinforcements stationed in the surrounding area of the cave entrance should the three of them encounter additional insurgents in the hills, as well as the possibility that some of the insurgents in the tunnels had escaped.

Major Khouri deferred to Brady's analysis of the situation and dispatched a platoon to spread out near and about the cave entrance and surrounding foothills. Ali, who had been treated and bandaged by the medics, insisted he be allowed to join his platoon, which Major Khouri had just ordered for Brady's backup. At first, Major Khouri denied the request, but seeing that Ali had 75 percent use of his shoulder and arm, and being short of battle-tested soldiers like Ali, he allowed him to assist the backup platoon by operating the field phone. A beaming Ali grabbed the rest of his gear and the field phone and fell into line as the platoon left for the area Brady and his men had just left.

As they began their trek through the foothills, Brady ordered them to take five. Brady took notice of how the boulders were sprinkled about the land as if someone had placed them there. Brady's mind, as if seeking some refuge from the immediate peril they faced, contemplated how this land had endured wars, natural disasters, and bore witness to the evolution of the Earth and its inhabitants. He wondered, what if these boulders, these inanimate objects, could communicate? Could they mentor us on the mistakes we make in life: the inhumanity invoked in the name of our God or a god; the prejudice created by uncertainty, lack of knowledge, our failure to persist in understanding, and most of all, to care and respect the rights of others who may have different beliefs, different cultures, and different ideas? These existential moments often found Brady examining his own beliefs and opinions with respect to the world around us.

This brief period of meditation by Brady was short-lived and violently interrupted by rifle fire coming from their twelve o'clock and about fifty yards out. Brady and Samu immediately returned fire while Sergeant Khalid pulled up his binoculars to see if he could determine from where the shots were coming. Khalid gave Brady hand signals indicating there appeared to be three men behind rocks in a slightly higher elevation.

Fifty yards being too far for hand grenades, Sergeant Khalid strapped an RPG to his M16. He aimed at the place he had seen the light from the gunfire and fired his RPG. It hit dead-on where Khalid had aimed. One insurgent was felled, and another began to turn and run in the opposite direction. Brady aimed and fired his rifle, dropping the fleeing insurgent in less than five steps. There remained one insurgent who they couldn't see and did not know if he was still in place, or if he too had decided to flee.

*****

Omar Saeed was a Syrian by birth, raised in Mosul, Iraq, by a lower-middle-class family of meager means. His father had worked himself up from rural poverty selling handmade linens provided by Saeed's grandmother. The grandmother had self-taught herself on the loom and had ingratiated herself to a cloth and fabric dealer in their village. Saeed's dad eked out a living for his wife, Saeed, and Saeed's younger sister, Shari. However, his dad always managed to put a little money aside in hopes that someday, Saeed would be able to finish high school and enjoy an advanced education somewhere beyond the borders of Iraq.

After the war in Afghanistan, known as Desert Storm, and prior to the outbreak of war in Iraq, Saeed had managed to get through high school with an adequate knowledge of academics and a fairly good grasp of English. Saeed had learned from one of his teachers in school that there was a program in America for students from foreign countries to come to the US to live in foster homes while continuing their education.

Saeed wrote letters to some of these families, one of which he had learned of from a Mr. Sullivan, an American arms dealer based in Baghdad and visiting Mosul to negotiate arms deals with local tribesmen. One day Mr. Sullivan came to his father's store shopping for sweaters to take back to his daughters in Blacksburg, Virginia. While Saeed's dad was showing Mr. Sullivan cashmere and cotton sweaters, Saeed stopped by the shop, having just returned from his last day of high school.

Saeed's dad introduced him to Mr. Sullivan, beaming as he bragged to the businessman that Saeed had just finished his last day of school and was looking forward to the high school graduation ceremony. Mr. Sullivan congratulated Saeed and his father and wished Saeed well in his future endeavors. Saeed responded that he had hopes of traveling to America to continue his education. He also explained to Mr. Sullivan what he had heard from his teacher concerning the foster family program for foreign students.

Mr. Sullivan, a well-educated businessman himself, having ubiquitous contacts back in the US, entered into a discussion with Saeed centering on the areas of interest Saeed had in the different fields of study. Saeed, not having given much thought to what his major field of study might be, felt he might enjoy politics and government and maybe the field of computer technology, although he had little understanding of what that meant.

Mr. Sullivan then stunned Saeed and his dad by offering the name of a family in his own neighborhood in Blacksburg who often had opened their home to foreign students. Their names were Mr. and Mrs. Potter. He wrote down the name and address and gave the piece of paper to Saeed.

He told Saeed when he wrote to the Potters to use his name, *William Sullivan*. Saeed then turned to his dad, who was smiling ear to ear, thanked Mr. Sullivan, and ran to tell his mother and sister the good news.

After many discussions with his family, they decided Saeed should contact the family in Blacksburg, Virginia, the home of Virginia Tech University, and see if they might entertain the possibility of Saeed becoming a resident in their home. Saeed's dad insisted Saeed apply for admission to the university first and determine what funds he would require for tuition, books, room, and board. Saeed, for the next week, said morning, afternoon, and evening prayers to Allah that he would not only be accepted for entrance to the school but be accepted by the Potters. For Saeed, his meeting Mr. Sullivan and obtaining the reference to the Potters was an epiphany in his life, and he prayed his hopes and dreams would all come true.

Before Saeed filled out the application for the school's registrar, his father asked that he sit down and prepare a budget on what he would need to survive while attending college. There would be the cost of boarding at the foster home, even though this amount would surely be less than the cost of living on campus. Then there would be the tuition. He had no idea what this would be but found out by using a student computer at the high school counselor's office. Saeed realized he had a lot of planning to do prior to contacting the Potters.

Once he had established his budget, Saeed contacted the registrar's office located in Blacksburg. Saeed considered many different curriculums but settled on a business major in the Pamplin College of Business. Then he inquired about grants and scholarships. He was told to submit his high school transcript, along with any recommendations or references he might have, and the registrar would get back to him.

Mr. Ransheet, Saeed's English teacher in high school, agreed to write a recommendation for Saeed. But what he didn't tell Saeed was that he would solicit the recommendations of each of Saeed's high school teachers to do the same. Saeed was unaware of Mr. Ransheet's efforts to secure a scholarship for him, but once the registrar had received and reviewed the recommendations and his high school transcript reflecting his A average, Saeed was awarded a full scholarship for academic achievement.

Saeed was overwhelmed when he received the notice of his acceptance and the award of the full academic scholarship. Now he needed only to find the source of funds he would need for the Potters, for his books, and for his daily expenses. His father had put aside a sum that would last through the freshman year, but Saeed would need to provide the rest.

Saeed then wrote to the Potters, introduced himself, and mentioned Mr. Sullivan as his sponsor. Saeed then heard from Mr. Sullivan, who wanted to be brought up to date. The Potters had called him for a reference on Saeed, and he wanted to know how things were proceeding. Saeed explained about the scholarship and the money his father had saved for him but that he would need a part-time job to cement the deal.

Mr. Sullivan laughed and assured Saeed that he would find a job when he arrived in Blacksburg. He guaranteed it. Saeed thanked Mr. Sullivan profusely, and when he hung up, he ran to his dad's shop to share the good news.

*****

Captain Brady motioned for Samu to circle to the left while Sergeant Khalid circled to the right. Brady hesitated to give them a head start, then he bolted along the same path as the last insurgent who had fled. In doing so, he cautiously approached the fallen insurgent he had shot, kicking away his weapon and kneeling to feel his pulse. The soldier was dead. Brady set out for the one that was trying to escape. A trail of blood indicated the last insurgent had been wounded; how seriously was the question. Brady did not want him to escape for fear he would alert any other insurgents that may have escaped the airstrikes or that may be amassed among the rocks and boulders.

Brady paused for a moment in hopes of finding footprints or other indications of the insurgent's path of retreat. Samu had taken a position slightly higher than Brady or Sergeant Khalid, and his view included a panorama of about fifty yards in front of Brady. The area seemed clear of movement, and Samu motioned to advance carefully. Sergeant Khalid, on the right side, darted forward some fifteen yards, and Brady did the same. Drawing no gunfire, Brady and Khalid continued their pursuit, zigzagging among the boulders as Samu kept watch above them.

Suddenly, their pursuit was interrupted by rifle fire. Samu saw the flash from the insurgent's rifle and lowered his M16 to fire. As he did so, he heard another shot ring out and simultaneously felt a sharp, hot pain in his thigh where the bullet had landed. Sergeant Khalid was first to Samu's side and applied a bandage to the wound. Captain Brady held his position but acknowledged Khalid's attention to Samu's wound.

Samu had seen the source of the gunfire, which was only twenty yards in front of Brady. Samu held up one finger, indicating there was only one insurgent involved. Samu saw no one else in the immediate fifty-yard perimeter. Brady ordered Khalid to assist Samu back to the Hummer. Khalid, being out of grenades and RPGs, was reluctant to leave Brady, but agreed, and using the boulders as cover, slung Samu's arm over his shoulder and proceeded to return to the Hummer.

Brady had decided that he would make one last attempt to capture the sole insurgent, and if he failed, then he would call in reinforcements to neutralize the area. Brady saw an opening in the boulders between himself and the last position where Samu had seen the insurgent.

As Brady ran to an area closer by about five yards to his adversary, he opened fire at his foe. Immediately, the insurgent returned the fire from his automatic rifle. As Brady hunched behind the boulder, he sensed a warm feeling of blood streaming down his leg. He had been hit in his right calf. It did not look as though an artery had been hit. Brady quickly pulled a bandage from his kit and wrapped it around his calf.

An Arabic voice from behind the rocks expressed satisfaction that Brady, too, had been wounded and was bleeding.

*****

The big day had come. Saeed was to board an airplane at the airport in Baghdad and fly nonstop to Richmond, Virginia. From there, he would ride a bus to the Potters' residence in Blacksburg, Virginia. His mother and sister, whom he would dearly miss, were crying as he hugged them one last time. Who knew when he would be able to return home? His father attempted to hold back his tears, but his control gave way to his emotions. His father told Saeed to always say his morning and evening prayers and live his life as Allah would approve.

Saeed promised his father that once in his new home, he would seek out the nearest mosque and introduce himself to the imam. He would keep up his prayers and his moral compass. Saeed tried not to show his anxiety, but his father could see through his attempts.

His father hugged him again, and Saeed jumped into the waiting taxi and was off to the airport.

The plane was a 757 jumbo jet with US Air across its fuselage. It was his first time aboard a plane. Saeed was amazed at the number of seats and how big the plane was inside. He stopped to pray silently that Allah would see that the plane safely reached its destination. The flight took approximately eight hours and was somewhat bumpy for most of the flight. Saeed enjoyed the free sodas and was taken aback by the amount of alcohol the passengers consumed.

They landed in Richmond without incident, and Saeed had no trouble securing his baggage at the baggage claim area. Once he exited the terminal, he checked the information for a bus schedule to Blacksburg.

The bus ride was a little over three hours. A taxi from the bus station took only fifteen minutes to the Potters' home. He was met at the door by Mr. Potter, a gentleman in his early fifties, with gray hair slightly receding, about six feet tall, and two hundred pounds. He was African American.

Mr. Potter welcomed him to his home. Behind Mr. Potter was Mrs. Potter, a slim, matronly woman in her fifties, and soft-spoken. She too gave Saeed a warm welcome. Inside the colonial rambler, Saeed met the children, Doris and Michael.

Doris was seventeen years old, very pretty, petite like her mother, and delighted to see Saeed. Michael, who was eighteen years old, six feet tall, and trim, took after Mr. Potter. Michael, less extroverted than Doris, shook Saeed's hand and simply said, "Hello."

After a nervous and awkward chat with the family, Saeed was shown his room, furnished with a nice bed, a desk with a laptop computer, a couple of chairs, a cabinet, a closet, and pictures of Lincoln and Roosevelt. After sharing dinner with his new hosts, Saeed retired to his room, where he immediately called his family to report his initial approval of his new home. Needless to say, Saeed's mom and dad were elated, as was his sister Shari.

Saeed unpacked his belongings, and immediately turned on the laptop, and utilizing the experience he had gained in his high school computer science class, began to fidget with the one item that would assist him the most in acclimating himself to this new environment.

In the next few weeks, Saeed familiarized himself with his surroundings, matriculated into Virginia Tech University, joined a local mosque, and dutifully made time for his morning and evening prayers to Allah. Saeed became aware of the fraternities and sororities on campus and, in fact, was invited to join the language club, which was mostly comprised of foreign students.

Saeed settled into his new world and buried himself in his studies. His freshman and sophomore years were hard, and he often contacted his mentor, Mr. Ransheet, to guide him through some of the more difficult subjects. Saeed was slowly leaning towards switching his major to computer science. He had also developed an interest in philosophy, especially as it related to religion. Saeed was interested in how science and the big bang theory correlated, if at all, with Allah's creation of the world, and the formulation and formation of our present-day ideas of ethics, moral conduct, reasoning, and especially man's relationship to man. So as he progressed into his sophomore year, he ended up with a double major in philosophy and computer science.

*****

Brady had one last grenade and figured now was the time to use it. He heard the rustling of movement just behind the boulders approximately five yards away. He pulled the pin and lobbed the grenade towards those sounds. He waited for the explosion, and when it happened, Brady pulled himself up to see if there was any activity where he had thrown the grenade. Nothing! He waited, hoping he had eliminated his target.

Brady's wound was merely a flesh wound, and apparently, no bones were broken. The tightly wrapped bandage had stopped the bleeding. He pulled himself to his feet and, with his M16 in hand, began to move to where he thought he had killed his enemy. No one was there. There was no sign of any remains, no clothing, but there were bloodstains on the rocks.

Brady took a few more steps and was suddenly surprised when the insurgent he thought he had killed, and who had taken refuge behind a boulder that had blunted the blast of the grenade, pointed his gun at Brady. Just as he was about to pull the trigger, the ground beneath both he and Brady gave way, and they tumbled into one of the tunnels some thirty feet below.

Apparently, the airstrikes had loosened the ground above the tunnels, and Brady and the insurgent now found themselves lying among the debris from the ground giving way. Brady had lost his rifle and found himself covered with rocks and debris up to his shoulder. The insurgent too was immobilized and detached from his rifle. Both men were somewhat dazed, just twenty feet apart, and unable to extricate themselves from their predicament. There seemed to be no outlet, and there was very little light emanating from the small opening in the ground above.

The two men faced each other, contemplating their next move. Both were buried up to their chest, and neither could move anything but their arms, head, and shoulders. The non-threatening wounds each had suffered prior to the cave-in were minimized by the dirt and debris pressing against their bodies, providing pressure on the openings in the flesh and stemming the flow of blood.

Both men, as if by instinct, began reaching for anything to hurl at the other. Brady pummeled his enemy with the small stones he could feel in the dirt around him, and his enemy did the same to him. Each quickly realized he was bleeding from the head injuries caused by the painful but innocuous missiles they were hurling. Brady, without uttering a word, was the first to stop the futile attempts to destroy the enemy. After tossing one more stone, Brady's foe did the same.

Both men stared at each other, blood streaming down from the superficial cuts they had inflicted. For the next hour, they struggled to dig around themselves, but encountering mostly hard rocks embedded in the dirt, they each acknowledged to themselves their attempts to extricate their bodies were futile, and they simply glared at each other.

Above ground, Sergeant Khalid had bandaged Samu and taken him back to the Hummer when suddenly they encountered four or five insurgents who had entered the area in hopes of rescuing their leader, Omar Saeed, who now lay partially buried no more than twenty feet from Captain Brady. The main contingent of the insurgents had vacated the area when they escaped from the tunnels during the airstrikes. Shots rang out from behind the boulders, and both Khalid and Samu returned fire.

Khalid and Ali had taken cover behind the Hummer, approximately fifty yards from the enemy. Brady had lost the field phone during the cave-in, and now Khalid and Samu were on their own with no way to contact Major Khouri and the reinforcements. Sergeant Khalid hoped that Major Khouri would realize the three of them were on their own and at least send a scouting party to search for them.

However, Major Khouri had led his troops in a pincer movement hoping to head off the main band of insurgents who were traveling north on the far side of the foothills. The small group of insurgents now confronting Khalid and Samu, had only their rifles, no grenades, and had an open space between them and the Hummer. Khalid surmised they could not circle him and Samu without exposing themselves to certain death.

Both sides began conserving their ammunition, and there were long periods of quiet interrupted by an occasional burst of fire when one side detected movement or sounds. One of these shots flattened the tire on the Hummer. Both sides found themselves without reinforcements and running low on ammo and no vehicles. It could be hours before a scouting party or flyover choppers discovered the predicament of Khalid and Samu, as well as Captain Brady.

*****

His senior year at Virginia Tech was the most joyful of his college experience, but it would prove to be his most sorrowful. Saeed had learned to fit in, to interface with his colleagues. He had become popular for his participation in extracurricular activities such as the Philosopher's Club, the Poly-Sci Group, and the so-called Nerd Club. His good looks didn't hurt, especially with the co-eds.

Saeed was known for his intellect as well as his respect and admiration for those students who were forthcoming with their ideas and beliefs. He had met Anna, with whom he had developed a strong affection. They had shared many interests and thoughts concerning the world situation, especially the turmoil in the Middle East, Africa, and Ukraine. Most of their conversations ended in heated discussions of race, religion, politics, and how these subjects seemed to monopolize their very existence.

Anna, a practicing Jew, had enlightened Saeed on Judaism, and the prejudice and hatred many held against them born out of ignorance and lack of understanding. Anna felt confident that these traits, prevalent among so many Americans, were the by-product of a lack of education coupled with the inability of most people to think for themselves. She and Saeed agreed that most people were unduly influenced by their upbringing and environment.

Saeed had observed the mannerisms and defensive mechanisms that African Americans exhibited when around white people. He had many discussions on this subject with Mr. Potter, Doris, and Michael. In many frank and heart-rending discussions, Michael had expressed the daily run-ins he would have, not only with fellow students but with white people in general, whose facial expressions, tone of voice, arrogance, and condescension seemed to permeate all their social interactions.

Michael had talked about his feelings around white people, how he had to learn to fight feelings of inadequacy, of sticking out in a crowd, of wanting to avoid any discussion that might lead to racial issues. Doris agreed with Michael. She too had to endure racial slurs from her white female colleagues, and her own feelings of not fitting into the white man's world.

The Potters often stated that times were getting better, that racial inequality and prejudice was being eviscerated, but it would be the following generations that would benefit, not the present.

Saeed had experienced his own bias. His appearance initially drew many jeers and taunts, causing him to eventually shed his Arabic attire and try to integrate as best he could into the college scene. He prayed often that Allah would forgive him for this concession he made to the non-believers. Saeed's English was near perfect, and he had learned the proper social graces. Saeed still attended the Mosque regularly for morning and evening prayers. This fact was not lost on many of those who knew him but did not like him.

Saeed, in his senior year, Saeed had taken advanced courses in Philosophy, Political Science, and Computer Science and Technology. He was mesmerized by the early Greeks and their studies of the different forms of government, especially democracy. But he was equally excited reading Machiavelli, St. Augustine, and such and their theories of how man should be governed, both spiritually and physically. He liked the idea put forth in Machiavelli's *The Prince* that the best ruler would be a benevolent dictator, one who could rule with an iron fist but still serve the needs of the people.

Saeed often wondered what would happen in his own country if democracy was instituted. Would his people accept this type of government? Would they take advantage of their right to vote, to assess and evaluate the candidates' qualities and platforms? He pondered whether the leaders in the communities could overcome the rampant greed and sinister desires that seem to infect those who rise to positions of trust and responsibility.

These questions and the answers Saeed would soon deal with in real-life situations. On the last day of his senior finals, Saeed received a phone call from Ransheet. Saeed was home at the Potters' when Mr. Potter informed him that there was a call for him. Mr. Ransheet asked that Saeed sit down as they talked. There had been an airstrike in the district of Mosul. Many houses had been destroyed. Saeed's family home had been demolished. His father, mother, and sister were killed in the bombing.

*****

"What do I call you?" Brady yelled at the insurgent. There was no answer, just an expression of disdain and hatred. Both men had grown weary of flinging stones and rocks at each other and had relegated to trading stares like two angry bulldogs. There was no sound from the small opening above. The rim of the cave-in was some twenty feet above them, and neither combatant wanted to risk yelling for help lest it be the opposition that responded.

Brady thought that Khalid and Samu would have found him by now and probably were captured, wounded, or worse. The insurgent wondered if any of his scouting party had survived and hopefully were somewhere in the area and would soon find him. Both of them had been clawing at the ground that surrounded and enveloped them, their hands bleeding and their fingernails torn. An hour had passed since the cave-in. Each man was tired, bloody, and fast becoming devoid of hope that their comrades would locate them anytime soon.

"Saeed," erupted from the mouth of Brady's adversary. "My name is Omar Saeed," he said.

"My name is Brady," he responded.

Saeed yelled in English at the top of his voice, "You are American?"

"Yes," responded Brady. This seemed to enrage Saeed even more, and he called Brady an infidel and murderer. Brady, at first surprised that he spoke English so fluently, let out a contemptuous laugh and bellowed, "Isn't this the pot calling the kettle black?"

*****

Saeed had slumped to the floor upon hearing the devastating news from Ransheet. His whole world seemed to crumble before him, and suddenly he felt an emptiness inside.

All those that he held dear, that he loved, that he had longed to return to since coming to America, was lost. He had no one, no one to turn to, to console him, to ease his pain.

Mr. and Mrs. Potter, Doris, and Michael were present but could offer nothing that would dissipate the hopelessness and helpless feelings now capturing his whole being. Ransheet had mentioned that

American jets had carried out the attack. None of the villagers could understand why their small community near Mosul had been targeted. Some blamed it on a few radical Islamists who occasionally let their feelings be heard. But these were generally old men who knew little about the outside world and what was occurring daily in the media.

Saeed immediately made reservations for a flight home to Iraq. He packed his belongings and headed for the airport without saying goodbye to the Potters. An anger was building in his mind and his heart, an anger that he could not control, an anger that would soon consume his mind, body, and soul.

Ransheet met Saeed at the airport in Baghdad, and from there they drove to Mosul. Ransheet insisted Saeed stay with him. But first, Saeed insisted on visiting the site that once was his home. The drive was long and treacherous. There were roadside bombs rumored to be along the main highway. Saeed sat silent but observed the devastation that had taken place since he had left for college.

Ransheet described the terror that quickly spread throughout their village when the local alert blared over the makeshift warning system, people scurrying to bomb shelters. Saeed's family, however, refused to leave their home and were found in each other's arms in the basement. Saeed could not hold back the tears at the thought of his father, mother, and sister being torn apart by the explosions. But quickly, the sadness was displaced by the anger that Saeed had begun to feel back in Blacksburg.

Upon reaching the village, Ransheet stopped at what remained of Saeed's home. Bodies had been removed and properly buried. But the horror that had taken place was reflected in the crumbling remains of Saeed's home. As he walked among the rubble, Saeed was approached by one of the elders in the village. His name was Maliki. He wore traditional garments and spoke of the bombings and how the villagers had been taken by surprise, having only seconds to seek shelter.

This old man expressed anger and hatred for the Americans. He denounced them for coming and destroying his country. He recited the Quran and how the American devils must pay for what they had done. How the American devils should be tortured and beheaded for their sins. Saeed listened without comment. His mind was blinded by his loss and engulfed with a wanting to strike back, to take revenge against those who had abruptly turned his world upside down. Saeed's grief for the loss of his loved ones had morphed into a feeling of extreme hatred for the Americans for what they were doing to his country.

Maliki mentioned a rogue insurgent group that some of the men of the village had formed. This group called themselves "Hezbollah," agents or party of Allah. Maliki said he could put Saeed in touch with their leader.

Saeed contacted the group Hezbollah. He met with a regional leader and joined his outfit. It was not long before Saeed began the rigorous training, both physical as well as technical. Saeed learned about operating rifles, makeshift bombs, and terror tactics, all while putting his body in its best shape since college. It was not long before the leader of the group realized the value of Saeed's education in America and his grasp of the English language. Saeed was made a leader of an attack unit that specialized in raids on enemy units, especially those run by Americans.

*****

Khalid and Samu could hear the sounds of artillery fire and explosions in the distance. Major Khouri was engaging the enemy and was closing the circle as he maneuvered around the insurgents who had fled the tunnels. Back near the cave entrance, there was a standoff between Samu, Sergeant Khalid, and the insurgents. Neither side was willing to risk an advance or retreat. Sergeant Khalid and Samu's survival seemed to be in the hands of Major Khouri and the success of his pincer movement.

Major Khouri decided to await darkness before he began his offensive to attack from all directions upon the insurgents' positions. Khouri ordered up his tanks, and his sergeants were ordered to replenish ammunition, water, and food rations. In three hours, it would be dusk, and Khouri would order his units to move in.

*****

Saeed was so furious at Brady's comment that he tried to expectorate at Brady but only succeeded in slobbering on himself. Brady tried to control his emotions and concentrate on what, if any, information he could extract from this adversary while Saeed was emotionally distraught. Brady knew from his training that during interrogations, losing one's temper meant losing one's rationale.

Brady asked Saeed why he was so hell-bent on killing and torturing his own people. Why did he lead his armed band of terrorists to attack his own army, comprised of his countrymen? Did not they too believe in Allah? Were they not also Islamists?

Saeed responded with his own onslaught of questions. "Why are you here? This isn't your concern. Why are you and your country trying to impose your form of government, your culture, your beliefs on my people?"

Brady wanted to ask about Saeed's unit, its size, equipment, its base of operations, and other intel, but he had quickly surmised that Saeed was not lacking in intelligence and had the presence of mind to avoid any conversation about such matters. Perhaps this train of thought could be revisited later, but now was not the time. The two combatants had just completed their first verbal skirmish.

Both men recoiled somewhat from the flurry of words they had just exchanged. Each paused to consider their present condition and how they might survive. Saeed hoped his roguish band of followers would somehow be able to discover the cave-in. Brady, in turn, rolled around in his mind what Major Khouri might be strategizing with respect to capturing the rogue insurgents, and whether Sergeant Khalid and Samu might still be in the area.

Brady recalled his Catholic upbringing back in Chicago and the dilemmas his religion had inflicted upon him. He had often questioned his faith, and the many unanswered questions were still buried in his subconscious. Early on, he had decided that he would keep an open mind when it came to religions. Right now, in this foreign country, he knew he was amidst a religious tug-of-war involving not only different religions but different sects and divisions in those religions.

Saeed, recalling the horrible manner in which his family had died, was having trouble controlling his built-up hatred and disdain for Brady and the American people. Brady represented to Saeed the epitome of all things evil. If it wasn't for the fact that he was now barely able to move up to his arms, he would be flailing and maiming Brady. Unfortunately, he was restricted to the worst vitriol that had ever passed through his lips.

Brady viewed Saeed as just another radical upon whom reason and logic were wasted. And now, Saeed seemed out of control with the epithets and disparaging remarks that spewed from his mouth. Brady was inclined to respond to some of the obscenities but decided to let Saeed tire of his maniacal ramblings.

Eventually, Saeed did tire, and the words came slower and less violent. Brady maintained his self-imposed air of silence. After fifteen minutes or so, Brady felt compelled to challenge Saeed on his political beliefs. Little did he know that Saeed was well-versed in the field.

"Why do you fight against the Iraqi army and the allied forces that are trying to bring democracy and freedom to your people?" Brady asked.

Saeed, still smoldering from his earlier tirade, fired back, "My country was better off under Hussein than it is now. At least then we had respect for our leader, and people were allowed to worship as they wished and conduct their lives as Allah would want. The only thing the Americans have brought us is death and destruction of all we hold dear."

Brady responded, "Hussein was a dictator whose men were no more than henchmen who took advantage of the people. Hussein was developing weapons of mass destruction to use on the people."

"Not true," responded Saeed. "Under Hussein, the people had water, sewer, and utilities. We had the ability to come and go as we desired. There was never any truth to the theory of his developing weapons of mass destruction. Since this war started, our banks have been plundered, as well as our museums and mosques. Cities in many places are reduced to rubble. Utilities, sewer, and public water are non-existent. How can you claim you are helping us when in fact you are destroying us?"

"The US has provided financial aid to help reinstate utilities, to build new schools, and assist in instituting democracy in your country," responded Brady.

"Yes, and all the while you kill women and children in your airstrikes, without regrets." Saeed was becoming more and more angry as the conversation continued. His mind strayed to his home, his sister and parents, and how they perished.

*****

Sergeant Khalid shook Samu, who had dozed off. Khalid had heard rustling in the area where the insurgents were dug in. Suddenly, all was quiet. Khalid listened intently and peered over the Hummer hood in their direction. Still no movement or sound. Ever so slowly, Khalid silently crept to a higher position where he should be able to see something indicating the insurgents were still present. Nothing!

Sergeant Khalid threw a rock to see if there was any response. Again, nothing. Khalid gave Samu a hand signal to position himself behind a boulder closer to the spot where the insurgents were last seen. Slowly, Samu inched forward while Khalid provided cover. Then, when there were still no sounds or movement, Sergeant Khalid juxtaposed himself in front of Samu, only a few feet from where he had observed rifle fire earlier during the day. It was apparent the insurgents had vacated the area and were no longer a threat.

Immediately, Khalid's thoughts were on Brady and where he might be. Was he captured, killed, or was he injured but still unable to contact them? After a brief search of the area, Sergeant Khalid and Samu headed back to the Hummer. Quickly, Samu changed the flat tire on the Hummer for the spare. Once finished, they headed back to join up with Major Khouri. Little did they know that Captain Brady was still in the area, but buried in dirt and rocks and only twenty feet separated Brady from the enemy.

Brady and Saeed each had dozed off into a deep sleep that both needed badly to regain their strength. Brady was the first to awake.

He glanced over to Saeed, who was still asleep with his face free of the contortions exhibited previously when Saeed had launched into his uncontrollable hatred of Brady and what he represented.

Brady lamented how this young man, somewhat handsome and obviously well-educated, could be so lost in his concept of what the Americans stood for and were trying so hard to accomplish in this godforsaken land.

*****

Brady reminisced about his days in undergrad at the University of Illinois. He enjoyed reminiscing about his days on the football field, and his studies in political science, social studies, and liberal arts had only increased his liberal biases and added fuel to his passion for justice and freedom for all. Until his tour in Iraq, he had little knowledge of Islamic teachings and its followers. He knew a little of Mohammed and the Quran but not enough to engage in a dialogue or criticism thereof.

In his upbringing, Brady loved the innocuous antics of Bud Abbott and Lou Costello and the dashing exploits of John Wayne and the Green Berets. He often jested that he was the all-American boy who loved his mother, apple pie, and baseball. He had been taught always to respect the rights of others and to dedicate himself to the love and defense of his country. His father had related stories of his own service during the Vietnam War. How the French had lost control of the Country, and the Communists had moved in. Brady recalled the visions he had watched on television of the rooftop evacuation of personnel from the Embassy in Saigon.

His father had also spoken of the Korean conflict in which the United States had defended South Koreans against the invasion of the Communist North. This action too had ended without victory or an ultimate solution to each side's problems. Now, the United States had ventured into a new arena, one in which religion seemed to be the underlying force. There had been many innuendoes about America's intentions for entering the present conflicts, wanting to protect the oil fields, gain control over the area, and take advantage of the unrest of some of the people. This was a war where the Americans, unlike in the past, were disliked and viewed as a necessary evil and temporary interlocutor to settle the country down and restore peace.

*****

Saeed was starting to stir, and his eyes widened as he caught sight of Brady. Brady waited, expecting a continuation of the wild, irrational rantings of Saeed. Instead, Saeed seemed calm, collected, and somewhat placid. Saeed spoke first, staring at Brady quizzically. But for the camouflaged uniform, Brady reminded Saeed of the typical college student he had met in Blacksburg. They were clean-cut, articulate, confident, and perhaps naïve when it came to the culture and traditions of the country where Saeed was raised.

"Why are you here?" asked Saeed. "Why have you risked your life to defend this land, to kill innocent people, and destroy our villages and cities?"

Brady was taken aback by this sudden change in the tone and nature of Saeed's dialogue. He answered Saeed, but first, he hesitated, collecting his thoughts so he might clearly and succinctly respond. "I believe in what my country is trying to achieve in this conflict. I believe that America wants to bring peace to this country. To rid its people of tyranny and gain their freedom. To preserve individual rights and install a democratic government in which these rights and freedom are protected."

Saeed could wait no longer. He immediately lashed out at Brady. "How can you be so arrogant to claim these motives for the United States when your country has its own troubles? Your people are not free. African Americans are treated as second-class citizens. Americans claim freedom for all but look down upon and condescend to all other races except the Caucasians."

Saeed had gained momentum in his rebuttal and continued on. "You claim freedom for your people, but elections are slanted in favor of politicians who are backed by the rich, by PACs with unlimited donations. Your electorate is separated between the haves and the have-nots. Your middle class is disappearing, mostly downward.

Less than two percent of the voters garner almost half of the income for your nation. Law enforcement is predominantly white, and their biases against minorities are depicted every day in the media. The jails are filled with an abnormally high percentage of people of color."

Brady suddenly realized that this insurgent spoke with apparent familiarity about American culture and its history. He collected his thoughts and responded. "America is founded upon the premise that all men are created equal and free, and these rights are protected by our Constitution and the Bill of Rights attached thereto. America was born out of a desire by our forefathers to ascend beyond the shackles of tyranny, of taxation without representation, and to have a say in how we would be governed and by whom."

Saeed could not resist interrupting Brady. "How can you say your people were free when a substantial segment of the population were slaves, who were not free and who had no vote in the newly formed government? Americans speak critically of our freedom fighters beheading the infidels, of a careless and reckless disregard for humanity towards others. How about Americans who castrated the negroes, who pummeled blacks in the streets of Selma, Alabama? How about your elite, the rich who squander huge sums on their own materiality while millions of Americans go hungry and without jobs? Your tax structure ensures that these conditions continue. Your Wall Street traders have been guilty of a gluttonous control over trading and investing on the stock markets, with no consideration for the devastating losses of homeowners, small investors, and everyday people."

Brady took advantage of Saeed's pause and immediately took the offensive. "Yes, we had slavery, and yes, they had no vote, nor did women. But much of this was corrected as our nation developed. Hangings, lynchings, castrations, and general abuse of minorities rightfully protesting conditions have been outlawed. Are there still abuses of minorities? Certainly, but we are slowly eviscerating this from our country. As to the division in our economic levels, yes, there are some inequalities, yes, some of our elections are bought, but these are isolated instances, many of which are reversed in due time. We have had an African American as our President, and we may soon have a female President. The problem America has with the division of classes and the increasing disparity between the rich and the poor is a normal phase of capitalism. It is a balancing act between encouraging investments via tax laws to boost the economy, thereby creating jobs, and providing for the public's needs and safety.

"We know there are no quick-fix answers. Our Constitution allows us to evolve in a civil manner. We continue to search for new solutions in a peaceful manner."

"Then why are you here in our country?" Saeed responded. "My people can solve their own problems. The regional wars amongst the various religious sects, the Shiites, the Sunni, the Kurds, and all the others, merely want peace and freedom for their people."

Brady responded, "Even if this means serving under a dictator, or worse, a thug like Hussein?"

"Unlike Americans, our people are devoutly religious. We worship daily, not just on Sunday. We follow the Quran and live by its tenets," responded Saeed.

Brady was somewhat taken aback by this enemy who was obviously well-educated, intelligent, and extremely articulate. Why, Brady thought, is this man fighting on the side of insurgents, especially this particular sect that enjoys beheading their enemies? Brady was having difficulty reconciling this brash young man, dressed in the familiar attire of the insurgents, with the head garb, scarves, and loosely fitted shirts and baggy pants, with the man with whom Brady was presently engaging in a dialogue about the morality of the battles being waged in this country Saeed called his home.

*****

Major Khouri had, with his troops, encircled the last known location of the band of insurgents, and the drone he had requested from the US Air Force was just about to fly over the area. Sergeant Khalid and Samu were excited and relieved to see their comrades coming up from behind them, and soon joined forces. Sergeant Khalid met with intelligence officers to be debriefed on any information he and Samu could provide that might lead to the whereabouts of Captain Brady, as well as the retreating insurgents.

After they were treated for their wounds, Sergeant Khalid and Samu zeroed in on a hundred-yard perimeter in which they felt confident Captain Brady could be found. Shortly after the drone had passed over the area designated by Khalid, Major Khouri received word from Air Force field command that the heat sensors on the drone had picked up the movement of two people below ground and approximately seventy-five yards from Major Khouri's position. Khouri ordered one of his sergeants and a squad of men to rush to the area and determine if one of the bodies could be Brady, and to report back.

*****

Brady, after pondering his next move, decided he would test Saeed's beliefs, especially his understanding of morals, the good, the bad, and the evil. Brady stated, "I have related my understanding of this war, why the Americans are here, and why Americans feel an obligation to assist your country to be free and to decide their own fates through democratic elections. So what are your convictions with regard to religious freedom, free elections, and the value of human life?" he asked.

Saeed hesitated before answering. He felt the need to choose his words carefully and to fully explain what he considered the schism between his and Brady's beliefs. "I believe that my God, Allah, is the only God and as such provides His people with guidance on how to live their lives, and when they do so, how they will be rewarded in the next world. I believe that those who are not believers will be punished for their actions and will not be admitted to the afterlife. I have dedicated my life to Allah. I pray to Allah in the morning and evening."

Brady responded by asking Saeed how his Allah differed from Judaism and Christianity's God. "Perhaps," Brady suggested, "we are worshipping the same God." Brady ventured further and asked Saeed to define Allah. Saeed responded that Allah was all-knowing, all-powerful, and ever-present in our lives. Brady acknowledged this belief and added that the non-Muslim world also believed their God was omniscient, omnipotent, and ever-present.

"Could it be that we believe in the same God?" Brady asked. "Both our religions—mine Catholic and yours Muslim—claim there is but one God and no other. Both our religions demand a righteous life, love and respect for our fellow man, and charity for those less fortunate."

Saeed seemed somewhat agitated that Brady could be so arrogant and presumptuous as to discuss Allah in the same sentence with belief in another God. Brady sensed he had hit a nerve with Saeed and decided to approach him from another philosophical direction. Brady asked, "Can you describe your Allah? Can you tell me what He looks like, where He resides, and how He came about?" At first, Saeed ignored Brady, but having nothing better to do, decided to verbally joust with Brady.

"My Allah has always existed since the beginning of time. Allah exists everywhere. Allah is in us all. Allah perceives our every move."

Brady interjected, "If Allah has always existed and is everywhere, why doesn't Allah speak to all of us, not just Muslims? Why doesn't he inject himself in our everyday lives to correct the crime, poverty, and wars that exist in our world today?"

Brady could sense the hatred and anger swelling inside Saeed. His face was flushed and contorted. Saeed went into a rant about how Brady's words were sacrilege and insulting to Allah and that Brady should be beheaded for this. Brady, not wanting to lose the opportunity for a dialogue with the enemy, lowered his voice and very calmly admitted to Saeed that he had thought of these subjects and had examined his own beliefs at times. Brady had often wondered how God was created, how something could come from nothing, how all the miracles of the Bible could have happened. Or did they? Why God did not reveal Himself in a manner in which we all could perceive without question. And why God did not intervene in our world to stop wars, crimes, and inhumanity towards man.

In his heart, Brady believed in God and the teachings of Christ. But he had often questioned whether Jesus was, in fact, the Son of

God. Could it be that Jesus was simply one of many men and women who had preached the gospel of love and understanding for our fellow man in the name of God because this is the only way we can coexist on this planet? Mohammed, Gandhi, Moses, Jesus, and many others gave us role models to live our lives by and to ensure that this world we live in will persevere.

Brady felt the slight tickle of something running down his calf. Although he could not see that part of his body since it was covered by dirt, debris, and a large rock the size of a wine barrel. The rock was abutting his stomach and buried atop his knee and calf. Brady wondered if his leg was broken and if this ticklish feeling was his blood streaming down the calf. Brady remembered how he often saw men buried up to their necks in the movies, and this is about how he found himself at present.

Saeed too was buried beneath debris and rocks the size of bowling balls, but enough of them so that he was unable to tell if any part of his body beneath his shoulders had been injured, broken, or bleeding. There was no immediate pain for him or for Brady. Both men tried to make out their surroundings, but there was no light and each could only see a few feet in front of themselves. Brady could hear Saeed saying his prayers. Brady thought he should be doing the same since there was little chance they would be found alive. Brady had faced death many times, but never as now where there seemed such a finality to his life. He couldn't help but think about his wife and children back home and whether they would be able to survive without him. He knew his wife was strong, but he wondered how his kids would grow up without a father and whether they would be able to attend college. Whether his wife would be able to cope with the burden of being thrust into the role of head of the household. He was glad that the lack of light prevented Saeed from observing the tears streaming down his cheeks.

Saeed finished his prayers, and his thoughts turned to memories of his father, mother, and sister. He relived the day when he first heard from Ransheet of their deaths and the manner in which they died. Saeed recalled how happy his father and mother had been when he left for school in Blacksburg. He recalled the long flight home, hoping by some miracle that one or all of his family might still be alive, only to arrive home and be faced with the reality of their demise. Unlike Brady, Saeed now experienced a confluence of feelings—those of anger and sorrow. Saeed wanted to strike out in his anger but had neither the energy nor means of doing so. His only weapon would have to be his words. He tried to collect his many reasons for hating Brady and the things he stood for. In Brady, he saw the embodiment of all that Saeed felt disdain for.

Brady's thoughts returned to the present. He asked himself why he was here, why he was risking his life for people that appeared to resent American assistance and hurled insults at American soldiers passing through the villages. Brady wondered whether the incursion into this land by American forces would bear any fruit. Would this simply be a waste of American lives for people who really didn't care who governed them as long as there were jobs and the simple amenities of life? Perhaps, he thought, the ideology of democracy was too advanced for them. Perhaps a dictator was what they needed.

Saeed's body from the shoulders down was now numb, and he felt a sense of desperation creeping into his psyche. He suddenly reminisced about Anna and the happy times they shared during his years at Virginia Tech. Anna had taught him to confront his biases with an honest search for the truth. Her interest in understanding Muslims and the Islamic religion seemed to lurk in the corners of his thoughts. He recalled her saying many times, "You can't tell a book by its cover," and adding that he should react to those who prejudge him and his people with the same attitude he would address his own biases towards others.

Saeed's thoughts drifted to the Potters and the many discussions he had shared with Mr. Potter about race and religion. Mr. Potter had related his own experiences of his childhood when he had seen firsthand the viciousness of a "redneck" venting his anger on a black man for no other reason than he was black and had stared too long at the redneck's girlfriend. Or the many times Mr. Potter had crossed the street on a dark night simply to avoid the obvious nervousness of some white couple coming upon him. Mr. Potter had drawn the analogy to how Saeed might find himself being treated by some of the less understanding on campus.

Saeed recalled how on one occasion, while he and Anna were attending a campus rally, one of the male students made slurs in reference to Anna associating with an Arab. Mr. Potter's prophesies had come true; the simple fact that Saeed was of dark complexion and Anna being fair seemed to be the fuel that ignited the anger in the male student. Anna, as usual, had ignored the student and encouraged Saeed to do the same.

Saeed lamented that once he had entered school at Virginia Tech, he had lost contact with Mr. Sullivan and failed to thank him for all he had done. He had inquired of Mr. Potter if he had any communications with him, and the answer was no. Saeed thought about the generosity Mr. Sullivan had shown him, and the trouble he had gone to just to help a young high school student whom he barely knew to get into college. On occasion, Saeed had asked Ransheet about Mr. Sullivan, and Ransheet had not seen or heard from him either. Saeed often thought how he would like to have thanked him for his assistance and how much it meant.

"Are you awake?" Brady's voice boomed out, still not sure how close Saeed was to him.

"Yes, why?" responded Saeed.

"Just wanted to know if I should be protecting against any missiles coming my way," Brady said, half smiling to himself.

Saeed, picking up on Brady's sarcasm, shot back that he was saving his energy for this large rock he had just dug out of the debris around him. Both men were weak from their ordeal and shared a feeling of anxiety and desperation. Neither of them had any desire to renew their pelting or verbal warfare with one another.

Brady was the first to proffer in a normal voice that they might be in this cave for some time. Even without food and water, they could last for several days. Saeed had started saying his prayers to Allah, and when he had finished, he acknowledged Brady's comments and expressed his view that Allah would save him, that it was only a matter of time. Brady felt similarly in that he had prayed God would spare his life so he could once again see his wife and children.

*****

The craters created by the recent airstrikes had left the ground difficult to navigate on foot. Major Khouri had requested a drone be sent back to double-check the two bodies that had been detected in the earlier flyovers. It took about fifteen minutes for the drone to return and search the same area as before. This time, the drone was destroyed by a ground-to-air missile before it could reach the area. Major Khouri furrowed his brow and sadly accepted the fact that Captain Brady must have been captured or slain by the enemy.

Meanwhile, the insurgents who had previously escaped through the tunnels, undeterred by the airstrikes, had regrouped. Their leader now, in the absence of Saeed, was a ruthless fundamentalist of Islam who had no regard for the value of human life, not only for the non-believers in Allah but for those believers he considered moderates who shunned the strict interpretations of the Quran. He was called Casab, the "Butcher."

One of the men, Micah, who had earlier encountered Samu and Khalid, passed the word to Casab that before he and his comrades had disengaged in the firefight, he had noticed a portion of the ground that had been disturbed by the airstrikes and appeared to have sunken in certain areas, indicating the ground may have given way. Perhaps these were cave-ins where the tunnels had been. Casab discussed with his men the possibility that Saeed was still alive and might be trapped in one of these areas. Saeed was extremely well-liked by his men, and upon hearing this news, they all argued to return to the area in hopes of finding Saeed alive.

Casab decided to wait until dark and then send Micah with a scouting party to the area to determine if there was any indication that Saeed might still be alive. As nightfall enveloped the area, Micah led the small band of insurgents back to the area where Saeed was last seen. Major Khouri and his men had moved further north of the site, believing the insurgents had hightailed it back to their base a few miles north. Major Khouri left behind only Sergeant Khalid and a squad of soldiers for a last effort to find Captain Brady.

Sergeant Khalid had his men fan out to cover every inch of ground where Captain Brady was last reported seen by Samu and himself. Samu had been transported back to the medical facility some ten miles away. Sergeant Khalid and his men were unaware that Micah and his band of insurgents were just on the other side of a small foothill about a hundred yards to the east. Sergeant Khalid had brought with him an army canine trained to sniff out enemy combatants. The dog's name was Finder.

*****

Brady had now concentrated his thoughts on his options for extricating himself from his present dilemma. He could try digging with his hands, or perhaps he could find a pointed rock to remove some of the dirt and debris covering three-fourths of his body. He considered yelling, but like Saeed, he was concerned that anyone who might respond could be the enemy.

Brady had noticed his breathing was becoming more frequent, and the air seemed thinner. It was apparent the space that Saeed and Brady now occupied was not ventilated, and the small opening in the top of their cave was not sufficient to provide enough oxygen, which was slowly diminishing. Brady had no way of knowing the size of the space they were in, but he now realized that it was confined and limited. Saeed, too, had now become aware of the limitations of their surroundings and that a prolonged stay in their present environment would be deadly for him as well.

Saeed hoped his men would return for him, but he was uncertain when that might happen. Brady knew Khalid or others would at least launch a search party to find him, but how long that would take was unknown.

In the meantime, the two men participated in small talk while listening intently for any indication that someone was near or at least in the area. Brady had been curious as to why an obviously intelligent, educated man like Saeed could be so devoted to what Brady considered a blatant disregard for human life and its values.

"So tell me," Brady asked, "what brought you to join the rebels and lead a life of terrorizing your own people as well as the Americans who are attempting to help them?"

Saeed thought for a moment. His first inclination was to ignore Brady, but he felt the need to participate in some discourse, if for no other reason than to help pass the time. Saeed responded by relating his journey to America, how he had been helped by a businessman his father knew, how he had been accepted into Virginia Tech University, had traveled to America, and settled in Blacksburg, Virginia. Saeed stated how he had ample occasion to witness firsthand the bias of whites against all minorities, especially the Jews and blacks.

He told Brady of experiencing humiliating taunts from fellow students, who referred to the color of his skin, his background, and worst of all, how many of these insensitive acts occurred in front of Anna, with whom he had developed a deep friendship. Saeed went on to mention that white boys had hurled epithets, including the word "nigger" both in private and public, against the black students, including the Potters, their son, and daughter. The N-word was even directed towards Saeed, referring to him as a "sand nigger," and "turban head." Saeed related how he had watched on television the many instances of police brutality against blacks, and what he saw as a breakdown of justice, especially when the offending police officers avoided punishment or suffered only minor reprimands.

But this was only part of Saeed's detest for Americans and what he considered their hypocrisy. Saeed had noticed how the religious attire worn by Muslims was the object of snickering and even disdain written across the faces of white people. He had seen articles written in newspapers, sacrilegious cartoons, and other debasing comments about Allah and the Muslims who worshipped him. Saeed couldn't understand how all Muslims could be held responsible for the acts of a very few terrorists and radicals. He felt that Americans were not only hypocrites, going to their church or synagogue on the weekends and then committing sacrilege against the beliefs of others during the week.

Brady was taken aback by the passion and vehemence contained in the tone of the words now erupting from Saeed. Brady sensed that Saeed had obviously harbored these feelings for some time. Brady saw a pause in Saeed's tirade and decided to interject his own feelings on the subject of bias in America.

"Americans," he said, "are no different from other people in this world. We all have built-in prejudices that we have absorbed from our particular environments, both in our upbringing and extending even into our adult lives. It always seems easier to accept the opinions and beliefs of those close to us than to form our own independent opinions and beliefs."

"Yes, we have serious problems in our society, but through our democratic process, we are trying to eliminate these social injustices. Albeit belatedly, we are expanding our educational facilities to serve all without regard to race, creed, or financial status. America is aware that prejudice is a cancer that grows from a lack of knowledge and understanding of those around us. How often have you encountered a person of different attire, different religion, or even a different color of their skin, and immediately formed an opinion of that person? It's akin to judging a book by its cover. Without ever reading it, you have no idea what it's really about." Saeed smiled to himself as he recalled these same words spoken by Anna.

"We need," Brady continued, "to get to know those we are judging so at least we have some basis to form that opinion. How often have you encountered someone and immediately surmised you didn't like them, or that you did not want to associate with them, only to find out after getting to know more about them, that they were not what you thought?"

"The thing we forget, or refuse to accept, is that the color of our skin, our intelligence, our physical makeup, etc., is simply an accident of nature. We have no choice of parents, of the social, financial, educational, or even religious environment to which we are born. If we, as humans, wish to occupy this Earth in peace and harmony with our fellow man, then we need to not only understand our own needs but see life through the eyes of those with whom we must share this world."

Brady continued, "It is the lack of knowledge about our fellow man that foments our fears and concerns for their motives and goals. If, by some work of magic, we could appreciate the fact that others may not share our own needs and desires, then we could work towards a true reconciliation of our differences and at least strive towards solutions. For us to turn our backs on those with whom we disagree, we might as well set off a chain reaction of nuclear weapons and blow up the world. After tiring of ages of wars, we began a League of Nations and eventually a United Nations to provide an alternative to war. These organizations were created to give a forum to those nations with grievances to resolve their disputes in a peaceful manner. As we know, these organizations have not solved all the problems, but certainly, they have kept us from destroying ourselves thus far. If someday all our representatives can approach the negotiating table with a sincere desire to reach a balance of the varying needs of all the peoples of the world, giving up our own selfish desires, we may all live in peace without fear of our neighbors. No easy solution but one that I believe is attainable."

Saeed had been listening intently to Brady's words. Brady was just espousing the American rhetoric that Saeed had heard many times in America. In Saeed's eyes, Americans did not follow their own teachings. Saeed believed that Allah looked after everyone who believed in Him and that every true believer would either enjoy the blessings of Allah during one's lifetime and/or in the afterlife.

Saeed felt that Brady had omitted one very important element in his dissertation on humanity, and that was religion. Saeed fervently believed that Allah was the only God, and that Allah would ultimately decide the course of the world and mankind's fate. Thus, Saeed believed it was essential in everyday life that homage and devotion must be paid to Allah, and worldly matters were secondary. He understood the problems this might create with those of different religious beliefs but discounted the value of these differences because, as he believed, Allah was the only true God, and all the nonbelievers would perish eventually.

*****

Micah and his men were searching in the darkness, listening for any hint or movement that would indicate Saeed was nearby. Khalid and his men were now unknowingly just fifty yards from where the ground had toppled Saeed and Captain Brady into their subterranean prison. Khalid's men were using searchlights to illuminate the area. Micah and his men suddenly spotted Khalid and his men and immediately took cover. Finder had picked up the scent of humans in the tracks left in the dust and sand and had begun barking to indicate such.

One of Micah's men slipped on a loose rock, and Finder heard him. Finder immediately pulled his handler towards the sounds. Khalid ordered one of his men to fire off a flare to light up the area. Micah's men were now exposed and opened fire on Khalid's men. A firefight rapidly developed, with automatic rifles and grenades pounding both sides. Micah had his men take cover behind the boulders, and Khalid did the same. The firefight raged on for almost fifteen minutes before Micah decided to order his outnumbered detail back to their camp. As the insurgents retreated, Khalid's force attempted to follow and engage them but lost them in the darkness. Khalid considered releasing Finder but did not want to risk losing him in the dark.

Micah, however, had remained hidden in the area after instructing his men to return to their home base. Micah made sure he was downwind so Finder would hopefully not pick up his scent. Micah had noticed a depression in the area of the firefight. He wanted to see if, by luck, Saeed might have fallen into one of the tunnels. If this were true, perhaps Saeed was still alive. Micah had been close to Saeed and was the most loyal of his men. On more than one occasion, Saeed had saved Micah's life by risking his own in the process.

*****

Brady continued, "Describe to me, Saeed, what Allah looks like. What is His form? Is it similar to man, or is it more like a spirit that permeates our every experience, much like a drifting fog across the land? And in doing so, please describe Allah's relationship to not only Earth and its inhabitants but the rest of the universe."

At first, Saeed felt he should ignore the grumblings of an infidel, but instead, he fired back at Brady. "Allah exists beyond our human experiences. He has always existed, before the universe which He created. He is spiritual in that He has no materiality and can be viewed only in our minds."

Brady pressed on, "How does Allah communicate with you, or your people?"

"Allah communicates through His blessings to those who worship and devote themselves to Him."

Brady was aware that the questions he posed to Saeed were questions he had long pondered himself, as to his own Catholic religion. Brady pressed on, repeating what he said earlier, "Maybe your Allah and my God are the same," spoke Brady. "Perhaps we are all the creation of the same deity. Can we at least agree that our respective religions have evolved from lore passed down through the ages and recorded by scribes in books that form the basis for the Old and New Testament as well as the Quran? Have you actually spoken with Allah? Have you witnessed his presence among man?"

Saeed quickly responded that Allah was not interested in proving he existed or dealing with the trivial matters that face all humans daily.

"So then, we are left with just our faith, are we not?" asked Brady. Mankind is supposed to obey the teachings handed down by men who claim their writings were the word of God or Allah. For instance, Mohammed, in the cave, when he listened and memorized the word of Allah which formed the basis of the Quran. Moses when he received the Ten Commandments which would lay the foundation for several other religions. Thus, we are asked to devote our lives to that supreme being of whom we know nothing except that which has been handed down mouth to mouth and book to book from our forefathers. What's even more difficult to understand is that mankind relies on these sources to justify their actions, even if it's beheading an infidel."

Saeed listened and quickly pointed out, "Brady and his fellow believers had done the same down through the ages. Just take the Crusades, the crucifixions, the nuclear destruction inflicted upon Hiroshima and Nagasaki during the end of World War II."

Brady knew he was treading on sacrilege, but he sensed that by exposing his own doubts and longing for answers, he might cause Saeed to examine his own beliefs. Saeed had listened intently to Brady's comments. Saeed was impressed that Brady would admit to doubts of his own religious beliefs, but he held vehemently to his dedication to Allah and his Muslim doctrine. Saeed's thoughts drifted to the many battles in which he had been engaged, the many infidels he had killed, and the innocent women and children who often had been slain.

Saeed recalled the many nights he lay awake thinking about the incongruity of it all, the contradictions that he often faced between right and wrong. Why would Allah create humans whom He knew would not be believers, some of which yet would live righteous lives, dedicated to doing good for their fellow man, and demand that these same infidels should be slain?

Brady, ironically, found himself engrossed in the colloquy between the two. Brady wanted to push further, hoping that Saeed might share some of his ideas to help enlighten the subject of mankind's creation and its purpose on Earth. Saeed, at first, felt a competition with Brady, but now he too, in what appeared to be their last moments, longed to delve into the taboo subject of the Creator.

"What is your best guess," he asked Brady, "as to what our creator is like?"

After a long moment of silence, Brady began, "Men are created with certain senses, five as far as we know. Our perceptions generated by these senses, as well as our ability to discern their meaning, is all we have to offer to any deity. Therefore, if the deity is in a form that exceeds our human abilities of perception, then it may not be feasible for us to fully comprehend His existence."

Saeed interrupted, "Tell me how you think the world was created. How the universe came to be, how we came to be."

These were questions pregnant with possible answers, but Brady had dealt with them before and proffered his thoughts. "The only true answers, for ourselves, come from one's inner being. We cannot feel, sense, or absorb what another is thinking, but only what he expresses that can be picked up by our senses. Therefore, we must rely on our psyche to supply the answers to these questions. Input from others still has to be filtered through our own intellect. Man is capable of reason, and by reason, we can produce certain truths. One truth is that I didn't create myself, but if I did, I don't remember. Thus, someone or something created me. This could be by accident, by the big bang theory, or by a greater power than myself. This greater power is what I believe is our creator. Physics partially explains the creation of the universe. Quantum mechanics delves deeper and deeper into a world beyond our present capabilities. However, man's ability to innovate seems to be opening the doors of the unknown, about a world whose mysteries are slowly being unraveled by modern science. Man first had to learn to live together, in order to avoid his destruction under the law of the jungle. For his protection, man formed unions with others. From these unions, man formed communities and later cities, countries, and even nations. All of these unions were the result of man's desire to live more comfortably and without fear of harm."

Brady continued, "As man evolved further, he searched for more comfort and consequently more pleasure. This led to selfishness and a desire to have as much if not more than his fellow man. Countries, in turn, reflected these same desires and this has led to wars. Early on, man realized this would happen and so they constructed certain rules for man to accept in order to avoid these confrontations generated by desires for more comfort and pleasure. In support of these new rules, some form of enforcement was needed to see that man abided by the rules. The enforcement took the form of a deity (or deities) that man would have to worship and offer a sacrifice to ensure that he would survive. The icing on the cake would be the promise of an afterlife if man fulfilled his devotion and dedication to such deity or deities or punishment if man failed. To give more credibility to these rules, it was recorded that the deity had personally given them to religious leaders, who in turn promulgated the rules to all of mankind."

Brady caught himself, realizing that he was espousing the doctrine of an atheist. Something completely abhorrent to him, and not at all what he truly believed. Brady quickly clarified some statements he had just made, to make certain that Saeed understood that Brady was still dedicated to his Catholic religion. Brady added, "Yes, I believed in Moses, the Mount, the fiery bush where God spoke to Moses, Lazarus emerging from the cave after three days." Brady quickly added that he believed in the Apostles, their teachings, and the benevolent spirit of God and His grace. "Why," he asked, as Saeed listened intently, "because I feel this is the proper path to please God, and at the same time, to care for our fellow man, to strive for peace, to protect and care for those in need."

Saeed listened quietly and tried to overcome the desire to unleash the vitriol that lurked in his head.

Brady realized he had delved further into his most inner beliefs than he had ever gone before. Saeed felt he was betraying his own beliefs by even listening to what he considered were Brady's ramblings. Both men simultaneously slumped into a period of quiet contemplation of what they had just discussed. Their silence was soon interrupted by the faint sound of rifle fire and grenades exploding. But within moments, the sounds stopped. Saeed and Brady grew solemn, not knowing what was coming next. They each hoped and prayed they would be discovered soon.

*****

Micah decided that the men under Sergeant Khalid had abandoned the area. He remembered an entrance to the tunnels that was hidden and only about fifty yards from the sunken ground he had observed previously. Micah hurried to the entrance, and once inside, he used his flashlight to guide himself through the tunnels to where he believed Saeed may have ended up if indeed Saeed was the victim of a cave-in. When Micah neared the approximate area beneath the sunken ground above, he encountered a sudden end to the tunnel. A mound of dirt had closed off a portion of the tunnel. He could see that this was newly disturbed earth, and Saeed could possibly be buried therein, or there was a slight possibility that Saeed was still inside the tunnel, separated from Micah by the mound of dirt.

Micah grabbed a discarded pointed piece of wood, probably used in the construction of the tunnels, and began digging to see if he could penetrate the surrounding mound of dirt. At the same time, he spoke Saeed's name over and over.

Saeed and Brady had retired from their dialectic and both had slowly begun to accept the fact that they would not be found. Saeed was the first to detect a faint sound. The sound was recurring over and over, and Saeed suddenly recognized the voice of his comrade and friend Micah. Saeed was jubilant and immediately yelled Micah's name. Micah acknowledged and asked if Saeed was injured. Saeed responded that he was unable to move but had no serious injury.

Captain Brady listened, turning his head towards the sounds that he now realized had been emanating from behind him, except that now the sounds became increasingly louder, and he heard Saeed's name shouted over and over. Brady now realized the help that had arrived was not for him but for his enemy. Brady began to pray, not for himself, but for Lois, Sara, and Michael. Micah continued digging through the blockage of dirt until he could poke a hole all the way through the dirt to an opening. He peered inside, but it was dark, and he was unable to see exactly where Saeed was located. Micah kept digging. It would be another fifteen minutes before he could make his breakthrough large enough for him and Saeed to slide through. Neither Saeed nor Brady could tell exactly where Micah was located. They spotted his flashlight that flickered from the small hole where Micah had punched through.

Brady was silent as Micah slowly made his way through the rubble to where he could crawl inside the opening he had made. Micah yelled, "Saeed," and Saeed responded, indicating his position to Micah. Micah crawled by Brady to get to Saeed. As he did so, he paused, and Brady assumed he would meet his fate at Micah's hands. Instead, Micah crawled directly to Saeed and began extricating Saeed from his entombment.

Once freed, Saeed and Micah began crawling back towards the hole Micah had dug and from which he had just emerged. As they passed Captain Brady, Micah looked quizzically at Saeed. Saeed paused and then told Micah to keep on crawling. There was no further communication among the three of them. Both Micah and Saeed reached the exit and within minutes had crawled through to the tunnel and then were gone. Brady knew he had been left to die.

Saeed, with Micah's help, made it out of the tunnel, and in minutes the pair caught up with their comrades heading back to their base. As Saeed revealed himself, there was a hushed cry of relief from his men. Saeed was back and safe. The small group headed north towards their camp to rendezvous with their main force.

Brady could feel the slow drifting of air coming from the hole Micah had dug to gain entrance to what Brady now considered his burial place. He considered the fact that he may never be discovered and most likely would suffer a slow death from lack of food and water. Brady felt a sense of panic fostered by the darkness, numbness in most of his body, and the inability to free himself.

Then, as if a gift from God, Brady, while frantically scratching at the dirt around him, felt a sharp pain in his one hand. It was the point of the discarded stick Micah had used to dig into the cavernous area where he found Saeed and Brady. Brady was ecstatic. He frantically began digging the ground around his body. After approximately fifteen minutes, he was able to slowly extricate himself from his predicament.

Brady slowly crawled towards the opening from which Saeed and Micah had recently exited. Brady had almost complete control of his arms, but from his waist down, he found himself too weak to run. Once free of the entombment, Brady followed the footprints left in the tunnel floor by Saeed and Micah just an hour or so before. Knowing that he may run into them, Brady slowly approached the exit from the tunnel, and after looking about, decided it was safe to stagger into the fresh air. His first impulse was to thank God for his deliverance. Brady hesitated, got bearings on his position, and headed in the direction where he was sure his unit would be located. Major Khouri and his men had given up on tracking down Saeed's men and had ordered his own men to regroup and head back to their base. Brady stumbled and walked about a mile before he was spotted by one of Khalid's men. Immediately he was assisted, and a Hummer vehicle appeared from nowhere to drive him back to the base.

On the way back to the base, Brady pondered over the ordeal he had just endured, and the conversations he had with Saeed. He couldn't quite understand how a man as educated and intelligent as Saeed could be so passionately committed to a belief in another God, a God that encouraged savagery and beheadings of non-believers. Brady sensed that he and Saeed had each been affected deeply by their own upbringing and environment. What perplexed him the most was how difficult it would be for them to ever reconcile the differences in their fundamental beliefs.

*****

Once back at the base, after receiving medical treatment for his calf injury, Major Khouri insisted on a detailed account of Brady's encounter with Saeed and details of their conversations, especially as those details may have provided any military insights into Saeed's unit. Brady was happy to oblige.

After the debriefing, Brady looked forward to a shower and lots of sleep. Not only was his body tired, his mind was also. He went to his quarters, stopped briefly at the mess hall for some soup, and hit the sack. Brady drifted into a deep sleep that lasted eighteen hours.

The next day, Brady awoke, dressed, and sought out Major Khouri. Brady wanted to begin his preparation for discharge, which meant he needed Major Khouri to sign off on his current assignment. Instead of this discussion, Major Khouri informed Brady that he had been up most of the night. Khouri's men had engaged in a commando raid on Saeed's unit, and after several hours of battle, Saeed's unit had been destroyed. Khalid had led the assault, comprised of the three helicopters, mobile artillery, and airstrikes from F-15 fighter jets. Brady was sorry he had missed the action but happy for Major Khouri and his victory. Brady learned that his debriefing with Major Khouri had provided valuable insight into the possible location of Saeed's men.

Brady felt the need to inquire whether Saeed had been killed. The consensus was that Saeed had perished in the initial airstrikes. Brady viewed this as a denouement. Somehow, he wished he had been able to communicate more with Saeed on their different philosophies.

*****

A few weeks later, Brady's tour of duty was over. He boarded an Air Force plane in Baghdad and headed back to Fort Dix, New Jersey, for his discharge. From there, he flew commercial direct to O'Hare Field in Chicago, Illinois. Lois, Sarah, and Michael met him at the terminal gate. Brady was enthralled with the sight of his wife and two children. He had prayed many times for this moment, a moment he knew he would cherish forever.

It had been almost two years since he had seen his family. Sarah was now a teenager in the eighth grade, and Michael was in his freshman year of high school. Lois made sure they maintained good grades in school and had successfully passed on to them her own moral compass. Their home was a simple, comfortable, two-story, four-bedroom split level located in the suburbs of Chicago. For the next few months, Brady would spend his time with his wife and children, enjoying the things he had often dreamed of doing when he returned home.

He would spend time taking them fishing on the lake and imparting his knowledge and love of sports to both. Sarah had participated, and was very good, in girls' field hockey. Michael had signed up for junior varsity football, which put a gleam in Brady's eye. Every chance he got, Brady threw around the football with Michael and taught him the ins and outs of the game. Lois acknowledged that both kids seemed happier since Brady was back. Sarah became closer to her mom, and Michael did the same with his dad.

Brady began contemplating what vocation he would settle into and started scanning the help-wanted ads in the paper. He had thought about maybe teaching, but this required a teaching degree in education. He also pondered over a position with an investment firm on the Chicago Exchange. This had always excited him, especially with his respect for economics as it affects the political establishments.

On a warm Saturday morning in October, Michael had an important game to play for the junior varsity championship. Brady was awakened by Michael at nine a.m., even though the game was not until noon. Brady jumped into his clothes, and he and Michael headed outdoors to go over Michael's assignments as quarterback. For the next two hours, Brady quizzed Michael on his passing routes, his checkoffs, as well as his play-calling. Not so much what play would be called, since the coach would do that, but what changes the defense would have for each play. Michael had developed his father's quick grasp of the game and had natural ability when it came to selecting his receivers and calling an audible when the defense dictated in favor of a better play option.

As Michael and his teammates gathered together before the opening whistle, they grasped hands, asked for the Lord's blessing, and tore onto the field to play. The game was uneventful, and Michael's team maintained a lead going into the final two minutes. Michael's coach sent in a play that called for the right flanker to run a post pattern downfield. Michael called the play in the huddle and clasped his hands, signaling the team to line up on the football.

Danny, a small African American, smiled at Michael, confident he could outsmart the defensive back and slip into the clear. Upon the snap of the ball, Michael dropped back five steps and let loose a perfect spiral towards Danny. Danny faked to his right, drawing the defensive back with him, and immediately turned towards his appointed spot to catch the ball. Just as the ball reached Danny, he reached up, grabbed the ball, and crossed the goal line.

The defensive back that Danny had beaten tackled Danny after he had crossed the goal line and intentionally dug his knee into Danny's neck. Danny lay there gasping for breath while Brady and Michael's coach rushed to the end zone where Danny lay. Danny's father, a tall muscular man, also rushed to Danny's side. Danny suddenly stopped breathing. Brady immediately began CPR, and Danny slowly began to breathe in air.

Brady consoled Danny's father and insisted the local firemen who attended all of the boys' games check Danny's vital signs. They did, and Danny was given a thumbs up to get up and join his family. The boy who had injured Danny stood on the near sideline, and Brady heard him remark to a man next to him, who turned out to be his father, that he was glad that he had "hurt that nigger." His father replied with a grin and said, "Nice hit."

Brady's first impulse was to respond to the insensitive and prejudicial comments, but instead, he simply looked at Danny and his dad and rolled his eyes in a manner that all could understand to be his contempt for that boy's attitude, and especially his father's comments. Brady had anticipated when he contemplated his return home from the war that he would encounter some racial prejudice, but nonetheless, hearing it so openly and without regard for the impact such hateful words could have on people like Danny and his family didn't make it any easier to comprehend.

On the way home from the game, Brady asked his son Michael if he knew the other boy who had tackled Danny. Michael said he did and that the boy was in his Sunday school class at church. Michael explained he is always bullying the other boys and girls and uses disturbing language when referring to the race and religion of fellow students, especially when the kid was around Blacks, Muslims, and other people of color.

Brady made a point to let Michael know that he must not allow a bully like this kid to influence him in any manner that would cause Michael to criticize others for the accident of their birth, their ethnicity, or their religion. Michael smiled and told his father he was okay with dealing with such prejudice, and his participation therein was not an option.

*****

Several months later, Brady accepted a position with a large bank with branches spread out in the suburbs of Chicago. He would start as a security officer for a local branch, and if he did well and exhibited supervisory skills, he was promised accelerated promotions. While earning his wings, Brady enjoyed observing the many types of customers that frequented the bank. He loved meeting new people and studying their different habits, cultures, and general demeanor when interfacing with them.

As part of his responsibility, Brady was required to frequently converse with the employees and brief them on security procedures, especially in case of a robbery or other disturbance that might affect the safety of the customers and their deposits. Because of his obvious congeniality and interpersonal skills, Brady quickly acquired a group of bank customers who regularly enjoyed some light banter and conversations with him. He often found himself assisting customers with simple matters like where the restrooms were located, who to see for loans and mortgages, and how to fill out some of their forms for various banking activities.

Although Brady appreciated the compensation he was earning and the benefits that went with his employment, he found himself missing the stress and strain of everyday action in the service of his country, especially his last year in Iraq. His thoughts often drifted to Major Khouri, Sergeant Khalid, and the rest of the comrades he had left overseas. He found he had blocked from his memory the details of the inhuman indignities and insensitivity that he had experienced—the atrocities that some men could inflict upon others. Somewhere, in the hidden corners of his mind, Brady wondered what might have become of Saeed. Had he met an untimely end? Would Saeed have become a leader of his country, a beacon for his fellow man in comprehending the complexity of the political and religious cultures of that part of the world? Or would he have become just another fanatic bent upon wreaking damage and pain upon his fellow man? Brady had convinced himself that the world would somehow be a better place if more Saeeds of the world would listen, analyze, and evaluate the intellectual discourse among opposing minds. Still, buried deep in his psyche, Brady understood that Saeed was a skillful, unrelenting killer and that the world was better off with him dead.

One Friday evening, when the bank was open until seven thirty, Brady was on duty and conversing with various bank customers standing in line to do their banking. A regular customer that Brady often encountered at the bank inquired of Brady as to where the men's restroom was located. The customer asked Brady to please save his place in line to see the teller. Brady acknowledged that he would, and the customer disappeared. Upon returning, the customer approached Brady, and Brady took him to his previous spot, which happened to be next in line to see the teller. When Brady had done so, a person at the end of the line yelled that the person Brady had helped back in line should return to the end of the line. Brady explained what had occurred, but the angry man at the end of the line blurted out a few expletives referring to the customer's obvious age and the fact he was African American.

Brady's first impulse was to lash out at the individual, but reason settled in, and he tried to explain to the rude individual that the customer helped back in line had simply gone to the restroom and Brady had saved his place in line. The angry man then turned his anger upon Brady, making fun of his security uniform and that Brady had a would-be cop's job. Brady then realized this was the same man whose son had tackled Danny beyond the goal line and had complimented his son for the nice hit. With this sudden realization, Brady, in a more forceful voice, asked him to calm down. The man challenged Brady with, "What you gonna do? You don't have a weapon." Brady asked the man to please leave the bank. This is when the man swung at Brady, and with one punch, Brady sent him to the floor writhing in pain with blood coming from his nose. Police were summoned by the branch manager and the man was escorted out of the bank.

The remaining customers applauded Brady's handling of a difficult situation, and the manager smiled at how quickly and appropriately Brady had reacted. Brady apologized to all in the bank that he had to resort to force. Inwardly, it felt good that he still had the ability to recognize danger and react accordingly.

*****

Several uneventful weeks passed by, and Brady realized that slowly but surely he was becoming bored with his job. During his Walter Mitty moments, Brady daydreamed about the days in Iraq and the battles with the insurgents. Though he had blocked out much of his memories of the devastation, hunger, and human misery, Brady still missed the action and the feeling of pride that he was serving his country to help these foreign people attain liberty and freedom for all.

It was during one of these days of dallying that Brady was approached by his immediate supervisor with respect to a possible job offer. Upon further discussion, the man explained that he had witnessed the way Brady had calmly handled the incident in the bank, and that had led him to think of Brady when the bank had created a new position, one which he thought Brady might be interested in. He explained the job title as Financial Intelligence Director for the bank and that it would require knowledge of banking, investigative skills, and working in unison with bank auditors and government regulators.

Not only was he interested, but Brady was also eager for the opportunity to advance his position with the bank. The Bank, Union International (UI), had expanded since Brady was first employed, and presently maintained and operated ten branches throughout the US and a couple of branches in Iran and the UAE. Brady had only recently experienced a few businessmen who came into the branch where he worked, who appeared Middle Eastern, and had business dealings with Iran. Brady's supervisor explained that the position had been created because of the bank's concern that certain transactions involving large sums had come under the watchful eye of the Internal Revenue Service, and it was only a matter of time before the bank would be audited. UI wanted to make sure that there was nothing going on at the bank that would not survive close scrutiny.

Brady applied for the position, hoping his undergraduate work in accounting and tax law, coupled with his intelligence training in the service, would be sufficient to qualify him for the position. He filled out the application and ran it by his supervisor (and his wife). Upon their approval, he submitted it to the bank's human resources department. He was informed that the review process would take about two weeks, and he would be notified to come in for an interview, if selected.

Exactly two weeks later, Brady received that phone call requesting him to sit for an interview with the bank's committee that had been assigned to select the person for the position. Brady was excited and yet alarmed that perhaps he wasn't qualified or that he was untrained in the nature and extent of the transactions that he would be reviewing. These feelings soon disappeared once his briefing for the position began. He was greeted by two intelligence officers from the US Banking Commission as well as one gentleman with the bank.

The interview went on for over two hours. Brady was questioned on everything from his childhood, marriage, education, and religious and political beliefs, as well as an intensive discussion involving his service in the Army. He was as honest and forthright as he had been with his superior officers in the service, conveying his own moral compass and passion for the ideals he valued. Brady, when asked what experiences stood out in his mind from his days in Iraq, immediately recalled the encounter with Saeed and especially the time he and Saeed spent disarmed and alone in the cave-in. The two intelligence officers seemed acutely interested in his description of this episode in his life and his conversations with Saeed.

After the interview was completed, Brady was told he would have their answer within a week. Brady was now excited and surprisingly optimistic about his chances of getting the position. He enjoyed the emphasis that had been placed on his experience with Saeed and the insurgent forces. Although it brought back many painful memories, the interview helped him revisit his goals in life, especially to provide a better and financially secure life for his family.

Back home, Sarah, Michael, and their mother Lois all supported Brady in his desire to succeed in the pursuit of this position. Although Lois secretly feared the job might require traveling away from home and perhaps even overseas, she kept this to herself, not wanting to spoil the excitement and enthusiasm that exuded from her husband. One week after the interview, Brady was called into the branch manager's office where he had been working that day.

The manager was short and matter-of-fact, perhaps knowing Brady would no longer be handling security for the branch. The committee had been unanimous in their selection of Brady for the position. The manager congratulated Brady on his selection and informed him he was to report for orientation the following day.

What followed were weeks of training in the criminal side of banking, including money laundering, identity theft, document falsification, and in-depth sessions dealing with hidden account owners and suspicious bank transactions. Brady was enjoying what he was learning and was eager to begin this new phase of his life. He discovered how little he knew about the ease with which ne'er-do-wells could manipulate the investment markets, how these people could bring a national and even global economy to its knees, as had been done during the 2007 and 2008 debacle in the housing market. He learned how stock market investors, hedge fund managers, and day traders were able to profit by manipulating the markets by spreading rumors via third parties, shielding themselves from charges of insider trading. He learned the true meaning of greed as he analyzed and digested case histories of large market swings and fluctuations in currency values, how hackers and con artists used identity theft to purge depositors' bank accounts, and so many other areas of concern for the banking industry. Brady was thankful for the economics courses he had taken in college.

At first, Brady felt overwhelmed, but slowly he realized that his training in Army intelligence could be applied to the new position. He recognized how similar his Army training in interrogation and processing of voluminous documentation was to the procedures used by the bank in his preparation for the job he was about to undertake.

After nearly three months of training, Brady was promoted to his new position of Financial Intelligence Director. His boss, Mr. Preston Jenkins, an ex-Army officer like himself, was a small man of five feet eight with a Van Dyke beard that caused him to look like a college professor, not the president of the bank. He was in his mid-fifties, somewhat nerdy looking, but with a sharp intelligence that Brady quickly discerned was why they had made him president ten years ago.

Brady wore no uniform but was surprised when he was handed his weapon, a .38-caliber snub nose with a shoulder holster. He was told to report for arms training, which brought a smile to his face since he had been trained with almost every hand weapon as well as rifles and automatic weapons in the Army. After one day of firing on the range, Brady qualified as expert with the .38-caliber snub-nose pistol.

Brady was briefed on his staff, which consisted of each branch location's security guard and their regional supervisors. He would receive a daily briefing from the regional supervisors on any unusual or suspected activities, as well as any information that the bank officials deemed important and relevant to Brady's responsibilities. One of his perks would be a company vehicle to assist him in routine visitation and inspections at the various branches.

For the days and weeks that followed, Brady became familiar with his day-to-day routine, which amounted to daily briefings, occasional visits to local branches, and meetings with people under his authority, covering everything from personal problems to ideas concerning how to improve the bank's security procedures.

*****

It had been over two years since Brady had assumed his new position. It was only now that he felt comfortable in the job. He had learned to read ledgers, balance sheets, tax returns, and other documentation as they applied to the bank's relationships not only with its depositors, but also the bank's officers and stockholders. Brady was astutely aware of the bank's obligations under the aegis of the Securities and Exchange Commission (SEC) as well as other governmental agencies providing oversight to the US banking system.

Previously, he had heard the bank officials he worked under complain about the ubiquitous nature of the rules and regulations governing the many different areas of finance and banking. Brady had been made aware that bank personnel had to be proficient and constantly alert for violations of these rules and regulations, as well as the numerous scams that they faced on a daily basis. These were the areas that both worried and fascinated Brady. In the two years he had enjoyed his job, he had evolved into an aficionado of the ways and means the scam artists utilized, especially cyber-attacks, to cheat people, banks, and credit card companies out of their money.

One area in particular that worried Brady was how easily fooled and vulnerable to intimidation the elderly were. They could be cheated out of their life savings simply by a phone call threatening arrest, or worse, if they didn't immediately send payment of an obviously fictitious debt or, even worse, a tax deficiency. Brady had seen how many senior citizens were very sensitive concerning their forgetfulness and reluctance to admit the same in the heat of such scams. No matter how frequently Brady distributed fliers and account notices of the most recent scams currently circulating and how to avoid these nefarious traps, the bank would still get voluminous calls and complaints of sad instances of such criminal activities.

In just one week, Brady had been made aware of several different accounts that were previously owned by persons who had passed away leaving no heirs or assigns. These accounts were dormant for various periods of time. Then the vultures, lying in wait, would come forth producing various forms of false identification documentation, all of which were easily obtained from public death records. They would then simply assign the account balances to a new account name, usually a business or other entity not easily traced. The new account was then depleted. In many instances, no one was ever aware of the illegal transactions.

But beyond the frequent attacks on the elderly and vulnerable, Brady was seeing more and more activities of a curious nature that didn't involve the day-to-day depositors. One bank account in particular caught Brady's attention in that periodically the account balance would fluctuate wildly from one to two million to as much as five billion. The deposits would be anywhere from two or three million to as much as half a billion dollars. The account owner was a large international corporation with its headquarters in Yemen, an area of extreme unrest and a melting pot of nefarious type individuals.

Brady had never met any of the principals of this corporation, and when he inquired about them to his employees at the bank, he was provided with names of individuals of whom he was unaware and who had never, to Brady's knowledge, visited any of the bank branches. A quick check on Facebook and Google proved futile. Brady could understand the bank being secretive about the identity of the account principals, but this didn't belie the point that they, like every other depositor, had to comply with all banking regulations, especially those dealing with foreign transactional activities.

Nonetheless, Brady reconciled himself to paying attention to the day-to-day operations of the bank, but promised himself he would keep an eye on that particular account. He was curious, to say the least, as to where such large sums originated and where they ended up.

*****

Brady had come to love Fridays. This was the one day of the week when he would visit various branches of the bank just to check with the local managers and security personnel for briefings on any abnormal activities. He especially enjoyed meeting with the managers who could be relied upon for gossip information on major depositors in exchange for any innocuous gossip Brady might have encountered on his excursions throughout the bank branches.

He made it a priority to occasionally sit down to lunch with one or more of the employees to get a feel for day-to-day activities. These lunches inevitably led to complaints about the bank's operations, but more importantly, the lunches afforded Brady an opportunity to discuss possible violations of security, as well as possible violations of the banking laws and regulations.

On one of these Friday tours of the branches, Brady met with Wayne Caldwell, the assistant manager of the west side branch of the bank. Wayne had asked to have lunch with Brady the next time he visited Wayne's branch. This was the next time, and Brady had called ahead to make sure Wayne was available. They left the branch and went to the sub shop on the corner. The shop was small, and luckily they found an unoccupied table, one of only four in the shop.

After ordering a Reuben sub and soda, and Wayne having his usual Philly cheesesteak, the two began exchanging amenities.

Shortly, the conversation turned to the purpose for why Wayne had requested the luncheon. Brady had pondered the question and had guessed that Wayne probably had a bone to pick with management and expected Brady might intervene on his behalf.

Brady had already reviewed Wayne's personnel file. Wayne had graduated from Maryland University with a degree in business finance. Wayne had been with the bank for almost eight years. He had aspirations for becoming a branch manager and then perhaps someday an officer and/or a director at the bank. In his file was nothing but praise from his previous and current supervisors, and he was well liked and admired by his co-workers.

Wayne explained he had been observing the activity of one account, an account that usually carried an eight-figure balance. The reason for Wayne's interest in this particular account was the swiftness with which money deposited was so quickly diverted to another banking institution. Always, the other banking institution was located in a foreign country. Brady quickly pointed out that this type of activity, though not that unusual, was seen a lot in transactions involving the sale and purchase of real property and businesses, both here and abroad.

Wayne acknowledged Brady's explanation but stated his concern was the fact that with each such transaction, the money coming into the account would be from one foreign country and would be transferred out to another foreign country within two to three days. The normal transactions that Brady was describing would be, for example, a deposit of a substantial sum with the bank to be placed into an escrow account, and then wired to another bank whether here in this country or another. Wayne excitedly interjected that he would not be as concerned by the example Brady gave, but the difference between Brady's example and Wayne's was that the money came in from one country to the United States and then was almost immediately transferred to a third country.

Brady's interest had been piqued, but his gut told him there was most likely a simple explanation. He agreed with Wayne that he would look into it and get back to him as soon as he could.

*****

Fall was here and gone, and cold weather was settling in. Brady looked forward to the Saturdays he would be spending with Michael and his football games. Michael was seventeen now and had been elevated to quarterback on the high school varsity team. Brady was amazed at how much Michael had retained from last year and how adept he was at figuring out defenses, pass routes, and how to anticipate (and read) an all-out blitz.

The first game came quickly, and Michael was ready. The team was playing the same team they played last year when Danny, who was still playing wide receiver, had been hurt. Michael stated that the kid who had injured Danny was again playing for the opposing team this year. When Michael and Brady arrived at the playing field, sure enough, there was the boy and his father. Brady recalled the incident at the bank when the kid's father had to be restrained by Brady. Brady chose to ignore the kid and his father. Brady was here to enjoy the game, as was Michael, and they would not allow this past incident to spoil the occasion.

Brady had learned the father's name during the incident at the bank after he had floored him. When the police arrived, they asked for his identification. He had an Arabic name: Farrid, Abbas Farrid. The game was uneventful until the last two minutes. Michael's team was winning by two touchdowns. His coach was now calling all running plays to run the time clock down. Michael ran a dive play with the fullback off tackle. Farrid's son flew in from the defensive back position and put his helmet into the fullback's helmet, knocking the fullback unconscious. It was an illegal hit, and the defensive back was thrown out of the game.

Michael and the coach rushed to the kid lying unconscious and barely breathing. They restrained the young player from twisting or turning while unconscious to make sure there were no broken bones or a serious concussion. Slowly, the player began to wake and started moving his legs and arms, which indicated the player had not injured his spinal column, or worse. Brady watched as the coach's aide applied smelling salts under his nose. The player was now wide awake, and blurted out that he was okay and reached out to Brady to help him up. Brady put the kid's arm around his neck and slowly walked him back to the sideline. As he did, Brady heard Farrid yell to his son, "Nice tackle," just as the referee signaled a fifteen-yard penalty for targeting the runner. Farrid smirked at Brady as he helped the injured player off the field.

Michael's team went on to win the game. The fullback recovered with only a mild concussion. Brady asked the coach as they were leaving the field if he knew this Abbas Farrid. The coach looked at the man, smiled, and answered that he did and that he had met and spoken to Farrid at his curio shop in town. Farrid had mentioned that he dabbled in stocks, securities, and investments and also operated an import/export business. The coach further added that he had heard from friends that Farrid had once been in trouble with one of the government's agencies, but nothing ever came of it.

*****

Time seemed to fly by. Michael was now eighteen and in the twelfth grade at school. Brady tried to spend as much time as possible with his son. Brady was very aware that these were the substantive years when a young man or woman begins to formulate ideas and tenets that will last them a lifetime. Lately, Michael had been dropping little statements about politics and religion that Brady took as his attempt to enter into a dialogue with his father. Perhaps it was Michael's attempt to alert Brady that he was of an age that required parental encouragement and enlightenment in various phases of life, becoming more aware of the world around him, and a desire to better understand that world.

This particular Sunday, once the family returned from church and dinner was finished, Michael turned to his dad and asked why some people dislike others simply because of the clothes they wore, the color of their skin, the accent when they spoke, and the religion they practiced. He also asked Brady why some kids and grownups felt the need to bully others less able to defend themselves, either verbally, physically, or both. Brady finished helping Lois with the dishes and sat down in his favorite chair for what he expected to be a discussion of prejudice and social injustices. Michael was obviously becoming a very inquisitive young man, and Brady felt the need to convey his own perceptions and analysis to help quench his son's thirst for knowledge and understanding in these areas.

Brady started by explaining that most people have an innate feeling of kindliness and generosity, a tendency to respect and appreciate their fellow man. He explained that, in his opinion, the bulk of the people, from all over the world, think optimistically and therefore believe in their fellow man. They believe in the golden rule that says, "Do unto others as you would have them do unto you." However, he continued, there are also those who have very narrow views of the world and their fellow man. These people are often only concerned with imposing their own view of the world and how it should function. These people often attempt to impose their opinions on others by force. Thus, you have religious and political wars, bullying, and aggression against those with whom you disagree. These are the people who degrade, debase, and insult those who might look, dress, or practice religion and politics differently.

Michael interrupted Brady often. He wanted to know how each person, even each nation, knew their way of living was the right way, and who defines "the right way." Brady realized Michael had the type of mind every high school teacher and college professor longed for. That fertile, virgin mind that can't quench its thirst for knowledge. That desire to understand the turmoil, the hatred, and the aggression that seem to permeate this world we live in.

Michael began looking glassy-eyed, a look Brady had learned indicated Michael's confusion and misunderstanding. Brady then summarized what he had told him by an example: Brady stated that if Michael met a strange homeless man on the street, Michael might think, *What can I do for this man?* or, *What can this man do for me?* The purpose of the first statement would be for the benefit of the strange man, and the purpose of the second statement would be for Michael's own self-gratification.

Now Michael was beginning to see some daylight. Michael went on to give his own example that when the majority of people he knew met someone new, they would react as in the first example, that is to say, by seeing what they could do for that person. But

Michael quickly followed by saying that he also knew several guys (and some girls) who would immediately try to degrade the stranger, or in some selfish way bully or even make fun of the stranger. Brady smiled, knowing that Michael had indeed understood what he had been saying.

Brady went on to expand on Michael's example, explaining that selfish persons would harass the stranger for their skin color, dialect, clothing, mannerisms, and even their intellectual capabilities. In other words, if a person acted in the way he had just described, that person would find untold ways to elevate himself above what he perceived the stranger to be, to satisfy his own self-image.

Then Brady reminded Michael of the incident last year when Farrid had congratulated his son for the late hit on Michael's friend and classmate. This, Brady explained, was a clear example of someone who did not know Danny but, because of the color of his skin, had to satisfy his own inner self by enjoying his son's illegal hit upon Danny. Michael nodded his understanding. The lesson had been successful.

*****

Brady had just set out for his usual Friday rounds, swinging by several branches of the bank for his weekly inspection and to review any new complaints or security breaches. When he arrived at the branch where Wayne worked, he was immediately met by Wayne. Wayne had something he felt required Brady's attention. It seemed that one bank account Wayne had been monitoring was showing large in-and-out deposits of several hundred million dollars. Though this by itself was not unusual for a bank their size, the manner in which the money was transferred caught Wayne's attention. The money had originated from a bank in Nigeria, then transferred to Wayne's bank, and within forty-eight hours, the money was transferred out to a bank in Dubai in the United Arab Emirates.

Wayne informed Brady that he had a friend in the bank's overseas branch in the UAE and that he had emailed him to see if there was anything in this bizarre transaction that Wayne should be concerned about. Wayne's friend told him he would look into the matter and get back to him. Wayne had waited a few days, and when he didn't receive a call back, he called his friend again. This time the friend in Dubai sounded a bit disturbed and told Wayne everything was fine and not to worry. The friend explained that the transaction was merely to buy gold bullion on the international market. The question of why was never answered.

Brady contemplated the information that Wayne had provided and reviewed the documentation of the transaction in question. Brady concluded that nothing illegal had transpired, nor had any banking regulations been violated. He complimented Wayne on his dedication to duty as well as his suspicions, but nonetheless, there was nothing Brady could determine that would compel further action at this time.

Brady shared with Wayne his own concerns that dealt with computer hacking into customer accounts. The main offices of the bank had circulated notices to alert branch managers to monitor closely any abnormalities in the bank's computer activities. Brady had already been advised that there had been instances, although not a pattern, where bank customers had noticed small amounts being deducted from their accounts that had not been authorized. Not wanting to cause an uproar among its depositors, Brady directed Wayne, as he had the other branch managers, to conduct a due diligence search of depositor accounts. He told Wayne to run a computer check for small amounts appearing as fee charges, credit card charges, etc. Usually, the amounts would be under ten dollars.

Weeks went by, and Brady concerned himself with the new government that had just been elected and was now running the United States. There had been much dissension among the electorate, and it seemed the country was equally divided. Brady had not voted for the new president but felt a duty to respect and acknowledge his leadership of the most powerful nation on Earth. Lately, the media had been concerned with the president's relations with Russia and the Russian leader. The two had met several times recently and had signed a pact pledging cooperation between the two countries on such topics as trade, currency support, and nuclear arms controls.

Brady questioned whether the new president was sincere in attempting to improve relations with Russia or was naively getting cozy with the Russians, believing their propaganda or perhaps becoming enamored with the leader's dictatorial powers. Brady had recently read of a glitch in an electric grid in the northeastern United States that caused a temporary "blackout" of an entire city. The cause was attributed to a computer error, but some in the media said it was the result of a Russian hacker testing our nation's cyber defenses and industry security.

Brady had recently called an intelligence officer that he had trained with in the Army, John Bradford. Brady had stayed in touch with Bradford, and occasionally they spoke, usually about security matters for the country as well as the bank. Brady had asked Bradford what he thought of the blackout, and he told Brady that he was relatively sure the hacker was in Russia, probably Moscow. Bradford also informed Brady that the National Security Agency (NSA), where Bradford had been employed as an analyst for the past five years, had evidence to back this up. Bradford disclosed this information to Brady, knowing Brady was cleared for access to top-secret information and documents.

Bradford too was an ex-Army Ranger and had served his country well for twelve years prior to being offered a job with the NSA as an analyst. After several years of black ops assignments, he found himself longing for less stressful employment. He was fluent in Russian and Chinese. He was presently stationed at NSA headquarters near Fort Meade in Maryland, right outside of the District of Columbia.

Brady felt comfortable with Bradford both as a close friend and as a confidant on security matters for the bank. During their respective tours of duty, the two had crossed paths in Afghanistan and Iraq on several occasions, usually in connection with intelligence raids on insurgent locations. On these occasions, Brady came to respect the bravery and common sense that Bradford exhibited. Each maintained a deep respect for the other and harbored a sense of reliance on each other borne out of the close encounters with death that they had shared.

Bradford had on several occasions warned Brady to be alert to any unusual activity with computer-generated transactions affecting depositor accounts, wire transfers, and any suspicious deductions from checking and savings accounts generally in deceptively small amounts. Brady had heeded this advice, and that was the advice he had given to Wayne as well as all security officers at each branch.

It was Friday, on a cold December day, and Brady was completing his rounds of the various branches. He had purposely made Wayne's branch the last stop. He could almost certainly rely upon Wayne to be prepared for the visit with an agenda of concerns and suspicions of certain banking transactions that had caught his attention. Today was no exception. The wind had been picking up, and Brady welcomed the opportunity to sit and talk and shake the chill he had from the cold, even if it meant listening to Wayne methodically and painstakingly cover his checklist of concerns.

On this occasion, Wayne was overly excited and began recounting the actions that had precipitated his anxiety. Several days before, Wayne had met with a bank teller who stated to him that she had been working on daily wire transfers when she noticed an incoming wire transfer for a hundred million dollars. The wire originated in Rio de Janeiro, Brazil. However, a few hours later, the same amount was ordered by the account owner to be transferred to Athens, Greece, to a large international corporation that, among many other holdings, owned a fleet of oil tankers. The bank teller had taken the liberty of tracing the sender from Rio and determined the money came from a shell corporation that listed only meager assets, and the registered owners and officers were obviously straw men since a quick credit check on each revealed only that each was employed in the trade of securities and municipal bonds.

Wayne, observing the quixotic expression on Brady's face, quickly related to him that two weeks previous, Wayne had a similar type of wire transfer, but this time the money came from Geneva, Switzerland, to Wayne's branch, and then was transferred to Hamilton, Bermuda. Wayne had no way of knowing whether the transfer referred to by the teller was related to the one Wayne had been briefed on previously.

Brady assured Wayne he would investigate these recent wire transfers and get back to him. He also complimented Wayne on being vigilant and inquisitive concerning these matters.

When Brady got into his car and began his drive home, he promised himself he would not only pursue the information Wayne had provided but would check with the bank's lawyers to make sure no banking rules or regulations had been violated. However, Brady's focus quickly changed from wire transfers at the bank to the black-tie dinner that he and Lois were to attend that evening. The bank threw an annual dinner dance for employees and invited guests. The latter usually being some of the more favored investors and professionals associated with the bank.

Brady put the car in gear and, in twenty minutes, pulled into his driveway. Lois met him at the door with that look he knew so well that said he better hurry and get dressed. Brady rushed up the stairs to their bedroom and quickly slid into his tuxedo complete with cummerbund and bow tie. Lois met him at the foot of the stairs and delighted in how dashingly handsome and athletic he looked. With a hug and a kiss on her cheek, they were out the door.

Once they arrived at the posh ballroom of the Jeffersonian Hotel, Brady checked their coats, located their table from the room map on the wall leading into the ballroom, and made his way to the closest bar. He picked up two drinks, one a glass of club soda and the other a whiskey sour. The club soda was for Brady. As he had explained earlier to Lois, he had some of his security men on duty that night to make sure all went well with the evening's events.

He delivered the drinks to the table and quickly excused himself to check on his men. Although Brady did not anticipate any trouble, he knew that at these affairs, sometimes the employees indulge a little too much, and one or more might become a bit rowdy. If this happened, Brady's men would be ready to usher the unruly out the door, hopefully without incident or too much commotion. After being reassured by his officer in charge, Brady returned to their table and sat down to hopefully enjoy a rare night out with his lovely wife.

As the night wore on, Brady and Lois shared dances and a scrumptious dinner consisting of rare filet mignon, baked potato, and green beans. Brady had selected a moderately dry Amarone that went perfectly with the dinner. Just when Brady and Lois had finished their baked Alaska dessert, Brady caught a glimpse of Wayne at a table across the dance floor from where they sat. Brady caught his eye and waved to Wayne. Wayne immediately left his table and approached Brady and Lois. After being introduced to Lois, Wayne turned to Brady and pulled him aside. Standing on the edge of the dance floor, Wayne asked Brady to look over his shoulder at the tall, stately looking man dancing with, apparently, his wife. Brady observed a tall gray-haired man with a white mustache gracefully moving about the dance floor to the song made famous by Glenn Miller, "Moonlight Serenade." When asked by Brady the significance of this gentleman who was enjoying his dance, Wayne proffered that this man had been associated with one of the wire transfers that he and Brady had discussed earlier that day. Brady pointed to a secluded part of the room for him and Wayne to continue this discussion.

Wayne explained that earlier that same day, one of Wayne's tellers at the branch had approached him with a copy of a wire transfer request she had received from a corporate account with a bank in Indonesia. The transfer was for three million dollars. The local bank account was in the name of Malcomb Securities LLC. The teller had run a credit check as well as reviewed bank records and determined that this LLC was created in the State of Illinois and was in good standing. The originator of the LLC was a Mr. John C. Malcomb, the man Wayne had pointed to on the dance floor. Wayne had recognized the man from a picture the teller had downloaded from the internet.

Again, Brady inquired of Wayne why the transfer was so unusual and what made Mr. Malcomb a person of interest to the bank. Wayne explained that the teller looked further into Mr. Malcomb's background and learned that he owned a small export/import business with overseas offices in Athens as well as Hamilton, Bermuda—the same addresses as two previous transfers of several million dollars. Brady was interested, but he wasn't quite convinced that there was anything illegal or unethical in these transactions that would require further due diligence. He told Wayne he would look further into this matter and contact him the following week.

Brady returned to the table where he recognized he was the focus of Lois's evil eye, the one she gave him when she felt neglected. He immediately swept her up out of her chair and hustled her to the dance floor. After all these years, he still loved his wife deeply and cherished those moments they held each other close and confessed their undying love for each other. This was one of those moments. Lois had consumed two whiskey sours, and as the two gracefully swayed to the music, he knew this night would end only after he and Lois had made passionate love and fell asleep in each other's arms. What he didn't expect was that the last thought he would have before drifting off was about the unusual wire transfers.

Sunday morning was usually a full breakfast of bacon, eggs, hash browns, and coffee. Then off to church and back home to relax with the family. Brady was finishing his breakfast when he heard on the television newscast that Russia had sent troops into neighboring Ukraine, alleging that the action was necessary to protect pro-Russian Ukrainians from radicals who wanted them out of the country and to bring Ukraine back under the control of Russia. Russia had been threatening this action since taking back Crimea. Brady was unsure from all he had heard and read why they were now suddenly sending their army into Ukraine. The Russians knew this action would compel some action on the part of the US and the NATO forces per existing US agreements with Ukraine as well as their pact with the NATO Alliance.

All this came with newspaper articles chronicling North Korea's Kim Jong Un's assertion that North Korea now had the capability of reaching the United States with its long-range missiles, possibly armed with a nuclear warhead, and evidence that China was creating islands in the South China Sea, possibly for military purposes or possibly to interfere with or control the commercial trade routes, which accounted for approximately forty percent of the world trade. Iran too was rattling its sabers by threatening Israel.

Brady pondered over these articles of doom and gloom, only to have his thoughts stray to memories of the fanatical groups such as the Taliban, Hamas, ISIS, and the ubiquitous terrorists, many unaffiliated with any groups or sects, that were now prevalent throughout the world. Brady fought back hard against the feeling of helplessness that crept over him from the realization that the present state of the world was unstable, both economically and militarily.

However, for the time being, Brady decided that world affairs, over which he felt he had little control, should be set aside while he dealt with the matter with which Wayne was so concerned. Brady thought of an investigative agency run by an ex-Marine Major that he had met when stationed in Iraq. Jim Fallon had served in the Marine Corps for fifteen years when he decided to resign from the Corps and start his own investigative service business. In the Marines, Jim had been an agent for the Naval Criminal Investigative Service and for years with the Office of Naval Intelligence. As such, he had gained invaluable experience both overseas and stateside. His background included counter-espionage activities and criminal fraud involving military and civilian contracts for supplies and services.

Brady knew Jim often did background checks on various persons of interest. Brady had decided he would see if Jim could give him a report on Mr. Malcomb that would shed light on Malcomb's involvement with the wire transfers, and what interest, if any, Malcomb had in the participating entities. Brady searched for his address book online, found the number for Jim Fallon, and made a note to call him on Monday.

*****

Brady, Lois, and the family returned from church, and rather than relaxing, he called out to his son Michael, and the two of them slipped into their sneakers and headed for their weekly jog. Brady enjoyed his time running with Michael because it gave him a chance to be mano a mano with his son and delve into the inner sanctum of his teenager's mind. Michael was ready when Brady challenged him to a race to the park and back. Both dashed off the porch and down the street. Recently, Michael had been inching up on Brady, and this day he gleefully flew by his dad and waited for him in the park.

Michael used this time alone with his dad to speak to him about the kid at school who had placed the illegal hit on his friend Danny last year. It seemed that that same kid was now pestering and even bullying Michael during class breaks and after school. Brady was aware of the kid's size, which was comparable to Michael in both height and weight. Brady listened while Michael explained that the kid had embarrassed him several times in front of his friends, including some of the female students with whom Michael had become friends. Brady knew Michael was not physically afraid of this kid. Brady had taught Michael to box, wrestle, and protect himself when necessary.

Michael didn't want to fight the kid if he could avoid it, but he didn't want to appear a coward as a result. Brady understood; he had himself often chosen turning the other cheek as an alternative to beating the heck out of someone deserving it. Brady wanted to know if Michael had sat down and talked with the boy. Michael had not because he was not sure if he would be sucker-punched. Brady pondered Michael's dilemma and suggested he wait until the kid and Michael were alone, or even with others, and Michael offer his hand as an act of peace. All the time keeping a stance that would readily lend itself to Michael's defense. Wary that this would work, nonetheless, Michael agreed that he would try it and, if it did, to start some dialogue with the kid. If it didn't, Michael would defend himself.

*****

Monday came, and Brady was up and about early. Too early, he decided to call his friend Jim Fallon at the investigative agency. So Brady drove to his office at the bank and began rummaging through various bank documents that were maintained on persons of interest to the bank. After several hours of searching, Brady came across the name of John C. Malcomb. The bank files listed him as a local investor who occasionally purchased certificates of deposit but usually for no more than ten thousand dollars and never for more than a ninety-day period. Malcomb was noted as having overseas contacts and as a beneficiary of a trust administered by the bank's trust department.

Brady quickly pulled up the trust on his computer to see if there was any connection with the wire transfers.

What he found was that the trust was discretionary, meaning the trustee had the discretion to distribute the corpus, or principal, of the trust in any manner he deemed necessary, including disposing of the trust funds and terminating the trust. Initial funding of the trust had come from an entity in Switzerland. Brady noted the principal of the trust was one million dollars, and the trustee was a holding company called Enius Ltd., a Canadian business organization. A further check by Brady into Malcomb's file revealed that he periodically, usually every three months, had a sum of ten thousand dollars deposited into his checking account with the bank. The multimillion-dollar deposits were sporadic and within two months before the money was transferred to another banking institution. However, each time such a large deposit and transfer occurred in the trust account, the regular ten thousand-dollar amount was then deposited into the trust account. Again, the regular smaller deposits as well as the multimillion-dollar deposits all came from Enius Ltd. Brady contemplated whether the ten-thousand-dollar deposits could possibly be payment for expediting the larger sum transfers.

Brady placed his call to Jim Fallon. Fallon was on assignment in the field but returned Brady's call that afternoon. Brady left a message as to why he was calling and that he was interested in any information Fallon might have in his files regarding John C. Malcomb as well as Enius Ltd.

When Fallon returned his call, Brady explained about the connection of Malcomb to the latest wire transfer as well as the information Brady had reviewed in the bank's files. Fallon assured Brady he would follow up on his request and get back to him shortly. Knowing it may take a few days, Brady turned his attention to the locations where the wire transfers had originated and terminated. It had become obvious that the United States was only a piece of the puzzle, a puzzle that Brady now viewed as probably legitimate, and yet possibly nefarious, or even criminal.

*****

The months and then years seemed to whisk by like leaves blowing in the wind. Michael was now eighteen and finishing high school. Brady and Lois had not enjoyed a vacation alone in years. So when his vacation period became available, he asked Lois to see if they could get away by themselves for a few days without the kids. Lois was ecstatic at the thought of having Brady alone absent kids.

For the next few days, while Brady was busy delving into the Malcomb matter, Lois began scanning travel brochures for resorts where they might fly and enjoy the warm breezes and white sandy beaches. She finally settled on a trip to the Caribbean, preferably Paradise Island in Nassau. After consulting with Brady and securing her younger sister Joyce's assurance that she would stay with Michael and Sarah, Lois booked their room and flights. Lois always enjoyed the days of preparation for their trip; this, to her, was almost as much fun as the trip itself.

It was late November, and the weather was changing from fall to winter in Chicago. Lois knew that by early December, when they would be leaving, the cold would have set in, and the warm breezes of the Nassau beaches seemed just that much more alluring. She couldn't wait for December 10, their departure date.

The next day, after Lois had booked the vacation trip, Brady received a call from Fallon. Fallon was following up on Brady's past request for information that might relate to Malcomb's wire transfers. Fallon told Brady that he had phoned Bob Bradford, their mutual friend at the NSA, and ran Malcomb's name by him. Bradford had immediately recognized the name and provided a plethora of information to Fallon, the gist of which was that Malcomb had been on a watch list of the NSA for years in connection with his import/export business.

It seems that Malcomb had been negotiating the sale of arms in the Middle East between arms dealers in Africa and Hezbollah in Lebanon. Malcomb only handled these negotiations outside the United States and never openly violated any arms regulations of the US. However, that's not to say Malcomb was not wanted by any Middle Eastern country; it's just that he was never caught crossing the line.

Brady asked Fallon if there was any indication in Malcomb's background that would explain the exceptionally large money transfers going to Athens, Greece, Hamilton, Bermuda, and Switzerland. Fallon responded that the wire transfers and the amounts involved would indicate one-time large purchases of material, equipment, or services. It might be fruitful to coordinate these transfers with any global acquisitions, public or otherwise, that occurred in close proximity to the wire transfers. Bradford would be the one with access to this type of information. Brady scratched his head and wondered just how far down this possible rabbit hole he was willing to go.

Unexpectedly, the suspicious wire transfers tapered off, and Bradford couldn't or wouldn't shed any light on the legitimacy of such transactions.

Weeks flew by, and except the curious large wire transfers that occasionally transpired, the bank's activities, with which Brady was concerned, were relatively normal. Wayne had not complained of any other unusual transactions, and bank customers had experienced only minor problems with hacking and intrusions into their accounts. Brady felt confident the bank was in as secure a position as possible.

It was early winter, and Lois couldn't wait to lay on the beach at Paradise Island, Nassau, in the Bahamas, with no worries but to ponder over what to eat for dinner and how much suntan lotion to apply. Even Brady, she noticed, had been mentioning the trip, indicating to Lois that he too was excited about their vacation. Things had quieted down at the bank. Brady briefly questioned whether this was an indication of a slowdown of activity with his bank or perhaps whether the questionable transfers had been channeled through another bank. In any event, he was looking forward to spending time with his childhood sweetheart and the mother of his children.

The flight to Nassau was about two and a half hours. Both Brady and Lois enjoyed cocktails on board and the very stingy snack the onboard hostess had offered them. The flight was uneventful, and Brady, as he often did during his service flights, counted the seconds it took for the Boeing 437 Jet to travel down the runway prior to liftoff, as well as the rollout upon landing. Roughly ninety seconds for the takeoff and one hundred twenty seconds for the rollout upon touchdown.

The cab drive from the airport to the hotel Atlantis took about thirty minutes, during which time the taxi driver expounded upon the more beautiful and interesting sights and things to do on the island. Particularly, he pointed out a restaurant and bar that he was probably being paid to hype. Nonetheless, Brady and Lois were determined to enjoy every minute of this trip and agreed that work and household affairs were to be kept out of their discussions.

Upon reaching the hotel, Brady immediately checked them in and summoned a red cap to transfer the luggage to their room. The room was on the tenth floor, just high enough that they had a clear view of the sea and the complex on which the hotel was located. It was a beautiful view, with the palm trees swaying in the warm breeze. They could hear laughter emanating from below, where several children and adults were riding inner tubes on the snake-shaped waterway surrounding the hotel complex. Lois and Brady agreed that riding the water on the inner tubes was a priority.

That night, the couple made reservations in the hotel at the steakhouse restaurant. They each enjoyed a medium rare steak, loaded baked potato, and a bottle of 2012 Chateau Margaux. At dinner, they reminisced about their early dating and how they endured the good times and the bad. Lois told Brady how much she had missed him during his tours of duty, but also how much she admired him for his patriotism and love of his country. Brady conveyed how much he had missed Lois during those times, but, as was his nature, stopped short of relating any of his wartime service experiences. They made their way past the casino and back to their room. They laughed the next morning, remembering how each had planned on an especially nice sexual encounter but then had fallen asleep as soon as their heads hit the covers.

For the next three days, Lois and Brady took in the sights of Nassau, had dinner at some of the nicer restaurants, especially Graycliffs. They enjoyed the local markets and the bazaar area with all the straw hats, colorful native outfits, and the people in general. They welcomed the warm breezes and the clear, sunny days. Only

STOIC REVENGE

once in those three days did it rain, and that was more of a squall that quickly passed.

Lois had called home two or three times a day to check on Sarah and Michael. She was scolded for doing so and told by Joyce, her sister, to concentrate on having a wonderful time. Unfortunately, the fourth day was their travel-back-home day. That morning, Lois packed their clothes, and Brady took the luggage downstairs to the Red Cap station in the lobby. While there, Brady purchased the first newspaper he had read since they had arrived. What had caught his attention was the headline that read, "Oil Tanker for Bahamas Missing." Normally, this would not be a major item in Nassau, but the oil tanker involved was destined for Nassau. The import of oil, Brady noted, represents 13–14 percent of the gross national product of Nassau.

Brady, while waiting with Lois for their ride to the airport, wondered just what effect the missing oil tanker with its cargo of oil would have upon the island of Nassau and, more importantly, the Bahamas in general. While on the flight home, Brady used the earphones to listen to the world news to see if there was any mention of the missing tanker. There wasn't, and Brady figured the ship had either sunk in a turbulent storm off the coast of South America or had been hijacked for ransom. He was sure there would be more information available later.

*****

When exiting the plane back in Chicago, Brady and Lois felt the chill of winter invade their bodies. Both remarked dreamily about turning around and going back to the sunny, warm, and beautiful island. They arrived in Chicago a little after 3:00 p.m., which allowed Brady time to check in with Bob Miller, his deputy security manager at the bank. Brady was anxious to hear if there were any incidents with the various branches that he should be aware of and that might need his immediate attention. His deputy stated that nothing unusual had occurred while he was gone. He gave Brady his phone messages, which included calls from Bradford and Fallon.

Miller added there was an interoffice memo on Brady's desk from Wayne.

Since none of the messages were marked urgent, Brady decided he would enjoy what was left of his vacation and relax on his couch and catch the Chicago Bulls basketball game. Once back in their house, Brady and Lois hugged their kids, thanked Lois' sister for watching Sarah and Michael, and while Lois went upstairs to unpack, Brady asked Michael to sit with him for a while. Brady had noticed an aloofness in Michael since he and Lois had returned from their vacation. Also, there was a slight bruise below his left eye. Brady had assumed it was from some athletic activity Michael had participated in at school. But coupled with Michael's apparent avoidance of conversation with Brady, Brady felt compelled to break the ice.

He asked Michael how he had hurt himself. Michael said he didn't want to discuss it and went up to his room. Brady waited until after dinner and joined Michael in his room. Brady asked if there was something Michael wanted to tell him. Michael, wrestling with his emotions, finally gave in and apologized to his dad for not telling him earlier. Michael had encountered the boy from the incident on the football field. Michael offered his hand as Brady had suggested. The boy proceeded to sucker punch Michael and began calling him racial slurs, like "Mick" and "—*** lover." When Michael tried to reason with him, he tried to hit Michael with a baseball bat he had been carrying. Michael quickly removed the bat from his grasp, threw it to the ground, and did the same with the boy.

Brady wanted to know if the boy was okay and if this ended the fight. Michael said it did then, but the next day, the boy and two of his friends had jumped Michael and roughed him up, leaving him on the ground after kicking him in the body and face.

Brady became enraged and wanted to know where the boy lived. Michael told him, and Brady immediately took Michael in the family car, and they drove to the boy's home, which was Farrid's residence. Upon arriving, Brady rang the bell, and Farrid answered the door. Brady gestured towards Michael and his bruises and asked if Farrid knew his son and his son's friends were responsible. Farrid did not seem surprised and, with a smirk, snapped that yes, he was aware of the scuffle and was told by his son that Michael had started it—and quickly added, but couldn't finish it. Brady recalled the episode in the bank when he had to use physical force to subdue Farrid and his aggression.

Brady was dangerously close to swinging at Farrid, but his self-control took over. With a stiff finger in Farrid's chest, he warned that this better not ever happen again or the police would be brought in and charges filed. The two drove back home, and Brady walked Michael to his room, where he sat on the bed and explained to Michael how proud he was of the discipline and self-control Michael had exhibited in handling this matter. And then, to break the tension of the evening, in jest, he chided Michael as to why he couldn't take care of both Farrid's son and his friends. Lois hovered outside in the hallway next to Michael's room, and when Brady came out, she admonished him for coaxing Michael into fighting.

*****

The next morning, Brady was in his office before eight, going through all his phone messages and office memos. His first call was to Fallon. Fallon answered the call and quickly began briefing Brady on what information he had found on Malcomb. Fallon had contacted a friend in Athens, Greece, who was in the business of importing oil into Greece. This friend told Fallon that Malcomb had negotiated the purchase of a large oil tanker capable of transporting up to two million barrels of crude oil. The purchase price was forty million dollars, with a down payment of three million dollars and the balance upon delivery to Hamilton, Bermuda. Brady realized the coincidence between this and the previous wire transfers. It would appear that Malcomb was the middleman for the purchase of the tanker. The dates and amounts fit the puzzle. However, Brady still saw nothing wrong with the transaction.

Later that morning, Brady returned the call from Bradford. Bradford stated that he had spoken with their mutual friend Fallon and had discussed with Fallon the oil tanker transaction involving Malcomb. Bradford, though, added a bit more information to what

Fallon had provided to Brady. Bradford had learned from the daily briefings at NSA that the tanker purchase negotiated by Malcomb was only one of several hundred such purchases worldwide. Bradford went on to tell Brady that there were roughly over four thousand oil tankers worldwide. Of these, more than five hundred are registered under the Panama flag. What had caught the NSA's attention was that in the last year alone nearly one thousand of these tankers had changed ownership. The purchaser was a limited liability company (LLC) located in Dubai. The actual owners of the LLC were believed to be affiliated with a little-known offspring of a group the Taliban called Jahaalat.

Brady absorbed this information and tried to put it in perspective to see if the bank had any interest that needed to be protected as a result of these transactions, more particularly the wire transfer by Malcomb. Brady concluded no action on his part was necessary at this time. At most, he would file a memo of the conversations he had had with Fallon and Bradford. He saw no reason to brief Wayne on what he had learned. Brady, however, harbored an uneasy feeling whether this information was related to the missing tanker in Nassau.

The next day, while making his rounds of the bank branches, Brady dropped in on Wayne's office. After exchanging pleasantries and answering questions about his trip, Brady asked Wayne whether any more wire transfers had occurred. Wayne answered in the negative except, as he said, this one transaction in which a bank customer complained that his checking and savings accounts had both been compromised and the customer could no longer access his own accounts. Wayne had investigated along with one of the bank's computer specialists. It turned out that in fact the customer had been hacked and the hacking had originated in the Middle East, exact location not known. Before the bank could change the accounts, give the customer his new account numbers, and replace the funds, which totaled ninety-seven thousand dollars, the link to the Middle East had been terminated. There was little more the bank could do other than check the malware that had been employed and see what firewalls could be deployed to avoid future attacks. Brady thanked

Wayne for his quick attention to the matter and, deciding there was little else he needed to do at this time, headed back to his office.

Brady decided he would see if there were any similar attacks on any of the other branches. Although the bank probably considered this breach minor in terms of the amount, to Brady it might be the tip of the iceberg. Brady put in a call to his deputy to circulate a memo to all branches to report immediately any instances of money being pilfered from customers' accounts either by computer hacking or otherwise.

*****

Several weeks went by, and the activities at the bank in which Brady was involved seemed to settle down. However, a phone call from Wayne soon interrupted the hiatus. Wayne informed Brady that an individual who was a customer at the bank inquired of one of the managers at another branch location whether he could open a checking account with a deposit of one thousand dollars and put the name on the account under an LLC. The branch manager assured him he could but that he would have to identify the person to be signing on the account, along with his address and social security number. The customer provided identification for a Mr. Jamal Thiri, with an address and passport from Panama, and stated he would be signing on the account. He also told the manager that he would be handling large amounts on a regular basis to fund his international transactions.

Brady listened intently to Wayne but failed to see why Wayne considered this so important to bring to Brady's attention. Then Wayne explained that the branch manager normally would not have been concerned, but he had recognized the customer, this Mr. Thiri, from another branch, where the manager had worked as an assistant manager. This was the same branch where Brady had started work as a security guard. In fact, the manager even knew the customer's name: **ABBAS FARRID**.

The same person who Brady had a confrontation with and the same person that had congratulated his son after the illegal hit on one of Michael's teammates, and whose son and his friends had attacked Michael. Now Brady was excited. Not only did he dislike this man, but what Brady had just learned about him possibly amounted to a criminal act of fraud, an intentional misrepresentation. His first impulse was to notify the local police. Although he knew that Farrid, just like Malcomb, had an import/export business and the opening of the new account might be connected to that business, Brady smiled knowing that he probably had good justification for alerting the authorities to what was obviously suspicious behavior. Brady assured Wayne he would investigate this matter further and keep Wayne in the loop.

Brady, always circumspect when delving into unknown waters, went back to his office where he immediately called Bradford. He felt Bradford would be interested in this recent activity, especially since it involved the nefarious activity of a person claiming international ties and large cash transactions. He was right. Bradford, trying to control his enthusiasm, blurted out that he had been investigating incidents of bank accounts involving large money transfers and false identities on the accounts. Bradford felt comfortable discussing these matters with Brady since he knew he had had top-secret clearance in the service.

Bradford related to Brady how he had seen in UI and other international banking institutions' records evidence of a pattern of activity whereby large sums were run through certain bank accounts. When the banks attempted to locate the owners of these accounts, they ran into dead ends because the bank's documentation proved to be unreliable. Meaning the names and addresses could not be verified. Bradford explained this was not just in Chicago, but throughout the United States. In many cities, the same scenario had taken place over the past several years. An account, Bradford stated, would be opened under a non-existent name and address, usually by one claiming to be a foreign citizen with false identification documents.

Brady became excited himself and asked why the proper authorities had not swept in and put a stop to this activity. Bradford answered that because the activity for the most part was international and involved several other nations, the only charges that could be brought against the participants would be fraud and misrepresentation. The federal authorities were more interested in determining whether there was any connection or common thread that the transactions shared. When Brady asked what action, if any, was being taken, Bradford then declined on the basis of a need to know. Brady was disappointed by this answer but fully understood from his days with Army Intelligence.

Bradford requested Brady keep him informed of future activities and promised, to the extent he could, to keep Brady up to date. When he hung up the phone, Brady leaned back in his chair, folded his arms and hands behind his head, and drew a deep breath. He felt in his gut that something was brewing; he just didn't know what. Brady wanted to call Wayne and Fallon to share the information Bradford had just provided, but Bradford had counseled against that.

Brady closed his office and headed home. He reflected on what all had occurred today and couldn't wait to get home, enjoy one of the ever-enjoyable dinners he knew Lois would have prepared, and rest his body and mind while watching the Bulls basketball game. Lois met him at the door with a hug and a kiss. Michael and Sarah were upstairs plodding through their homework. At dinner, Lois asked about his day, and Brady answered, "Nothing important," and enjoyed the meatloaf she had prepared for him.

The next day, Brady instructed Wayne to circulate the memo for each manager to be on the alert for similar type activity that he and Wayne had discussed the day before.

For the next several months, things seemed to slow down for Brady. Activities that had concerned him suddenly tapered off. The large transfers appeared to disappear, and the fraudulent attacks upon depositors' bank accounts were few and far between. Brady mused that he sometimes felt his work took him on a roller coaster ride, up and down, fast and furious. He only hoped he could hang on long enough to see daylight at the end of what seemed like an endless tunnel.

Brady had mixed emotions during these months; on the one hand, he felt himself becoming bored with his position with the bank, while on the other, he felt somewhat relieved that hacking of customer accounts and the large dollar amounts of suspicious transfers had ceased. Brady had had little contact with Bradford or Fallon, and Wayne had been relatively quiet these last few months.

*****

Michael, now a senior in high school, was about to graduate. He had only a few games remaining on the varsity football team. Brady enjoyed Michael's Friday night games. He and Lois, along with Sara, attended the games. Lois and Sara sometimes complained that Brady was embarrassing them with his boasting of his own days on the gridiron.

Michael's team was on a winning streak and needed only one more win to go to the city championship. It was late December, and Lois made sure she and Sara had enough blankets to cover them for the big game. They knew it was senseless to worry about Brady since he would be up and down throughout the game. Michael was excited, playing under the lights and in front of the anticipated capacity crowd. Once the game started, the butterflies left his stomach, and Michael settled into his duties as quarterback.

It had rained earlier in the day, and the field was muddy. Michael kept the ball on the ground, running the ball along with his fullback and halfbacks. Both teams played relatively even through three quarters. With only twenty seconds left on the scoreboard clock and the score tied at 7–7, Michael, with no more timeouts, pondered whether to call a running play or try to surprise them with a pass to his wide receiver. It was fourth down and five, and the ball was on the opponent's 35-yard line. Michael's team did not have a very good field goal kicker, so the coach deferred to Michael to call the fourth-down play. Brady, Lois, and Sara each held their breath, trying to guess just what play Michael would call.

Michael opted for a pass play. Just as Michael was about to call for the snap of the ball, the rain began pouring again. Michael whispered to himself that he had made the wrong call. Too late to change, the ball was snapped, and Michael dropped back five steps and turned to face his receivers. The defensive end came charging, running over the tight end trying to block him. The safety, too, anticipating a pass play, blitzed up the middle, hands held high. Michael shrugged off the defensive end and, just before the safety raised his hands, spotted his receiver crossing the goal line. With a perfect spiral, Michael let go. His receiver found the spot vacated by the blitzing safety, and Brady went berserk as the official signaled the touchdown and winning score.

Time had run out, the game was over, and Brady left the stands and, with many of the fans, rushed the field to congratulate Michael. Brady could not have felt any more proud of his son. Michael, spotting Brady, ran to him and jumped up on him, forgetting the mud that also covered his dad. Brady didn't mind. He knew the mud would eventually be washed off, but the memory of his son's accomplishment would last forever. Back in the locker room, the coach awarded Michael the game ball, and later Michael would bestow that honor upon his dad during their ride home from the game. Brady would remember that night for a long time.

*****

It was a rainy, cold day in mid-December, and Brady was on his Friday inspection trips to the various branches. When he entered Wayne's branch, he was immediately approached by Wayne's secretary, who asked if Brady would follow her to Wayne's office. Wayne was sitting behind his desk and stood up to shake Brady's hand while blurting out that he was concerned by certain unusual activities he had been made aware of by some of the tellers.

Not only had the hacking of customers' accounts started up again, but there was also a deluge of calls from customers who demanded to know what was happening. Needless to say, these customers were angry as well as afraid of what they may have lost from their accounts. No sooner had Wayne reported this news to Brady than Brady received a text marked urgent. Brady quickly telephoned his secretary, and she informed him that several of the bank branches reported basically the same information that Brady had just heard from Wayne. Brady put in a call to the bank's president and briefed him on the situation.

Mr. Preston Jenkins had been a banker since he was twenty-one. Fresh out of Princeton University, he had started as an assistant teller and came up through the ranks as teller, chief teller, assistant manager, manager of a branch, officer, director, vice president, and finally president. Mr. Jenkins knew the hard times as well as the good times, steering the bank through many recessions and one or two panic runs on the bank.

Fortunately, Brady had kept Mr. Jenkins abreast of the previous hacking activity, but this time Mr. Jenkins could read Brady's expressions and sensed how serious this new situation was. Mr. Jenkins wanted to know how many accounts were affected and how much money had been siphoned from the bank's customers. Mr. Jenkins spoke on the phone with the bank's Chief Financial Officer, Jim Butler, who informed him that so far, there were approximately twenty-five hundred accounts involved from which roughly two and a half million dollars had been lost. Mr. Jenkins quickly did the math in his head and determined that the bank could survive the amount of money that would have to be put back into the customers' accounts, especially since the bank's deductible was only a million dollars before the FDIC insurance kicked in.

Jenkins ordered all overseas withdrawals to be monitored by bank employees to determine which might be legitimate and which transactions might be a result of the hacking. He also asked his internet specialist what options were available in addition to the usual firewalls the bank already had in place. The internet specialist assured Mr. Jenkins he had already shut down some entrances into the customers' accounts and had notified the Federal Bureau of Investigation, who were on the way to assist.

With the FBI on board, and the bank's IT division working full force into the night, the hacking activity suddenly stopped. The FBI had indicated similar activity was occurring elsewhere in the nation, but other than that morsel of news, they were mum.

Brady had instructed the bank security crew to alert every branch manager as to what was occurring and to monitor their customer accounts closely, especially those with higher balances. The employees were also instructed to keep this to themselves lest the bank experience a run on withdrawals. Nonetheless, a partial run did take place, and by the time the bank's internet specialists and the FBI declared the illegal activity thwarted by the government's intervention using highly secret maneuvers to intercept the illegal hacks, Mr. Jenkins informed Brady that the total sum drained from customer accounts was over two hundred million dollars. Mr. Jenkins had already informed the Federal Insurance Corporation of the bank's need for a replenishment of most of the amount lost.

Brady fretted over these different events that seemed to be intertwined, but as yet he couldn't see a connection between them. He could understand the greed of wanting to steal money, the arrogance of interfering with the world's internet, and the psychotic pleasure of watching people's retirements and savings being drained, but what he didn't understand was whether these assaults upon our society were simply an expression of sinister minds at play or if indeed we were experiencing the early stages of an onslaught of monumental proportions against our very way of life.

He decided to call Bradford to see if he would go to lunch, somewhere secluded, where Brady would be able to bend his ear about his concerns. To his surprise, Bradford stated he was about to call Brady to brief him on some nonclassified data of which he felt Brady would be interested.

The two met in a little café in suburban Montgomery County, a hole in the wall that Bradford often frequented with assets of the NSA. It was late in the evening on a cold February day, and Brady and Bradford had on their overcoats and scarves. About twenty minutes passed with the two getting updated on each other's lives. Bradford now had a family with his high school sweetheart and three kids—two boys and a girl. Brady filled Bradford in on his own family and the exploits of Michael on the football field.

With amenities out of the way, Bradford asked Brady how things were going with the bank and whether there had been any more activity with the sizeable money transfers as well as the hacking into the customer accounts. Brady related the recent run on the bank and the near panic that had occurred. He also mentioned the unusual money transfers that he had noticed coincided with the news of several oil tankers being sold around the world that he had read about as well as the incident in the Bahamas with the missing oil tanker. He inquired of Bradford whether there was any connection.

Brady also mentioned his own suspicions, with some basis in fact, concerning Mr. Farrid and Mr. Malcomb. Brady didn't want to go too far for fear he might be overemphasizing Farrid's and Malcomb's participation in these activities.

Bradford, in turn, seemed very interested in Brady's assertion he had a gut feeling, with no factual verification, that all these current activities somehow were related. How? Brady had no idea. Bradford leaned over the table as if to make sure no one else could hear their conversation and whispered to Brady that he was not too far off in his analysis of the current events. Bradford explained that NSA specialists had been able to trace much of the hacking into banks and other financial institutions to a small band of nerds located in Southeast Asia, probably in Burma. The feeling at NSA, after careful analysis, was that these hackers had somehow joined together to form an alliance referred to as Shadow Brokers, selling the glitches they found in the algorithms in computer programs, called Zero Days, for the purpose of compiling extensive amounts of money. What NSA had not determined was what, other than personal use, these criminals intended to do with their hacking expertise and all that money.

*****

As Brady rose from his chair in his new office, he inspected his surroundings. Six months had gone by since his last conversation with Bradford. The Bank had promoted him to Vice President in Charge of Security, including all fraud activities as well as security of all transfers of bank funds, other than normal banking procedures, especially the sending and receiving of large transfers of cash and valuable securities. As part of his new duties, Brady attended seminars on encryption methods, including corresponding malware and firewalls, especially quantum key distribution (QKD) systems utilized for the transfers of large bank transfers.

Brady was pleased with his new office, the mahogany inlaid desk and the riveted leather high back chair. He also enjoyed the bookcase matching his desk, which he had filled with family pictures of the wife and kids. He was especially proud of the trophies he displayed, that Michael had won in football and baseball in high school. These pictures and trophies reminded him that the coming weekend would be spent visiting College campuses since Michael would graduate from high school in two months. Michael had made the all-star team the past football season and, as a result of that accomplishment as well as his superior academic work, he had received several scholarships from Division One colleges.

Brady had pushed for Michael choosing the Naval Academy in Annapolis, Maryland but swore that he would accept Michael's decision whatever that meant.

The coming weekend would be enjoyable he thought since he, Lois Sarah and Michael were visiting the Naval Academy. Brady had always wanted Michael to attend a military school and the Naval Academy in Annapolis was closer than West Point. That evening, after dinner, Brady retired to his favorite chair, and asked Michael if he would like to know a little of the history of football at the Naval Academy.

Michael was eager to hear about the school and the history of its football team, especially the days of Joe Belino and Roger Staubach, that he had heard so much about. Brady slowly but deliberately related the stories he had heard as a high school player. Brady told of how Bellino and Staubach, not only starred as outstanding football players, but each went on to serve their country. Brady emphasized the tradition of the school and how each student took pride in not only the academic aspect of the school, but how religion, ethnicity, and race cut across the current enrolment like a slice of life. Michael took it all in, and Brady could see he had made his point, Michael was hooked. Brady was confident that Michael, with a 3.8 grade point average, his proficiency at quarterback, and Brady's own service as an Army Ranger would help him to be accepted.

That weekend Brady, Lois, Sara and Michael made the trip to Annapolis, Maryland for a tour of the campus. The campus was beautiful, and the assistant football coach couldn't have been nicer. He treated Michael like the top high school player in the United States, but then he did so with all new recruits. A perfect fit for Michael, were the words the coach used, and they had the desired effect. Michael would attend and play ball for the Midshipmen and Brady could not have been any more proud.

*****

During the following weeks, Brady had much to do at the office. There were some minor security problems with idiots trying to smash an ATM, even dragging it by car off its settings. Then there were the forged checks, a snatch and run at one branch with no injury to the teller, and an episode of a major transfer of funds through the bank and onto a foreign bank located in Indonesia. What was strange about the transfer was the amount—ten million dollars—and that the transfer was handled through the account of Abbas Farrid! Brady not only disliked Farrid, but he also suspected Farrid's allegiance lay outside the United States.

Brady, wanting to know more about this recent transfer, decided it was time to meet with Farrid to discuss the transaction. Brady knew that he was stepping on thin ice, given their past history, but he felt that gut feeling again that something smelled, and it wasn't rotten fish.

Brady first ordered a copy of the documentation relating to the transfer and sat down in his office to review it. The transfer originated in Rio de Janeiro, Brazil. It was sent by an international company based in Riyadh, Saudi Arabia. A notation on the original transfer order had a notation: "For purchase of WDGC." Brady made a note to ask Farrid about the notation. Further review revealed that the ten million dollars had originally been in Saudi Riyal currency, but was converted to US dollars at the bank and sent on to be converted back to the Saudi Riyal at the final destination.

Brady had his secretary contact Farrid at the number the bank had for the account. She later informed Brady that she had placed the call and had to leave a message on the answering service. Brady figured he would wait a while to see if Farrid called back.

Several days had passed since Brady had attempted to contact Farrid. Farrid had not returned the call. He looked up the address the bank had in the file and decided to contact his friend Jim Fallon. When Fallon answered, Brady and he exchanged pleasantries, and then Brady explained in detail his concerns about the transfer and especially about the participation of Farrid. He informed Fallon of his secretary leaving a message to contact Brady's office and Farrid's failure to respond. Brady wanted Fallon to visit the address Brady had taken Michael and report back whether Farrid was there, and if not, who was.

Brady put his feet up on his desk, leaned back, and began revisiting the various events of the past two years that had concerned him. He remembered the multimillion-dollar transactions his gut had told him had the appearance of being underhanded if not illegal. He wondered if the run on the bank and the hacking of customers' accounts were all related to the international transactions.

Then there was the concern he had involving the oil tankers and whether there might have been a global attempt to monopolize the tankers for the purpose of holding them hostage from countries that relied heavily on oil imports and exports. The incident of the oil tanker headed for Nassau that had gone missing again came to mind. This could very well affect oil imported by the USA.

Brady was drawn back to the present when his secretary opened his office door to tell him that Mr. Fallon was on the phone. Fallon was calling from his mobile and was at the address Farrid had provided to the bank when he opened his account. Fallon reported that the address was an old abandoned warehouse on the south side of Chicago. There was no one located on the premises and no vehicles about the site. Fallon also reported he had visited the house Brady and Michael had visited, but it was vacant and there was no forwarding address at the local post office.

Fallon had checked with the city building inspections office and was told the export/import business site had been vacated years ago when a publishing company located there had gone out of business. Brady's first reaction was that now he had cause to further investigate Farrid and his business dealings and to confront Farrid with the possible fraud created when he knowingly lied to the bank about the location of his business. Banks, for obvious reasons, needed a correct address to contact him should there be trouble with his bank dealings. Even the phone number he listed had since been disconnected.

After finishing with Fallon, a quick check with the chief teller of the bank disclosed that the bank account for Farrid had been closed, the same account that had been involved in the ten million dollar transfer just days before.

Brady was angry, irritated, and frustrated, but mostly curious about the international transaction, Farrid's nefarious activities, and what, if any, effect all of this might have upon the bank as well as the nation.

When Brady discussed these events with the president of the bank, he was told that since there was no obvious banking problem with the transaction, the bank saw no reason for Brady to be further concerned or involved. Brady acknowledged the bank's position and vowed he would act accordingly. As he left the boss's office, Brady knew he could not ignore or dismiss the stench swirling around Farrid and his activities.

Brady decided to call his old buddy Bradford at the NSA. If for no other reason, Brady felt a need to pass along the information he had on Farrid and the suspicious nature of the bank account and the multimillion-dollar transfer. Now Brady was beginning to wonder why the amount had been run through his bank and then forwarded to Indonesia. And why had so many previous transfers been run through the bank only to be forwarded elsewhere overseas? And what, if any, effect did this have on the oil tanker issue? Many questions, too few answers, he thought. Perhaps Bradford could fill in some of the blanks.

He was mistaken. Bradford couldn't help. Bradford knew about the transfers Brady had previously related, and he added that NSA had been alerted to similar transfers all over the country. Not only was this happening in America but in most of the Western world. Was the NSA alarmed, Brady asked? Bradford answered that NSA had not yet been able to find a commonality among the transfers. What Bradford and the agency had been working on was where the money transfers ended up. Most went for the purchase of the oil tankers, but many went to the purchase of real estate, businesses, and stocks and securities.

There seemed to be no rhyme or reason to these activities. Bradford seemed to lose interest in Brady's concerns and switched the conversation to some other incidents that were concerning the agency. He had previously mentioned to Brady about the sudden blackouts in the electric grids in various parts of the country. It appeared that these blackouts were becoming more frequent and the cause had not been established. This knowledge had not been distributed to the public. Bradford stated that more and more officials in various jurisdictions were insisting on answers.

After he hung up with Bradford, Brady wondered if perhaps he was reading too much into the Farrid problem and that perhaps he should concentrate on his job of protecting the bank and its customers from the day-to-day problems.

*****

He called Lois to see if she would like to go to dinner that evening. Lois was delighted; it had been months since Brady had done so, and she was dying to try out a new restaurant in the city. Lois made reservations at the Sans Souci Restaurant for dinner at eight o'clock. Brady rushed home to change his clothes and pulled out his favorite suit. The restaurant was small, dimly lit, and specialized in French cuisine. Each table had its own candle and red-and-white checkered tablecloths.

While studying the menu, Brady's eyes peeked over at Lois and realized just how much he adored this lovely creature across from him. Her eyes caught his, and he could tell the love was mutual. Brady suggested the chateaubriand, for two, and Lois, knowing that was his favorite, closed her menu in respectful acquiescence to his selection. Much to their surprise, mingling among the tables was a trio of gentlemen playing violins and quietly singing Italian love songs. Brady requested his favorite, "A Volia Bene," and winked at Lois.

On the way home, Lois noticed Brady's reticence and suspected his mind was elsewhere. She often noticed this mood and decided not to bother him with her curiosity as to what was going on in the complex corners of his mind. She relaxed and even nodded off. Upon arriving home, Brady went into his study, and Lois retired to their bedroom.

That night, something had been toying with his brain, and no matter how he had tried to concentrate on enjoying this rare evening alone with Lois, he couldn't avoid thinking about the conversations he had had with Fallon and later Bradford. He thought of Farrid and his involvement. Somewhere in the dark alcoves of his mind, Brady's gut was telling him there was something he was overlooking. Something both ominous and foreboding. Something bigger than just the recent events involving the bank.

The next few weeks kept Brady busy with the usual forgeries, hacks into accounts, and one bank robbery. He had little time to devote to his gut feelings and to ponder the importance of the unusual money transfers. What did catch his attention was a couple of newspaper items. One was a story about flooding in Tennessee due to an unexplainable outage of the computer network that regulated the Tennessee Valley Authority, which in turn provided electric power to most of Tennessee, Georgia, and Alabama. The outage only lasted eight hours before being reinstated, and the computer system put back in operation. There was no further explanation as to how this occurred and whether this might have been the act of terrorists.

The other news item dealt with an unexplained interruption of one of the main pipelines that carried refined oil across the middle of America from Canada. Again, this involved the computer systems that controlled the ebb and flow of oil so vital to much of the United States. Only this time, the outage only occurred for four hours before technicians had everything back to normal. The newspapers explained the incident as a glitch in the system.

Brady wondered if Bradford was aware of these events and, if so, whether he was concerned. Brady hoped there was an easy explanation and that Bradford would alleviate his anxiety. He called Bradford and was surprised when he answered on the first ring. Brady first let Bradford know he had Fallon still trying to locate Farrid to see if he had fled the country and whether he had closed down the import/export business. Bradford wanted Brady to keep him posted.

Brady then asked Bradford about the two shutdowns in the national pipeline and the TVA computer systems. Bradford hesitated; there was an uneasy pause. Bradford had been taken aback by Brady's interest in the computer disruptions and was contemplating what, if anything, he could reveal to Brady without compromising classified information. In short order, Bradford factored in Brady's prior top-secret clearance in the armed services, coupled with his recent knowledge of activities in the banking industry, and decided to give a little information in hopes of Brady providing him with collaborative information. Bradford answered affirmatively that he and the agency were aware of the strange events Brady had mentioned, and that there was concern that someone had hacked into the respective computer systems. But they were not sure of the purpose of these actions. More importantly, they were concerned that these actions might be part of a much larger conspiracy, of which this paradigm of events may only be a small part.

Brady needed to bifurcate his feelings. On the one hand, he was concerned with the events involving money transfers and bank-related hacking, but on the other hand, he was concerned with what might be going on in the global scene. Bradford, out of the blue, asked about Farrid and whether Brady knew that the last money transfer he had told Bradford about, and that Brady had thought went to Indonesia, had actually ended up in a small town in western Dubai.

Brady acknowledged that he was not aware of the final destination but inquired why Bradford was interested. Bradford explained that over the past several years, and after things had settled down in the Middle East, the agency had been tracking literally thousands of money transfers similar to what Brady had experienced with his bank. Many of these types of transfers were innocuous, but many more ended up being forwarded to various financial institutions in Pakistan, Afghanistan, and Dubai. So far, according to Bradford, the agency had not been able to tie these transfers into any coordinated or correlated enterprise.

Brady's mind was now flittering among thoughts of some global conspiracy by some evil organization, or country, that could only be foreboding for the United States. However, he had full confidence in the American intelligence agencies to sniff out and thwart any such intentions. Still, Brady knew, in order to protect his bank, he must now look at a broader picture of events taking place within the banking industry as well as throughout the world. Brady's inquisitive mind told him he needed to step up his game.

A few days following the conversation with Bradford, Fallon contacted Brady to let him know that he had run down some of the credit references Farrid had listed in the bank's records, which contained information on a couple of credit cards in Farrid's name. A check of these credit card statements revealed that Farrid over the past two years had traveled extensively throughout the Middle East. Some of the countries he traveled to were Pakistan, Afghanistan, and Dubai. Brady's mental antenna brought to mind what Bradford had stated about where some of the large money transfers through the banks in America had ended up. Asked whether he had located Farrid, Fallon answered in the negative. Brady told Fallon to continue his search for Farrid. Brady had many questions concerning the bank's hacked accounts, and maybe Farrid could shed some light on these accounts as well as the suspicious large wire transfers.

*****

Brady spent the next few weeks attending to various security breaches within the bank and its branches. Mostly minor break-ins, ATM thefts, customer identity theft, etc. He had reached a point in his job that a feeling of frustration was setting in, and he couldn't shake it.

He had pored over the situations with which he had been confronted since taking the job. The many cash transfers involving millions of dollars; the hacking into customer accounts to steal money from literally thousands of people, amounting to millions of dollars. Brady also felt an obligation to determine if any of the bank's problems were intertwined with the unusual nationwide events that had taken place: the suspicious transactions involving oil tankers, the blackouts in electric grids throughout the United States, and, more importantly to the bank, the suspicious behavior of Farrid and what part he played, if any, in all of this.

The weather in Chicago was changing from the hot, humid dog days of August to the cooler days of fall. The leaves were starting to change to beautiful shades of reddish brown, orange, and yellow. Brady mentioned to his wife, Lois, that this time of the year always reminded him of football. Especially the smell of fresh-cut grass brought back his memories of violent encounters on the football field. Brady confessed to Lois that he had enjoyed aggressively blocking, tackling, and even being hit by opposing players.

Michael was just starting his first semester at the Academy, and even though classes had not started, practice for the varsity and junior varsity was well underway. The first game was in two weeks, and Brady couldn't wait. Michael had proven his ability at quarterback and was in close competition for the starting job. Michael had worked hard since graduation last year, and under the tutelage of his dad, he had emerged as both a scrambler ala Fran Tarkenton and an accurate passer ala his dad's namesake, Tom Brady. Brady couldn't be happier for his son and spent as much time with him studying various defenses as well as game strategies. Brady had not only played football in high school and college but he was also a student of the game. He enjoyed passing this expertise on to his son.

But this particular day, Brady's mind was on a series of events that had been brought to his attention by Bradford. Bradford phoned Brady to alert him to certain activities that the agency had been monitoring. Several instances of counterfeiting US one hundred dollar bills had been discovered across the world, especially in the Middle East. Brady questioned why Bradford felt compelled to pass this information on to him since counterfeiting these bills was not new and had been going on for some time. This is why the bank, as well as other banks, constantly applied tests to these bills. Tests that are furnished to all major banks with classified information as to how to determine the validity of the bills.

Bradford interrupted Brady by stating that the difference between now and before was that the new counterfeit bills were so close to the valid ones that even the tests required by the Federal Reserve could not distinguish the bad from the good. It seemed, said Bradford, that the counterfeiters had almost precisely duplicated the plates used for the printing as well as the paper and ink. The various watercolor imprints, specially hidden variations in the designs, figures, and letters had all been replicated.

Bradford went on to explain that although the Treasury Department was already in the process of reprinting the hundred dollar bills, it would take a week or so to sufficiently replace those in circulation. During this time, Bradford informed him that the banks were being instructed to weigh stacks of fifty of the bills with scaling equipment being distributed worldwide. The one thing the counterfeiters had failed to do was replicate the exact weight in grams of a stack of fifty of the one hundred dollar bills. Although the difference in the weight of one bill was not significant to detect a variation, the weight of fifty or more was detectable.

Brady sarcastically asked if that was all Bradford had to tell him, and Bradford responded that was all for this day; tomorrow might be a different story. Brady mused that Bradford was right—these days seemed to bring new and different emergencies, and this day had been no different. What Bradford did not tell Brady was who they suspected of creating the counterfeit bills or from where they emanated. Immediately upon hanging up with Bradford, Brady contacted the president of the bank to see if he had been warned by the Treasury Department about the currency problem and was told he had.

Brady's mind was swirling with various scenarios streaming through his head. He needed to clear his mind, and the best way to do that, especially since it was Friday and there were no plans for working that weekend, was to get Lois, pack up the car, and head to Annapolis, Maryland, to watch the open practices of Michael and the rest of the Navy football squad. He phoned Lois, asked her to have her sister Joyce come over to stay with Sara, and to join him. She was thrilled to both spend a weekend with Brady and see her son in a Navy football uniform, even if it was just a practice uniform.

Brady and Lois made the long drive to Annapolis and checked into a motel. After awakening and going out for breakfast, Brady and Lois headed over to the Academy stadium. Brady was impressed at Saturday's practice. The varsity first string was scrimmaging the second team. He saw Michael taking turns calling signals with the varsity squad, both the first and second string. He seemed to read the defenses well, and the coaches complimented him on some of his passes delivered to the open receivers. Only once during practice did Michael get sacked, and then only because his right guard failed to pick up a blitz by the safety. That evening, Michael took his parents to a nice Italian restaurant in town and was nice enough to let his dad pick up the check.

After dinner, Michael returned to his room at the dormitory while Brady and Lois went back to the motel. The trip had worked; not only had Brady been distracted from the pressing problems of his daily routine, but he and Lois enjoyed a wonderful night in each other's arms watching old movies and making love until they both fell asleep.

The following Monday, Brady was back at his job, scanning the daily bank memos and his phone messages. Everything seemed normal except there was a call from Bradford marked urgent. Brady quickly dialed his number. Bradford answered, and Brady apologized for not returning the call sooner. Bradford informed Brady that there had been another run on one of the Federal Reserve Banks located in Los Angeles, California. The cause of the financial panic was a video on social media showing crowds of people trying to get into banks in

Los Angeles and being turned away by police officers. The video gave no reason for the panic, nor did it proffer any explanations.

Brady, though interested in the information provided by Bradford, questioned why this was being brought to him since it was obviously a federal matter. Bradford stated further that on another video on social media, a Federal Reserve Bank in Minneapolis, Minnesota, experienced a similar occurrence, with a video displaying long lines of cars at service stations implying a shortage of gasoline. Again, there were no explanations or text overlays to indicate exactly what the video was showing.

The only conclusion that made sense to Bradford and the NSA was that the videos were being used to implant fear in the minds of viewers that there were inexplicable outbreaks occurring across the nation caused by implied shortages in US currency as well as fuel at the service stations. As soon as these videos were seen by NSA analysts, the social media networks were notified that this was fake news and to edit out the videos as well as censor any future submittals for airing.

Bradford told Brady that when the social media companies were informed, they also were asked to identify the customers who ordered and paid for the videos to be aired. Citing First Amendment rights, many declined to divulge the sources without a court order. Bradford said that the agency was in the process of obtaining the court orders, but in the meantime, the agency was rapidly spreading the information to banks and national media that these videos were fake and that there was no concern for either a shortage of fuel or a shortage of currency.

Brady responded by thanking Bradford for the information and promised that he would contact Bradford if there were any unusual disturbances at his bank and its branches. Before he hung up, Bradford let out a sigh of frustration and stated that simple little episodes like these taxed the manpower and resources of the NSA. Bradford expressed his opinion that all of this commotion was probably the work of some misguided computer nerd who enjoyed seeing people panic. Little did Bradford know that some elite hacker or hackers capable of decrypting the source code of the Federal Reserve and Department of Transportation computers were the culprits.

Brady then called the bank president and briefed him to be on the lookout for any indication of customer concern for a shortage of currency within the bank. Then Brady contacted Fallon. When Fallon answered his call, Brady inquired about the search for Farrid. Still nothing, responded Fallon. Fallon said he had searched on the internet, through telephone guides, power companies, credit card companies, obituaries, etc., but so far there were no leads. All he could add was that Farrid had used the export/import business as his front in Chicago and perhaps he would do the same wherever he may have relocated. Fallon promised to keep looking.

The next day, at breakfast, Brady read in the newspaper how several cities reported a misinformed run on their banks. In other cities, it was reported that hundreds of drivers lined up at service stations, fearing a shortage of gasoline reminiscent of the shortages caused by the oil embargo in the late seventies. All of the present shortages were proven to be unfounded. The article went on to state that the people involved had seen videos on the internet depicting such scenes, but the videos proved to be doctored and used intentionally to misinform the public.

Brady left his office and began his rounds at the various branches. There were no signs of any concern or fear among any of the bank customers at the various branches he visited. However, when he came to Wayne's branch, Wayne met him at the entrance. He wanted to inform Brady that one of the bank's customers had asked him if he could exchange five million US dollars into euros. Wayne had recommended the customer go to Wells Fargo bank, that this bank didn't carry that much foreign currency. Brady asked why Wayne thought this was important enough to report to him, and Wayne responded that the man had told Wayne that the US dollars were in cash because he had kept them in a vault the man had installed in his home. Now Brady was interested. Why would anyone keep that kind of cold cash in his home and not in a bank? Brady was aware that if the man did try to exchange that much cash for euros, it would have to be reported by a bank to the Treasury Department.

Though this matter didn't seem to involve the bank since Wayne had referred him elsewhere, Brady deemed it important enough to pass on to Bradford at his next opportunity. Brady thanked Wayne and continued on his rounds.

The following week, Brady called Bradford. He relayed the conversation he had with Wayne and mentioned the currency exchange that the customer had requested of Wayne. Bradford was very interested and asked Brady if the customer gave any identification information to Wayne, or any indication of how they could track him down. Brady promised to press Wayne further and get back to him. Later that day, Brady contacted Wayne by phone and asked him if he knew the customer or if he had any way of knowing where to get in touch with him. Wayne replied that he had seen the customer around the branch before and was sure that he did his banking with them. Wayne agreed to search his and the bank's records and report back to Brady.

*****

It was Saturday, and Navy was playing the University of Michigan that weekend. Brady was excited because Michael not only was dressing with the varsity for the game, but Michael told his dad that he might get in the game if they were ahead or losing by a large margin. Brady, Lois, and Sara set out for Annapolis to attend the game. On the ride there, Brady received a call on his cell phone from Fallon. He had contacted a realtor that had the listing for the leasing of the premises where Farrid had operated his import/export business. While under the pretext of inspecting the premises as a potential lessee, Fallon had noticed behind the building what looked like trash that had been discarded in a trash bin by the previous tenant. After completing his walk around, and after leaving the premises, Fallon had returned to the trash bin; and after rummaging through the trash, he discovered a piece of paper with Farrid's name and a notation that read, "Forward my mail to 600 Beauregard Street, London, England." Brady was excited at this good news. He would pass it on to Bradford right away.

STOIC REVENGE

Navy was listed in the top ten football colleges in the NCAA, and their biggest rival was the United States Military Academy-Army, which was also listed in the top ten. That game would be for the prestigious President's Cup, to be played in Philadelphia, and was the last game of the season.

Today, however, Navy was ahead 21 to 0 in the last two minutes of the game with Michigan when suddenly Michael ran onto the field to take his place at quarterback. With the ball on the 10-yard line, he was instructed by the coach to keep the ball on the ground to run out the clock. The first call he made as a player for Navy was a quarterback draw where the quarterback dropped back as if to pass and turned and ran straight back up the middle. After shrugging off two hand tackles by the linebackers, Michael glided across the goal line. Brady and Lois were ecstatic and couldn't control their urge to shout out, "That's my boy!" Later, at dinner, Michael would have to repeat for Brady every step of the play so Brady could savor every detail. Brady hoped everyone else in the restaurant could see the immense pride he had for his son.

On the drive back home, he, Lois, and Sara shared how proud they were of Michael and how much happiness he had brought them that day. But slowly, as they neared home, Brady's thoughts turned to the news he had received from Fallon's phone call. Brady wondered if Farrid was somehow involved with the counterfeiting operation that Bradford had referred to, as well as some of the nefarious activities the bank had experienced in connection with the strange and unusually large money transfers that had been run through the bank, only to be forwarded to foreign banks.

Brady's mind was all over the board. He now wondered if there was any connection with the money transfers, the counterfeiting operation, the seemingly orchestrated runs on the banks, hacking of customers' accounts, siphoning of millions of dollars from accounts, the electric grid outages and bogus fuel shortages that Bradford had been concerned about, and more recently the attempt to exchange millions of cash dollars for euros.

To Brady, the world had seemed to be turned upside down, and he wondered where it would end. He felt himself sinking as if in quicksand, but the more his mind tried to find some logic to all that was happening, he hoped that somehow he could provide meaningful assistance that might lead to meaningful solutions.

That Monday, Brady was back on the phone with Bradford. He related his conversation with Fallon and provided Bradford with the address left in the trash, apparently by Farrid. Bradford, after thanking Brady for the new information, asked Brady if he had ever heard the word *enius* before. Brady replied that Wayne had mentioned the name previously in discussing a trust account in which Mr. Malcomb had been involved. When asked why the concern, Bradford stated that in the chatter that the agency encountered on a daily basis monitoring certain phrases and words in the myriad of communications throughout the world, this particular word or at least this sound had been repeated often by curious and suspect sources. Bradford quickly added, "Forget I mentioned it." Bradford stated he would run the address through intel and keep Brady informed to the extent he could on additional information for Farrid.

For the next few weeks, things appeared to settle down at the bank. There was no further communication with Bradford, and none from Fallon. Wayne had not heard further from the man wanting to exchange dollars for euros, and there were no unusual activities at the bank. But the lull was not to last. It had been a while since Brady had last communicated with Bradford, and Fallon had been busy with other clients, which probably meant he had no news about Farrid.

Wayne called, very excited. He blurted out that the man who asked about the exchange of dollars for euros was back in his branch. Wayne thought Brady would like to see him and even inquire into his recent request for information on the dollars for euros exchange. Brady pulled his car to the curb so he could collect his thoughts about what he might ask about the monetary exchange request, but his intelligence training in the Army told him he should clear this first with Bradford.

Brady called Bradford but could not get him on the cell phone. Brady decided to simply stop at Wayne's branch, go up to Wayne's desk, and have Wayne point out the gentleman.

Brady walked into the branch, into Wayne's office, and sat down. Wayne started some idle chatter, and without pointing or looking at the man through the glass partition, whispered to Brady that he was at the number two teller's booth. Slowly, Brady turned towards the teller booths and glanced at the gentleman who was leaning in towards the teller window out of sight of Brady. Brady almost fell out of his chair; the man was the same man Brady had seen at Michael's high school football game, and the same man Brady had an altercation with in one of the branches. IT WAS FARRID!

Farrid had not noticed Brady, and Brady did not want him to. Brady turned to Wayne and softly whispered that he wanted copies of any documents Farrid may have given the teller, and Brady immediately phoned Fallon. Fortunately, Fallon answered on the first ring. Brady insisted he come right over to the bank so he could tail Farrid if necessary to determine where he might be staying. Fallon hung up; he was only fifteen minutes from the branch and headed over immediately. Farrid was opening a new bank account and had to execute signature cards as well as fill out some bank forms. By the time Farrid had finished, Fallon was at the bank. Brady pointed out Farrid so Fallon could follow him upon Farrid's exit from the bank.

Farrid finished his business with the bank's teller and exited the bank. As Brady peered through the front windows of the bank, he saw Fallon's car follow Farrid out of the parking lot. Brady phoned Fallon to make sure he was behind Farrid. Once assured Fallon was tailing Farrid, Brady went over to the teller, along with Wayne, to see what business Farrid was transacting at the bank. The teller, a petite Italian lady, revealed the documents she had presented to Farrid, and that he had executed. The teller explained that Farrid wanted to open a new business, and in doing so, needed to open a checking account. He filled out the forms listing himself as the sole signer, and the name on the business listed on the checking account was "The Enius Project LLC" (a.k.a. WDGC). Now Brady was able to tie the previous money transaction with the notation WDGC to Enius LLC and Farrid.

Brady pondered over the documents and remembered Bradford had mentioned this word Enius several times, once when discussing

Mr. Malcomb, and later when he asked him if he had ever heard this word before. Brady knew that this was extremely important information that Bradford should have right away. Once he left the bank, with copies of the documents Farrid had filed with the teller, Brady was on the phone calling Bradford.

Brady left a message for Bradford that when he returned, Brady had some interesting information to give him. Then Brady contacted Fallon by cellphone to see where Farrid was taking him. Fallon answered and let Brady know he was still two cars behind Farrid in south Chicago and would keep him posted. Brady then asked Wayne to have one of the clerks do a rundown on the internet to see what the Illinois Department of Assessments and Taxation had on an LLC called the "Enius Project." The clerk, after ten or fifteen minutes, came back to Wayne and Brady with information he had copied off the internet. The business registration department of the State of Illinois listed the LLC as being formed just one year earlier, and the organizer was listed as Abbas Farrid.

The resident agent for the LLC was a commercial business that provided a service of using their offices as the main office and one of the officers thereof as the resident agent in the State of Illinois, both of which were required to do business in the state. Abbas Farrid was listed as the only member for the LLC.

Fallon called Brady back to report that he tailed Farrid back to a hotel on the south side and was able to enter the hotel lobby long enough to get the room number for Farrid when he requested his room key. All this information was relayed to Brady. Shortly thereafter, Brady received a return call from Bradford, and Brady reported to him the information on the LLC derived from the registration with the state. Bradford seemed pleased with what Brady had uncovered and thanked Brady for his promptness in contacting him.

Bradford sat at his desk at the NSA, pondering over this new information and yet feeling a growing sense of frustration generated by the seemingly endless enigmas he and the agency were facing on the global scene. The CIA and the FBI were closely monitoring the counterfeiting of the US one-hundred-dollar bill; the agency was monitoring the overwhelming number of hacks being carried out every hour against large government defense contractors and others. Bradford was aware the Treasury Department was not only concerned with the counterfeiting, but with hacking of bank accounts as well as the fake news about the "runs" on the banks due to false information indicating a cash shortage, and what part, if anything, the oil tankers might have in this conundrum. These concerns Bradford viewed against the backdrop of the unusual number of "blackouts" in electrical grids for large areas across the United States. And on top of these worrisome events, Bradford feared for a national panic if the public became aware of these activities. Bradford's thoughts were abruptly pushed from his consciousness as he reasoned that all of the many intelligence agencies, the CIA, the FBI, the NSA, and others, formed a stalwart defense against all who might attempt to destroy this powerful country.

Brady, mentally exhausted after the Farrid episode and his discussions with Fallon and Bradford, decided to call it a day and headed home. It would be a nice diversion, he thought, just to see Lois and Sara and find out the latest news from Michael. Lois greeted him at the door with a kiss and a hug. Later, after enjoying pork chops, sliced tomatoes, and succotash, Brady put his feet up on the footstool, and before he could ask about Sara and school, and Michael's days at college, he was fast asleep. Lois, knowing something or someone had apparently had him upset that day, smiled and lowered the lights. She covered him with a blanket and knew when he was ready, he would come upstairs to sleep.

The next couple of weeks, Brady split his time between the day-to-day security business of the bank and piecing together the tangled web that had been woven by Farrid. Brady had ordered Wayne to monitor the Enius Project bank account and to report to him any unusual transactions and to identify any parties other than Farrid that might be involved. Wayne, a week or so later, contacted Brady to report that Farrid had deposited the sum of six million dollars, which was transferred the next day to Islamabad, Pakistan.

Brady immediately informed Bradford of this new information. Bradford told Brady he would track the transfer through the bank in Pakistan and determine the ultimate destination for the transfer.

A few days later, Brady received a call from Bradford. He told Brady that the money had ended up in a bank in Dubai. The account where the money was sent was under the name Omar Saeed.

Bradford declined to expand on this information, citing a need to know for Brady. Brady understood, but in his mind, he wondered how this Omar Saeed might be associated with Farrid and who or what was Enius? Fallon called Brady to let him know that Farrid, whom he had been tailing, had checked out of the hotel the next day. Brady surmised he may not hear about Farrid for some time or perhaps forever.

A few days went by, and Brady allowed himself the luxury of forgetting the problems of the world and concentrated on the day-to-day business of the bank. The only time these worries intruded into his consciousness was when he received a phone call from Bradford to check on any further contact or information Brady might have regarding Farrid.

*****

Bradford made such a call on a cold and wintry Friday as Brady was about to head home to enjoy his weekend. When Brady answered the call, he noticed Bradford seemed unusually upset. Bradford first asked if Brady had seen or heard anything more of Farrid. Brady answered no and asked Bradford why he seemed so upset. Bradford quickly added that there had been some disturbing news regarding the Enius Project. Apparently, the agency had uncovered a possible terrorist plot to attack the US, but when, where, and in what manner was unknown. Bradford had been reluctant to share this information with Brady, but given Brady's intelligence training and his involvement in this matter, Bradford had decided that sharing the information with Brady could only help. Brady, in turn, had visions of reliving nine-eleven all over again. He crossed himself and murmured a silent prayer.

Brady decided to check again with Fallon to see if there was any possibility that Fallon might be able to pin down a forwarding address or any kind of data that might reveal where Farrid might be located.

Fallon answered Brady's call and explained that he had checked the hotel where Farrid had stayed, but to no avail—there was no forwarding address, and the hotel bill was paid in cash. However, Fallon had noted the tag number on the car Farrid had driven, and sure enough, it was a rental. A quick check with the agent for the rental revealed a copy of a driver's license in the name of Shakkar Abbas, the same as Farrid's first name. Unfortunately, when Fallon checked the address on the driver's license, it was the old premises where Farrid had operated his import/export business.

Just when Brady was about to hang up with him, Fallon proffered that the rental car agency had also required insurance data before renting Farrid the car. Farrid had given them a false insurance company and policy number. Once Farrid had left the rental car office, the agent had checked on the insurance company, discovered the discrepancy and possible fraud, and immediately called the telephone number Farrid had left them. When no one answered, the rental agency contacted the local police department, and they, in turn, put out an all-points bulletin to locate the car. Apparently, Farrid had checked out of the hotel and drove directly to O'Hare Airport, which is where the police found the rented car. Fallon had run a timeline on when Farrid had checked out of the hotel and about when he may have arrived at the airport. In doing so, he ran down at least twenty-five possibilities of flights that were scheduled to leave O'Hare shortly thereafter. Fallon read the possibilities to Brady, and it wasn't until the list was almost finished that Fallon mentioned a flight with United Arab Emirates direct to Islamabad, Pakistan.

Brady thanked Fallon for doing an excellent job and immediately called Bradford. Bradford was in his car when he took Brady's call. Brady related the investigative work that Fallon had done and the ensuing flight that might have been taken by Farrid. Bradford discussed his concern about Fallon and the part he was now playing in this extremely serious and very delicate matter. Brady assured Bradford of Fallon's undying devotion to the US and the many years he had known Fallon and shared with him the hardships and the dangers of combat while serving in the Iraqi War.

Bradford felt comfortable with Brady's recommendation of Fallon and Fallon's trustworthiness. He also knew he could use Fallon for unofficial snooping in areas where the agency's personnel could not go. Besides, there was no time to run background checks.

Bradford informed Brady that Farrid was on the way to O'Hare Airport and his destination was Islamabad. Brady's information on Farrid had only validated an analysis of certain chatter the agency had picked up in its monitoring of suspicious communications and wire transmittals. Apparently, the analysts had determined that something important was going on in Islamabad, and it centered around this Abdullah Saeed. Taken together with the information Brady had just provided on Farrid, it may also involve Farrid.

Brady wished Bradford a safe trip and couldn't shrug off his desire to accompany him, especially since it might involve Farrid and his business dealings with the bank. Nonetheless, Brady hung up and turned his car for home. It had been an exciting day, but at the end of the day, Brady felt somewhat melancholy. Somehow, his mind drifted to the days of the sand burning through his boots in Iraq and the smell of sulfur from artillery fire, air-to-surface missiles, and the many fellow soldiers that never returned. He silently prayed that Bradford would not join that cadre of brave men.

*****

Brady reached his home just in time to hear Michael's phone call. Lois said Michael had called several times for Brady to tell him about the big game coming up in two weeks. Navy was playing Army at Lincoln Financial Field in Philadelphia, Pennsylvania, for the President's Cup. Michael said he was hoping his mom, dad, and sister could come to the game. Brady called Michael to tell him that he had already purchased three tickets for himself, Lois, and Sara. Brady spent an hour on the phone with Michael, discussing school and football. Brady welcomed this brief hiatus from the problems of the world. He assured Michael that the Brady family would be at the game.

Brady went to sleep that night with Bradford on his mind. He wondered what he might be doing, if he was trying to locate Farrid, or if he was concentrating on locating others that might be part of a cabal formed to do harm and render destruction and annihilation to the non-Muslim population. Brady drifted off knowing that Bradford had the backup of the most powerful intelligence agency in the world, and the support of the most advanced technology and equipment known to man.

Early the next morning, around eight (Eastern Standard Time), Bradford called. He wanted to know if Brady could describe Farrid. The pictures of him that Bradford had received in his briefing before leaving the US were sketchy, sandy, and it was hard to distinguish faces. Brady went on to ask Bradford if there were any leads as to what, if anything, was about to occur. Bradford was silent, and Brady knew not to push further.

Bradford had to go. He had people meeting him at the airport to support a surveillance operation of the arrivals from Chicago. Via an intercom system they put into place, Bradford's agents signaled that no one had seen anyone resembling the description of Farrid that Brady had given to Bradford. After several hours of checking passenger lists on flight arrivals with the help of the Pakistani secret service, Bradford directed his men to retire to a safe house the CIA had available where they could establish a game plan for what to do when they located Farrid.

What neither Brady nor Bradford knew was that Farrid always traveled in disguise, wearing a glue-on mustache, beard, and facial makeup to lighten his skin. Farrid's passport was Canadian, created by Farrid's cronies, and bore the name Anthony Baldwin, one of many names and passports he had acquired in the last few years. What Brady also didn't know was that the agency had placed Farrid on the no-fly list a year back, but this had never deterred Farrid because of his access to bogus travel documents.

Brady, hanging up with Bradford, decided activity in Islamabad did not concern his duties and concerns for the bank, and decided to concentrate on his business at hand. He decided to check with Wayne and other managers to see if there had been any abnormalities in connection with customers' accounts, currency balances throughout the branches, and any experiences with counterfeit hundred-dollar bills.

Wayne stated the only instances he had heard about were a computer virus which could have been a result of someone trying to tap into the bank's customer account files, or it could have been simply the work of a rogue hacker having fun seeing just what havoc he could generate among the customers by stealing their identification information. Wayne added that the bank's technical staff immediately identified the intrusion into the bank's programs and almost immediately neutralized the malware virus.

Brady checked in with the bank president to see if he had become aware of any suspicious banking activity and was assured that everything was satisfactory. With those reports from both Wayne and the bank president, Brady turned his thoughts to home and what Lois might be preparing for dinner.

When he arrived home and settled down in his favorite leather reclining chair, Lois informed him that Michael had called and wanted to make sure they would all be coming to the Ohio State football game that weekend in Annapolis. Brady smiled his assurance to Lois that yes, indeed, they would all be there for the big game. Brady smiled to himself, realizing that he would be enjoying these days for three more years of Michael's journey through college.

Several days passed, and Brady began to be concerned whether Bradford and his agents had turned up any information on the whereabouts of Farrid. Brady decided to try and reach Bradford by phone, but was not sure he would answer. Much to his surprise, Bradford did answer. After exchanging amenities, Bradford asked if Brady had experienced any more unusual activity at the bank in connection with the fake rumors on social media, any currency shortages at the bank, or any intrusions into the computer programs of the bank. Brady responded that there was only the incident with what he described as a rogue hacker, which was neutralized, but nothing involving the currency on hand or counterfeiting.

Bradford stated that the agency had identified many sources of the fake news, but they operated in separate cells, and as soon as one was shut down, another popped up. The same was true, he said, about the hacking. The agency had swooped in on several locations from where these hacks originated, and again they seemed to be located in many sites around the world, and more importantly, they all seemed to be independent and not tethered together. When we try to extract information as to their financial backers, everything is done by computer, including cryptocurrency wire transfers, totally untraceable to any one person or organization. Bradford's voice reflected his obvious frustration with not being able to terminate or even effectively interrupt the activities of these criminals.

Bradford then turned the conversation to Farrid. He indicated that he and his operatives had located Farrid in Islamabad, and he was under surveillance. Bradford wanted to determine with whom Farrid was communicating and/or associating. The one thing Bradford decided he could share with Brady was that Farrid had met Abdullah Saeed, the man whose bank account Farrid had transferred the six million dollars into. Brady was curious about this Abdullah Saeed. Brady pressed Bradford for more information on this new character, but Bradford would only say that he was under close scrutiny, as was Farrid. Brady thanked Bradford for the update and warned him to stay safe. Once off the phone, Brady couldn't get the name Abdullah Saeed out of his head.

What Bradford had not told Brady was that a phone conversation between Farrid and Abdullah Saeed hinted at an important event that was soon to occur. However, even with the best deciphering of their conversation, which was riddled with code words and innuendoes, the agency still had not determined what the big event was and when it was to occur. Bradford had surmised that the event might be tied into the fake rumors, the constant hacks, unloading counterfeit dollars, or maybe a combination of these. Bradford also wondered what significance the large money transfers the agency had tied back to Farrid, including the one he made to Abdullah Saeed, might have. Bradford knew if he followed the money, he might begin to understand.

It was Friday, and Brady and the family would be going to see Navy play Ohio State in Annapolis the next day. Brady was so looking forward to it and the pleasant distraction it provided. Brady asked

Lois if she would like to take Sara to see a movie and enjoy dinner at their favorite Italian restaurant, and she answered with a big smile and loving hug. The three of them had a warm family evening that all enjoyed.

At seven o'clock Saturday morning, the day of the big game with Ohio State, Brady was awakened by his cell phone ringing. It was Bradford. He did not realize the ten-hour difference in time between Islamabad and Chicago. Brady quickly arose, and Bradford could tell from his voice that Brady had just awakened and was straining to clear his head. Bradford apologized for not considering the time differential and the fact it was Saturday and Brady's day off.

Bradford slowly began bringing Brady up to speed on the movements of both Farrid and Omar Saeed (a.k.a. Abdullah Saeed). Bradford related this information to Brady because he needed Brady's input concerning Farrid's past dealings with the bank, especially the money transfers. Bradford stated that the agency's analysts had traced bank accounts in the name of Enius to at least fifteen major banks throughout the world. The balances in these accounts ranged from fifty million to over one billion dollars.

Intelligence background data revealed that Farrid, up until just a couple of years past, was involved in arms deals, including automatic rifles, surface-to-air rockets, bombs, and other weaponry useful to various insurgent groups throughout the world. This was the connection to Abdullah Saeed. Saeed had led the uprising in recent years in Libya and more recently in the southern part of Turkey. Analysts further found that the sums of money Farrid had accumulated over the past five years were well into the billions. This money was hidden in some of the most credible banks in western and eastern cities around the world. Coupled with this information, the agency had intercepted transmissions that tied many of the money transfers from Farrid to bank accounts throughout the world controlled in one way or another by Saeed.

*****

Bradford then asked Brady if he had any additional data regarding Farrid. Brady had just experienced an epiphany regarding Omar

Saeed. Could this be the same person that Brady had fought against in the Iraq war, the same person with whom he had been trapped in a cave and spent hours quarreling and hurling objects at one another? Brady's mind revisited the many conversations with his adversary and the many times they had attacked each other by hurling whatever objects were within their grasp. He wondered aloud, could this Saeed be the same Omar Saeed that Brady met in the cave?

Brady packed up the family SUV, and within half an hour, the three of them were on their way to Annapolis. They arrived there half an hour before kickoff. Michael was on the field and looked to the section of seats where Brady had told him they would be sitting. The game was exciting, and Michael did get in, but only for a few plays. Navy led from the first quarter, and at the end of the game, the score was Navy 37 and Ohio State 21. After the game, the four of them went to a small restaurant in the city. Brady and Michael discussed much of the game and the fact that Navy had done pretty well against the number one team in the nation. Later, after dropping Michael off at the Academy, the three of them headed home.

On Monday, Brady was tied up with the theft of a file reflecting a customer's bank account information, including identification and access data. Fortunately, the incident proved to be a lone wolf event and limited to very few invasions of privacy.

Brady headed home, hoping for a good home-cooked meal coupled with a nice cabernet to rid his mind of the sobering thoughts he had experienced that day. Upon entering his house, he immediately took in the aroma of something broiling in the oven, and after a hug and kiss from Lois, Brady slipped into his slippers, picked up the newspaper, and flopped into his leather chair. Lois smiled, announced that dinner was in fifteen minutes, and left Brady to his newspaper.

At dinner, with Lois and Sara present, Brady inquired about Michael and whether Lois had heard anything. Lois, happy to see work had not occupied so much of Brady's mind that he forgot about his son being away at college, informed Brady that Michael was extremely excited about the Army game and the possibility that he might get in the game again if the score was lopsided. Michael knew how much that game meant to his dad. Brady wondered out loud whether Michael had impressed the coach enough with his unexpected trip over the goal line in the Michigan game that Michael might get another chance. Brady, after completing two helpings of Lois' prime rib and mashed potatoes, decided to call Michael. He and his son talked for twenty minutes discussing football and Michael's grades. Michael assured his dad that all was well and he would not disappoint him. With that, Brady leaned back in his recliner and Lois watched him fall fast asleep.

Upon reaching his office, he was met with two phone messages: one from Fallon and one from Bradford.

Brady called Fallon first. Fallon answered, and before Brady could exchange amenities, he blurted out that he had additional information on Farrid. Apparently, according to Fallon, Farrid had contacted the rental car agency to see if anyone had found a satchel that he had left in the car. The rental agency had not found the satchel, but they had Fallon's card with his telephone number and thought Fallon might be interested. They told Fallon the call came in from overseas, more specifically from Islamabad, Pakistan.

Brady hung up and immediately phoned Bradford. When Bradford answered, Brady relayed the information he had just received from Fallon. Bradford seemed excited because he and his operatives had lost track of Farrid in Islamabad and were frantically searching for his whereabouts. Bradford stated his people had become suspicious whether Farrid was still in the city or had left for parts unknown; now they knew he was still there. Bradford told Brady he would let him know if they found Farrid.

Brady sat back and contemplated the odds of whether Omar Saeed was the same person Brady had encountered in the Iraq war, and if so, what role he was playing on the world scene, as well as the nature of his relationship to Farrid. Later that evening, Brady's phone rang, and it was Bradford. Bradford's team had located Farrid at an international bank branch. The Pakistani intelligence organization had contacts in this bank and discovered that Farrid was transferring a large sum of money to a Swiss bank into an account titled Enius LLC. Bradford said he did not apprehend Farrid because one of the

Pakistani agents had planted a GPS locator in Farrid's rental car. The plan was to monitor Farrid, see who he contacts, and determine if those contacts had any relationship to the important event that NSA had been monitoring in the chatter on tapped wire communications.

Bradford called Brady two days later to inform him that they had again lost contact with Farrid. Bradford wanted to know if Brady had anything new on Farrid. Brady recalled what Fallon had discovered in the trash bin behind the building where Farrid had run his export/import business. He told Bradford that Fallon, while rummaging through Farrid's dumpster, had found a piece of paper that had written on it in someone's handwriting to forward his mail to an address in London, England. Bradford yelled thanks, hung up, and Brady knew he had given him useful information that might help relocate Farrid.

In Riyadh, Saudi Arabia, Omar Saeed, also known as Abdullah Saeed, sipped his morning tea and browsed through Al-Riyadh Arabic newspaper. Saeed was particularly concerned with the international sections that also covered the US college football games. He well remembered the competition in the Atlantic Coast Conference between Virginia Tech and Virginia. Although the information was meager, Saeed cut out an item referring to various college playoff games, in particular the President's Cup game between Navy and Army. Saeed was about to finish his tea when this morning ritual, after morning prayers, was interrupted by an alert on his cellphone. Someone was trying to reach him, and the phone screen simply said Farrid. Saeed answered the call, and Farrid said hello after offering praise to Allah.

The brief conversation was full of cryptic phrases and pseudonyms. Farrid told Saeed that the Enius account was almost complete and to go ahead with the final preparations for the upcoming festival. Saeed frowned at what he saw as a careless communication by Farrid, but blew it off as what he expected from a man he little admired and did not trust.

Saeed texted Farrid that he understood. That was all. Farrid was in London, England, and had just arrived there from Islamabad, Pakistan. Farrid hung up with Saeed and called one of his contacts in the terrorist underground in the city. There was a plan underway to set off a bomb in a railway station in the inner city during rush hour in two weeks. Farrid was the organizer, and a group of three Arabic men and one English woman were at his command.

Bradford had put out an alert to his contacts as well as MI6, the English intelligence agency, for Farrid, giving alternate descriptions that Brady and Fallon had discovered Farrid often used. Bradford had asked that if they locate Farrid, they not make contact or arrest him but keep him under surveillance for the present. Bradford knew it would only be a matter of time until either NSA or MI6 located Farrid. If so, he hoped they would be able to discover his contacts and get some indication if in fact a big event was planned and, if so, where and when.

*****

At Blacksburg, Virginia, the campus now seemed calm, and the years of unrest that followed the shooting that left several students dead had faded as time went by. Saeed recalled the warmth extended to him by the Porters during his time at Virginia Tech. Saeed also recalled the snide remarks and embarrassing moments when a few students hurled racial slurs at him. He had tried to reconcile the benefits of the fine education he had received there with the anger and hostility he had sealed inside, a result of the meaningless deaths of his sister and parents at the hands of US pilots when they recklessly destroyed his village with their bombing.

Saeed reprimanded himself for allowing his mind to return to those days. He now had a mission, one he had planned for several years, and now it was time to put his plan into place. Saeed had learned over the years many of the tactics of the various terrorist groups that he had encountered and with whom he had aligned himself. He had promised himself, and Allah, that he would someday vindicate his family by making the American infidels pay for his loss. This thought ate at him like an aggressive cancer spreading throughout his body. For years, he had thought of nothing more important than this personal vendetta that he would soon inflict upon the Americans.

*****

Brady had not heard from Bradford for several days but he was kept busy with several break-ins at the branches, including the hijacking of an ATM machine. While investigating the latter incident, Brady was contacted by Bradford. He wanted to know if Brady had any further word on Farrid. The reason for the call was that Farrid had fallen off the grid and no one knew of his whereabouts. Apparently, Farrid had stopped off in London but had left London, flown under an alias to Bern, Switzerland, and from there the trail grew cold. Brady questioned whether Bradford and the NSA were really that efficient since they had now lost Farrid more than once.

Bradford wanted to warn Brady in case Farrid might head back to his old neighborhood. Brady acknowledged he would do what he could. After the call, Brady contacted Fallon to alert him in case Farrid suddenly reappeared.

Farrid left the city of Bern, Switzerland, and flew a series of short flights to Sweden, Riyadh, and on to Chicago. Farrid had met Saeed some years earlier in Afghanistan shortly after Saeed had returned there to fight in the war with the US. Farrid had also fought against the Americans as an insurgent, but his reasons were different than those of Saeed. Farrid came from a very wealthy family in Mosul, Iraq. His father was a financial advisor and an executive in the National Bank. When war broke out and the Americans invaded their land, Afghans like Farrid's father were often kicked out of office and ridiculed by their peers. Farrid went from having financial security to poverty overnight. He even begged on the streets to survive. When he heard of Saeed and the insurgency he led, Farrid joined his cause.

Farrid and Saeed had grown close over the years since those days. The relationship, however, was akin to a general and his aide. Saeed was the brains, and Farrid provided the financial expertise he had learned from his father. Where Saeed wanted revenge for the loss of his family, Farrid wanted the promise of wealth and power. Farrid harbored the thought that one day, after Saeed had successfully neutered the USA, he would enjoy immense power and be equal to Saeed in controlling a vast empire. This fantasy of Farrid was well noted by Saeed. Saeed had little respect for Farrid. This feeling went back several years when Saeed's father, who had operated a retail linen store in Mosul, Iraq, had several dealings with the bank run by Farrid's father. When it became obvious war was about to break out with the US, Farrid's family was discovered absconding with several million US dollars belonging to local depositors.

Unfortunately for them, the local police, put in power by the Americans, summarily tried and executed Farrid's father. Farrid, after joining Saeed and his terrorist group in Afghanistan, and after planning many of the terrorists' attacks as means of accumulating funds for the insurgents, left Afghanistan, at Saeed's orders, and traveled to America. The plan was for Farrid to create corporate fronts to conceal the cash Saeed and Farrid would accumulate so those funds could be used by Saeed to further his burning desire for vengeance against America. Thus, Enius Project LLC and other entities were created. What was not expected by Saeed or Farrid was the swiftness of success in acquiring capital from sympathizers to their cause, as well as the ease with which Farrid could organize a network of hackers to siphon money from individual bank accounts without getting caught. Farrid was careful to keep two or three barriers between him and those with whom he was associating. These barriers were usually cronies he had hired who knew little if any information that could lead back to Farrid. Saeed, in turn, kept the trail from Farrid to himself just as difficult. Farrid had learned how easily strategically placed hackers, from South Africa to North Korea, could invade everyday checking accounts, withdraw small amounts of funds from literally millions of these accounts, and funnel the money to Farrid's hidden accounts, only to be transferred ultimately to Saeed.

Saeed had used many of Farrid's hackers in the United States to cause temporary shutdowns of some of the most critical utility grids, computer-operated dams, the New York Stock Exchange, and oil refineries. Over the last several years, Saeed had set in place the means of utilizing disruptions in America's electric grids in all major cities, disrupting computer controls over water flows through the nation's major dams, and causing panic on Wall Street exchanges by creating false information injected into the New York Stock Exchange and the futures market, as well as controlling a substantial number of the world's oil tankers, which if taken out of use would disrupt the flow of oil to the USA. All of which was mistakenly viewed by Farrid as Saeed's greed for money and power.

Saeed had married since the war in Afghanistan, and his one child, Kareem, was now eighteen and a freshman at the University of Riyadh in Saudi Arabia. Saeed had kept Kareem outside the circle of his activities, and except for his religion, Saeed had not attempted to sway Kareem in his political philosophy. He had never mentioned to Kareem the days he fought against the US troops as an insurgent in Afghanistan, the many battles he survived, and the many men he had slain. Saeed only allowed Kareem to know how much he hated America for the loss of his parents and his sister.

Kareem had grown into a handsome lad and was intelligent like his dad. Kareem aspired to become an astrophysicist and maybe one day join the space program and become an astronaut. Saeed smiled to himself whenever Kareem spoke of his dreams of the future, knowing that the future for Kareem and the rest of the world was not guaranteed.

*****

Brady had worked all week assuring the management of the bank that the hacking of depositors' accounts was sporadic at best and would soon be eliminated by new malware that he had had the techs install. This seemed to calm the powers that be for the time being, but Brady knew he would have to show progress in the prevention of the hacking to quell the customers' complaints and suspicions. It was Friday, and Brady was heading home tired and hungry. On the way, he called Michael to see how school was going. Michael, surprisingly, answered on the first ring, and Brady could tell he was out of breath. Michael told his dad that he had just entered his dorm room after two hours of football practice. The coach was making doubly sure that Navy would be ready for Saturday's game against Army. Brady listened to Michael describe his various classes and the practices on the field and thought to himself how nice he remembered his days in college with no responsibilities and little if any worries. Brady loved Michael and prayed often that he would see him graduate and become a success one day. Brady told Michael he couldn't see him this weekend, but that he definitely would be there for the Army game. As he turned into his driveway, he saw Lois standing on the porch in her apron, which meant dinner would be ready shortly.

That evening, after dinner, Sara came into the living room and sat down next to her dad's favorite chair. Brady lowered the newspaper he had been reading and looked at her with an expression that asked, "Do you have something to say?" Sara did. She had won the relay race at the girl's track meet. She beamed when she showed her dad the blue ribbon she had been awarded. Brady felt bad that he had not paid more attention to Sara lately, mainly because of his job and Michael's activities at school. Lois came into the room after finishing the dishes and smiled at Brady. Lois had told Sara to inform her dad of the accomplishment, and she too beamed, not for Sara, but for the look on Brady's face. He was sincerely proud of his daughter. Brady hugged Sara and told her she was without a doubt the bright star in his life. When they were alone later that night, and before going up to bed, Brady hugged Lois and expressed how proud he was of the two children his lovely wife had brought him.

Brady asked Lois to pour him a shot of Courvoisier VSOP, his favorite, before she and Sara headed up to the bedrooms. He pushed back in his favorite chair, sipped his cognac, and reached for the phone. He wanted to tell Fallon about Farrid and that he might be back in the US and to keep feelers out with his contacts should Farrid suddenly reappear in Chicago. During their conversation, Fallon informed Brady that there had been an explosion at an electric plant on the south side of Chicago. The authorities had no idea why or how it had happened, but there was concern that it had been a terrorist attack. Brady gulped down the rest of his cognac and turned on the nightly news. The explosion was on all channels, and the police chief, bomb squad, and others each were giving their opinions of what had transpired.

Brady called Bradford. Bradford was in his office, having returned from Islamabad, and sounded tired when he answered. He asked Brady if he had seen the news of the explosion at the city's electric plant on the south side. Brady answered that he had and that he wanted to know if this might be the event that Bradford had previously referred to in connection with the chatter NSA had intercepted. Bradford was silent, and Brady realized he had stepped out of bounds with his question. Bradford switched the conversation to Farrid and whether there was any word on Brady's end as to Farrid's whereabouts.

Brady related his conversation with Fallon and assured Bradford he would contact him with any news. Brady slowly climbed the stairs on his way to bed, all the while worried that this incident with the electric plant could be just the beginning of something greater. Lois was still awake, but the expression on Brady's face told her that conversation was not advisable.

Bradford was still at his desk at NSA and had the same feelings and concerns as Brady. Could this be the tip of the iceberg? Were any other plants going to be attacked? Or was this simply a failure caused by faulty equipment, a power surge, or computer failure? Bradford knew that very shortly one of their field investigators would report in with reliable information on just what had occurred. About an hour later, Bradford's supervisor advised him that the investigation revealed there was a surge from a pole transformer which caused an automatic alert to the mainframe of the computer that controlled the power distribution within the plant. This in turn caused the mainframe to direct an extraordinary amount of power to one section of a distribution line. When the line reached its maximum load, it simply exploded, thus shutting down a large segment of the city's power.

Bradford absorbed this information with a suspicious mind—that was the nature of his job. His supervisor seemed to accept the explanation, and so Bradford set his suspicions aside for another day. Perhaps it was in fact an innocent incident attributable to human and/or computer error. Bradford called it a night and headed home.

At this same time, Farrid sent a wire to a go-between in Riyadh that simply read, "We have a firstborn." This go-between then cut out from the daily newspaper letters that spelled out the same statement. This document would then be left in an envelope in a lock box at a UPS store in Riyadh where Saeed would normally check on a sporadic basis. But now Saeed, knowing he had given the go-ahead for initial actions in his master plan, would stop there regularly for the next few days. Saeed now knew that one of Farrid's minions had carried out Saeed's orders and facilitated the explosion at the southside plant. The first domino had fallen; there were many more to follow.

The next day, cable news reported the explosion and recited almost word for word the explanation given by the authorities the night before. The public received the explanation as nothing unusual, and the matter was not repeated in subsequent editions. NSA officials had met with Homeland Security and the FBI to warn them to conduct their own investigation to make sure nothing suspicious was connected to the explosion. Bradford, the next morning, had an uneasy feeling in his gut that told him something was amiss and that he should use NSA assets to inquire further. One of those assets was Brady, whom he trusted as a confidant and to whom Bradford could convey his suspicions without causing an uproar in the agency.

Brady received the call from Bradford while enjoying his lunch at Lion d'Or, a French restaurant across the street from his office. Bradford asked him to stay there and he would join him, and that he had something personal to discuss with him. Brady suspected Bradford may have some information related to the grid failures and anxiously awaited his arrival. When Bradford arrived, he asked Brady to join him at another table, one in a somewhat secluded area of the restaurant.

Bradford ordered his usual vodka and club soda and took a long drink before opening up to Brady. Bradford explained his gut feelings about the explosion the night before and that he suspected foul play. Given the chatter NSA had been following of some event about to take place, Bradford told Brady he had an uneasy feeling that this may not have been human error but the act of an individual or organization, an act possibly meant to make a statement. When Brady questioned exactly what Bradford thought the act to mean, Bradford rolled his eyes, indicating he knew nothing beyond his gut feeling. He was perplexed and had no precise answer. He just knew somehow that someone somewhere had just discarded a glove as done when our forefathers would challenge one to a duel. Bradford knew this metaphor was only in his mind and that he would have to find hard evidence if he was to convince his superiors of the urgency of this matter. Bradford completed his briefing of Brady on his concerns and was anxious to hear Brady's feedback. Brady confided in Bradford that he had harbored these same suspicions and that he wanted to help any way he could. Down deep inside, Brady felt there was very little he could say to ameliorate Bradford's concerns, so he merely offered to Bradford that he and Fallon would keep their antennae up and report back if anything unusual surfaced.

The two finished their lunch, shook hands, and left the restaurant, neither taking any comfort from their meeting. Back at his office, Brady sifted through the documents on his desk to see if Fallon had called and left a message. There was nothing from Fallon, but there was a message from one of the branch managers concerning a large payment from one of the flagged accounts belonging to Farrid. The amount was one hundred thousand dollars, and it was transferred into an account overseas. The significance of the transfer was that the account to which the money was wired was in Islamabad, Pakistan. What interested Brady was the fact the money was transferred within twelve hours of the explosion at the electric plant.

Brady immediately contacted Bradford on his mobile phone and relayed the information he had, as well as his thoughts on what this might mean. Could it be, he thought, that this might be payment for the sabotage of the plant? Bradford thanked him for the call and assured him it would be looked into.

Brady left his office and headed home. Once there, he asked Lois if she had heard from Michael. She had not, and Brady decided, while waiting for dinner to be prepared, to call him. Michael was in his dorm studying for his differential calculus exam but was happy to interrupt his study to speak with his dad. Brady realized that his discussions with Michael were his therapy, a distraction from the uneasiness Brady was becoming accustomed to given the daily calls from Bradford. Brady wondered to himself whether Farrid's sudden resurfacing in Chicago had any connection with the plant explosion. They chatted for a half hour about Michael's grades, his campus life, and finally how he was doing in football practice. Brady could tell Michael was excited about the game this coming Saturday with Ohio State University but did not think he would see much action. Brady knew Michael was more hopeful that he would see some action the following week in the game with Army.

Although Michael was always thrifty with his spending habits, Brady finished their conversation with a promise to wire Michael some cash to cover the following two weeks. As they sat down to dinner, Brady asked Lois if she had made hotel reservations for the weekend in Philadelphia for the big game with Army the following weekend. Lois smiled and answered affirmatively, knowing this was about the fourth time Brady had asked the same question.

*****

Farrid had checked in at a small hotel in central Chicago, nothing fancy but one where he had spent time before and one he knew would not question his identification. He checked into his room and immediately opened his laptop. He typed in a website for an import/export business located in Islamabad and scrolled down to employees. He selected a name and typed in only the word "Receipt?" He awaited a reply, and after twenty minutes, the alert on his computer indicated a response. The response had only the word "Thanks." Farrid knew his mission and payment were now complete. He lay down on the bed, smiled at the ceiling, and praised Allah. The plans that had been conceived years before were finally underway.

Fallon had not heard anything of Farrid, but he had run down a lead on him from a neighbor near the location of the import/export business that Farrid had abandoned. The neighbor had seen Farrid several times over the years conversing with an Arabic gentleman in his store. The neighbor had been in the store on several occasions and on one occasion overheard the Arabic gentleman mention to Farrid that he worked for Chicago Power and Electric Company (CPEC). When asked, the neighbor said the last time he saw the Arabic man was a few days ago. Fallon had noted this meeting between the two had occurred just prior to the plant explosion.

Fallon called Brady and related this new information concerning Farrid. Brady passed it on to Bradford, who said he would see if he could identify the Arabic man that had spoken with Farrid. Bradford immediately left for the main office of CPEC. The office manager, after Bradford had identified himself, invited Bradford into his office. Bradford explained he was trying to locate an employee of the company. He stated to the manager the employee may have left the company unexpectedly just recently, and the manager narrowed his search accordingly. They quickly determined a Jousef Pouri had taken off the day of the explosion and had not returned since. Pouri had only been employed for six months. Bradford thanked the manager and returned to Fort Meade. Bradford was confident he had located the tie-in to Farrid. What he didn't know was whether the plant explosion was the event that was the subject of the chatter that had been heard on the communications monitored by NSA.

Bradford knew if he had his men in Islamabad arrest Pouri, then the most that could be accomplished would be the additional arrest of Farrid. But this would not answer the questions of whether there was another incident planned, and whether the players were limited to Farrid and his accomplice Pouri. Bradford knew refraining from arresting Farrid immediately could lead to a much greater risk. There was much for Bradford to ponder, but in the end, he opted for the bigger picture, knowing he could reel in Farrid and Pouri whenever he thought it was necessary. Farrid and Pouri had been identified; it was the unknown persons that Bradford feared.

Farrid lay in his bed at the hotel pleased with himself but contemplating the next phase of the master plan that had been put into play by Saeed. Pouri had fulfilled his usefulness, and it was time to disassociate him from the operation. Farrid would have another associate in Islamabad see that Pouri met with a fatal accident in the next few days. Farrid looked forward to the chaos that he anticipated would ensue from the confusion created by the explosion at the electric plant, as well as several more disruptive actions that Saeed had designated to be carried out by Farrid and his radical Islamists. Little did Farrid know that Saeed had something far more nefarious in mind.

Neither Fallon nor Brady was aware that Farrid was back in Chicago, and Bradford had decided not to inform either of them that he had identified the probable perpetrator of the plant explosion. Bradford would keep this knowledge on a need-to-know basis. Bradford had been promoted regularly on an annual basis the past few years and now enjoyed the title of Group Leader for the Counterintelligence Branch of NSA that specialized in domestic terrorism, even if it involved foreign participants.

The next day, Brady made his rounds to the various branches just to check and see if all security measures were in order. All was well until he came to Wayne's branch. Brady had not communicated with Wayne for weeks and decided he would sit and chat with him awhile. Wayne always enjoyed it when Brady took notice of him; it made him feel important, especially when Brady took interest in Wayne's opinions and suggestions.

On this particular occasion, however, Wayne was anxious to inform Brady of some information he had just discovered. He reminded Brady of the prior wire transfers of large sums of money that involved some oil tankers. Wayne stated there had been another such transfer, and this time the money was sent to Hamilton, Bermuda, seemingly to purchase a medium-sized oil tanker. When Brady inquired why Wayne was concerned over this particular wire transfer and the possible connection with the purchase of the oil tanker, Wayne mentioned that the wire transfer came from a corporate business account, one on which Farrid was the signer.

Now Brady was interested. He was bewildered as to the connection between the purchase of the oil tanker and Farrid. He also pondered whether this could have anything to do with the plant explosion. Brady thanked Wayne for his perspicacity and said he would see what he could find out. Brady left Wayne's office feeling as though he was in a dark tunnel and had no idea where it would lead. Brady was not sure

STOIC REVENGE

this last bit of information was necessary to pass on to Bradford, so he decided to sleep on it. What did seem logical was that Farrid's peripatetic travels opened innumerable possibilities for dastardly deeds.

*****

Saeed couldn't wait for the door at the restaurant to open and Kareem to enter. Saeed had not seen Kareem for several weeks, and he was anxious to be with his son and hear how he enjoyed college and how his grades were going. Kareem was lean and handsome, about five feet ten and maybe 150 pounds. Kareem hugged his dad and whispered how much he missed him. Saeed had grown close to Kareem, especially since his wife, Kareem's mother, had fallen ill several years after Kareem was born and had succumbed to an aggressive form of leukemia that had rapidly spread through her body.

Kareem had been close to his mother but was only eight when she died. Since then, he was devoted to his dad and respected and admired Saeed. Kareem had heard the stories from others of Saeed's bravery and dedication to Allah during the Afghanistan war with the United States. Kareem did not hate Americans, but he did not respect them for what the American pilots had done to destroy his father's home, his grandparents, and his aunt. Kareem never brought up the day when the bombs were dropped inadvertently on the house, killing Saeed's mother, father, and sister. The one time when a friend from the old days brought up the subject with Saeed was the only time Kareem had actually seen his dad break down and cry.

Kareem and his father spent the better part of two hours catching up on each other. Kareem knew his dad loved to hear how he was doing in college, his studies, as well as his social life, especially if that included any potential bride.

Kareem related that his first year ended with him achieving a 3.6 grade point average and that he had enjoyed his courses in math and science and looked forward to the present year and his introductory courses in his major field of study, computer science.

Kareem told his father that he had decided that computer science and its possibilities for the future would certainly be one of the leading areas of concern for the defense of many nations, as well as a challenge for those who were visionaries of what the future and computer technology could and would bring.

Kareem blushed when his dad asked about his social life, knowing his dad really meant to ask if he had met any girls who might have captured his interest. Kareem responded that there was no one so far that had met his approval but he was still looking. Saeed simply smiled, knowing that he had raised Kareem well and that he would not hastily enter into a serious relationship without being extra circumspect in his choices.

As Saeed was paying the check, Kareem told his dad that a friend and colleague had invited Kareem to spend a long weekend with him and his family. The friend, Ahmed Jabar, was Iranian, and his family presently resided in a little town called Annapolis, Maryland. Ahmed's father left Iran when the Shah departed in 1979, and the Ayatollah Khomeini was invited back to Iran. Ahmed's father started a small textile business similar to Kareem's grandfather. The family business had grown over the years, and Ahmed's family had prospered as a result.

Kareem told his dad that Ahmed has a brother two years older who was attending the US Military Academy at West Point, New York. Ahmed wanted Kareem to meet his family, especially his older brother. Kareem was excited because he had never been to the United States, and Ahmed had promised to show him how a typical family resides there.

Kareem could see the frown that came over his father's face at the mention of the United States. Saeed started to express his disdain for Kareem going but decided that perhaps Kareem should see firsthand how the American infidels live. Saeed was assured by Kareem that Ahmed's family were deeply religious and practiced their Islamic faith daily. As they exited the restaurant, Kareem hugged his dad, holding him close as he whispered in his ear how he loved him. Saeed squeezed Kareem to his breast and wished his mother was there to share the moment.

*****

STOIC REVENGE

Brady had just looked at his alarm clock when suddenly the telephone rang. Brady grabbed the receiver, hoping not to awaken Lois. The voice was that of Bradford. He wanted Brady to know that there had been an explosion at a railway station in downtown London. Twenty-some people had been killed, and another seventy or so injured. MI6 had two men in custody. One English woman had been shot by the police. Bradford suspected that Farrid had something to do with the bombing since chatter had been detected concerning an "event" several days before, about the same time Farrid had stopped in London.

Brady was wide awake, and his mind was racing through the last few days. He asked Bradford if the bombing in England could have been avoided or intercepted had they arrested Farrid. Bradford explained to Brady that he had asked himself that question over and over, but he had surmised that this particular act of terrorism was not the big event that the intelligence community believed was yet to occur. Brady asked if Bradford was going to have Farrid picked up. The response was not yet, not until the NSA could be certain when, where, and how the suspected big event would unfold.

After he had hung up with Bradford, Brady was comforted in his own mind that the entire intelligence communities of the major powers, at least the US, England, Germany, Israel, France, and many others, were all concentrating and coordinating their efforts to intercept and diffuse whatever action the terrorists had in mind. Bradford had been including Brady on a need-to-know basis. Brady not only understood but also realized that there was much more that Bradford had not shared with him.

Meanwhile, Brady asked Wayne and the rest of the branch managers, as well as employees, to keep a sharp eye out for any unusual activities, especially inordinate amounts of money transfers. Brady then checked with Fallon to see if there had been any evidence of Farrid's activities in Chicago. Fallon had nothing to report. In his office alone, Brady leaned back in his high-back chair with his hands to his face and uttered to himself that time had to be running out on whatever was about to happen. Sitting in his chair, Brady felt a sense of alarm that the safety of his family and the nation rested on the shoulders of intelligence agencies worldwide.

Saeed had planned for many years and amassed a sizable fortune to expedite an event that Saeed hoped would please Allah. Saeed was the sole architect of this event and had restricted knowledge of the event to a very select few, and even then, this knowledge was parceled out to each confidant so no one person, save himself, had a complete understanding of where, how, and when the event would occur. Saeed had earned his nickname Enius (meaning "Genius") in the world of terrorists because of the intricate and important disruptions he had designed to be carried out around the Western world.

Saeed, after the Afghanistan and Iraq wars, had enrolled in Cambridge to study under a staff that followed in the steps of Isaac Newton, Hawking, and other giants in the field of theoretical physics. Saeed had impressed his instructors in many of his subjects. The internet and ubiquitous cyber world, as integrated with quantum physics, which had erupted since the 1990s, had created an insatiable appetite in him to comprehend all he could in this emerging field. Saeed indeed was now an expert in understanding the intricate ways in which the weapon and financial industries protected their proprietary intellectual properties. He was specifically adept in his ability to decipher those protective firewalls, malware, and encrypted passwords.

Saeed had learned from an elite few of the world's hackers how to find errors in the source codes of many worldwide entities with intricate malware. These errors were referred to as Zero Days. These hackers were Shadow Brokers, or persons who sold these Zero Days errors to the highest bidders, many of whom were countries like the USA, Russia, and China. The errors found by these hackers usually hacked into the program Logic Controllers, and by doing so, could allow the hacker to set traps or redirect the instructions from the Logic Controllers to disrupt or even cause failure of the system. This was how, allegedly, the USA caused the Iranian centrifuges to be corrupted, leading to the signing of the nuclear pact with Iran. Saeed was patently aware that the knowledge he had acquired and deducted from his expertise at inflicting havoc on the most sophisticated computer systems, storage links, and applications in the world must and would be his and his alone. He would be the one who would ignite the firestorm that would unite the world under and for Allah and against the American infidels.

*****

Kareem had met Ahmed Jabar in his first week on campus at the University of Saudi Arabia. They found they had similar backgrounds, both as a result of their parents' businesses and in the fundamentalist teachings of Islam. Kareem had conveyed to Ahmed the tragedy of the American bombing of his parents' village and the mental anguish that his father had suffered. Ahmed's father had suffered too under the regime of the late Shah, who had abdicated Iran in 1979.

Kareem telephoned Ahmed a few days after meeting his father in the restaurant to let him know that he would be arriving in Annapolis, Maryland, that coming Friday.

Brady had been reminiscing a lot lately about the person he had fought in the Afghanistan War many years past. Brady often wondered whatever happened to him. Saeed, on the other hand, had occasionally thought of Brady, but in doing so, felt a fury come over him, recalling the fatal day when he had received the phone call that American fighter jets had bombarded his parents' village. Saeed would push the memory out of his mind by concentrating on the day when he would have his revenge. Saeed anticipated anxiously the day when that revenge would be consummated in a sad denouement for Americans.

Although Bradford had never met Saeed, he knew his past history fairly well. Bradford knew that after the war, Saeed had gone to Cambridge University to complete his studies but had left the school early to enter the field of cyber studies. Saeed, in a short period, had mastered cyber studies and had opened his own data collection company. What Bradford had not determined was the nature and depth of his knowledge in artificial intelligence.

Saeed had collaborated with a limited number of elite Arabic students in computer technology to explore and detect a common thread through cyber technology that would be able to interplay with the major computer networks of the world by infiltrating the major data banks (i.e., clouds) as well as through the routers that interconnected these data banks.

This enterprise of Saeed's was financed by the vast amounts of money that his well-paid nerds, supervised by Saeed, extracted from unsuspecting depositors, investors, and even Wall Street brokerage houses. The reason he had not been detected was due to the complexity of his strategy. His people would only make small, unnoticeable deductions, and their activities were spread to numerous financial sources throughout the world. People could not identify or even describe Saeed because they never saw him.

Saeed came up on NSA's radar because of the seemingly unlimited sums of money he had been spreading across continents in carefully concealed bank and investment accounts. NSA had identified many of these accounts but was only sporadic in the ability to identify and freeze some of the funds. Saeed and his people had been successful in opening literally thousands of accounts in untraceable names and businesses. Attempts to tie these accounts back to Saeed so far had been impossible. Because of the vast amounts of cash available to Saeed, many of the second and third in command of several nations and countries were easily bribed into carrying out Saeed's plans. Exactly what the ultimate plan was, no one except Saeed seemed to know.

In the intelligence field, one way to segregate and isolate functions of an intelligence operation is into cells. This is done for various reasons, one of which is to make sure if one cell is compromised, there will be no obvious connection to the others. In addition, very few individuals are privy to how the other cells function. This is how Saeed had organized his businesses and money gathering/laundering activities.

Saeed was moving from country to country frequently these days. Seldom did he settle in one location more than a few days, and he only visited his main office when absolutely necessary.

Kareem had flown into Annapolis and met up with Ahmed and his family. Kareem was treated as a VIP and shown the limited sights there were to see in Annapolis. Ahmed's family had planned a trip that Saturday to see the game between Navy and Army in Philadelphia. Ahmed's dad had obtained tickets for the game, including one for Kareem. They would make the trip early Saturday morning, and they had planned a typical American Saturday football outing, including tailgating in their SUV Cadillac.

Kareem was excited and looked forward to his first visit to America and an American college football game. He felt like a teenager as thoughts ran through his head of American hot dogs, barbecue ribs, etc., that he had heard so much about. Ahmed too was excited and looked forward to sharing this weekend and the game with his friend Kareem.

Farrid had spent the last few days flying to various cities around the United States under assumed names and false passports. Farrid had contacts in Pakistan that could create a passport that would be acceptable in any country, including the USA. First, he had flown into Chattanooga, Tennessee, the center of operations for the Tennessee Valley Authority distribution center for all the dams built since 1933 (sixteen in all). Next, Farrid had flown to Hoover Dam, in Boulder City, Nevada. And finally, he flew into Spokane, Washington, where, just outside the city, is located the Grand Coulee Dam. Farrid was under instruction from Saeed to covertly take pictures and generally describe antenna locations, main buildings, and the latitude/longitude for each site. Farrid was proud of himself and the successful completion of Saeed's instructions.

Saeed received this information from Farrid by circuitous means, piecemeal, encrypted, and nonsequential, all according to Saeed's preset instructions. Saeed smiled at the completeness of Farrid's submittals. His smile was partly due to Farrid and his aides' successful scouting trips, but also due to Saeed's paradigm coming together. A paradigm that included two other soldiers Saeed had recruited who also had carried out their instructions. These two were brothers, Saul and Sou Ankar. Saeed had met Sou, the oldest brother, at Cambridge, and each found a kinship in their beliefs, especially

Islam. Saeed had slowly learned to trust them, delving deep into their fundamental beliefs and dedication to Allah.

Saul was an environmental engineer who had studied at the University of Wisconsin at Platteville. Saul had a strong academic background in the oil industry and had been instructed by Saeed to visit oil refineries in Texas, Louisiana, and California. In each state, Saul was to take pictures, identify the main refinery plant, and include the latitude and longitude of each of three different locations in the three states.

Sou Ankar had studied communications at Cambridge, England, and was well-versed in the number, types, and locations of both government and commercial defense satellites that were vital in protecting the United States. Sou had been sent to Seattle, Washington, Greenbelt, Maryland (home of NASA), and Maine to hack and record data received by the large satellite dishes in these areas, including times and routes of satellite orbits, as well as communication methods for the related computer location.

Saeed was confident that he had now assembled the information that he required for his master plan to be put into place. Farrid, now in Chicago, had amassed a small fortune, for and under the direction of Saeed, that was deposited in several banks around the world.

Money seemed to be the easiest problem for Saeed to resolve. He had strategically placed his paid mercenaries in various cities with instructions as to their missions, which were to be activated upon twenty-four hours' notice.

Each of these mercenaries was well-paid, and Saeed had certain sums set aside in each of their names that could be accessed with the appropriate passwords. These passwords were only known by Saeed. Each of these mercenaries knew they were to act only upon direct notice from Saeed, and even then, only if that individual had completed his assigned task. Saeed had made sure none of them knew any of the others, and no one person knew any other's mission.

Farrid, unlike the others, was not involved with Saeed just for the money but also for what he visualized as the ultimate placating of Allah for all the sin and corruption he saw in the world. Farrid, more than even Saeed, wished to be able to destroy a multitude of infidels, mainly Americans, and in doing so, to secure a place in Jannah and perhaps even into Firdaus, the Islamic equivalent of Heaven. Yet Farrid would not have joined this jihad without the promise of huge sums of money.

Saeed had promised himself not to allow Farrid to make any major decisions for fear that in doing so, Farrid might inadvertently interrupt or even nullify Saeed's master plan. Saeed allowed himself a small measure of pride and satisfaction that his years of planning, sowing the seeds of unrest, accumulating large sums of money, and placing his soldiers in strategic geographical areas, with only isolated knowledge of how the events soon to take place would unfold.

*****

On Wednesday, before the big game between Army and Navy was to take place, Brady received a call from Bradford. He seemed upset and more worried than usual. Bradford informed Brady that the intelligence agencies had moved to a high alert status as a result of internet communications through social media, as well as intercepts of numerous telecommunications that NSA had reviewed. Islamabad, London, Riyadh, and several other cities were reporting an increase in "chatter" indicating some imminent action that seemed to be put in place. But there was no consensus among the intelligence community as to what that action might be.

The reason for the call to Brady, on the protected telephone line that Bradford had previously installed in Brady's office, was to see if Brady had seen or heard anything from Fallon concerning Farrid. Bradford related to Brady that Farrid was now on the CIA's most wanted list. Apparently, a person fitting Farrid's description had been seen on one of his trips to acquire the information Saeed had requested. He was observed taking pictures and making notes when he thought no one was paying attention. But a military man on vacation had seen Farrid through binoculars while observing wildlife near Spokane, Washington. The soldier had taken a picture and sent it to the NSA as a precaution. Brady was not much help but agreed to check with Fallon as well as Wayne and the various bank branches to see if there was anything unusual occurring. Brady forwarded the picture of Farrid that Bradford had sent him to each of the branch managers and asked that each of them contact Brady immediately if Farrid was spotted.

Simultaneously with Brady hanging up with Bradford, Fallon called. Brady immediately relayed the request by Bradford for any information on Farrid. Fallon, in a high-pitched voice that took Brady by surprise, began describing some investigative work he had been doing on Farrid. First, he had secured copies of two credit cards and the account numbers that had been provided by a source Fallon had at the airport. Then, Fallon had contacted a fellow who Fallon knew to be an expert at hacking into mobile computers. Fallon's source could not decipher what Farrid had typed into the throwaway computer, but he knew Brady would know someone who could. "Zowie," exclaimed Brady, and asked Fallon to meet him at his home at 6:30 p.m. so he could pass the information on to Bradford.

Michael, that same day, had called his mom to see if she had reserved a room for her, Dad, and Sarah to stay overnight that Friday so they would not have to drive and be rushed the Saturday of the game. Michael was excited because he had taken equal snaps with the first-string offensive line. The first-string quarterback was nursing a high ankle sprain from the Ohio State game, which meant there was a good chance Michael would see action on Saturday. Lois smiled knowing Brady would be beaming if indeed Michael did get into the game.

Brady arrived home around 6:00 p.m., and before Lois could tell him about Michael's call, Brady told her to set an extra plate for dinner because Fallon was coming. Lois could tell Brady was preoccupied and decided to tell Brady about Michael later. Meanwhile, she set another place setting at the table for Fallon. Fallon was due there at 6:30 p.m. so Brady called Bradford on the secure line that had been installed in his home by Bradford's people. Brady left a message for Bradford that he would call him with some news when Fallon arrived.

It was now 7:30 p.m., and Lois had kept dinner in the oven to keep it warm. Brady was nervous and kept looking out the dining room window onto the street anxiously awaiting Fallon's arrival. At 8:00 p.m., Brady tried to call Fallon, thinking he had car trouble, an accident, or some other cause for the delay. Finally, failing to get through to Fallon, Brady called Fallon's part-time secretary Lori with whom Fallon always stayed in touch. She answered the phone, and when Brady identified himself, she was at a loss why Fallon had not shown up. She was aware that he was meeting Brady. She told Brady that earlier that day, before Fallon had called Brady, Fallon had been communicating with this person she only knew as Dan. Dan, she knew, was the computer nerd who was assisting Fallon's investigation. It seems that Dan had broken into a computer for Fallon earlier, and that was when he called Brady. When Brady explained Fallon's no-show, she promised to look into Fallon's files to see if she could identify this Dan. Brady thanked her, and after he hung up, turned to Lois in a worried voice, to serve dinner. It looked like Fallon would not be coming.

Early Thursday, around 7:00 a.m., Bradford called Brady to inform him that the body of Fallon, along with an unidentified person, had been found in a waste dump outside the city. Brady was taken aback. Not only had Fallon been his confidante and hired investigator but he was also his closest friend with whom he had shared many combat missions and memories. Brady suddenly recovered from this unexpected shock and bombarded Bradford with questions. Bradford merely said that Fallon had died of a bullet to the back of his head, as had the unknown person found with him.

Brady, now composed, filled Bradford in on the discussions he had recently had with Fallon and that a man named only as Dan had accessed Farrid's computer and that was the information Fallon was bringing to the meeting. The meeting that Fallon failed to attend. Bradford then acknowledged that the unknown person had been identified as Dan O'Reilly, a computer specialist employed at a data processing business in town. When the bodies were found, neither the computer nor the information that Fallon had promised to bring to Brady's house the previous night had been found. Bradford surmised that whoever killed Fallon and O'Reilly probably took those items with them.

Bradford felt it was time to bring Brady up to speed with all that had taken place in just the last few days. Intelligence had discovered Farrid had been visiting various sites in the US where vital dams were located. NSA had additional information on two questionable persons who had been spotted visiting different sites in the US where oil refineries were located. The two, known to be associates of Farrid, had been described as Arabic using perfect English and masquerading as tourists. When Brady inquired what our intelligence agencies believed was afoot, Bradford, not wanting to discuss this matter over the phone, suggested they meet at the Hyatt Regency that night at 10:00 p.m. Brady agreed and hung up.

That afternoon, Brady had purchased the latest Tribune edition when passing the newspaper stand outside his office. He had noticed the headline "Many oil tankers stranded in Hampton, Bermuda." As he read through the articles, Brady learned that someone or some entity had somehow secured control over these tankers and without explanation had taken the tankers out of commission (i.e., left them idle). Brady wondered if this had anything to do with the money transfers that had been detected not only in his bank but also in banks around the world. Puzzling, he thought to himself.

It was late afternoon and Brady decided to head home knowing he would be out late to meet Bradford. On the way home, his mind tried to put together the puzzle that seemed to be floating around in his head. A puzzle that had to be solved if this catastrophe, whatever it might be, was to be avoided. He wondered just how much Bradford knew about what was going on, hopefully a lot more than Brady. As he pulled into his driveway, Lois was waving from the porch. Michael was on the phone and was asking Lois whether they had confirmed their reservations for Friday night at the Hilton. Brady yelled to her to tell him that it was done and they all were excited about going to the game and hopefully seeing Michael play. Brady planned on leaving for Philadelphia around 7:00 a.m. Friday and arriving at the Hilton around 6:00 p.m. Brady told Lois to make sure she requested a late check-in.

It was now 10:00 p.m. Thursday, and Brady was just pulling up to the Hyatt Regency. He left his car with the valet and headed to the bar. He spotted Bradford in the far corner sitting alone. He sat down in the corner booth and shook hands with Bradford. Bradford looked a little disheveled, his hair somewhat mussed, and he had not shaven. Bradford spoke first and asked how his family was and expressed his condolences for the death of Fallon.

Bradford seemed to be perplexed about something but then blurted out that NSA had information concerning Farrid's latest movements and that he had been contacting various contacts around the United States, but to what purpose NSA was still in the dark. Bradford expressed concern that an attack, for the purpose of causing harm to America and its citizens, was imminent. Brady could sense that Bradford was perplexed, even confused as to exactly what catastrophe or disaster might be planned by unknown assailants against America.

Bradford told Brady, earlier in the day, apparently after speaking with Brady, that Fallon and Dan had been spotted while tailing Farrid back to his motel. Farrid waited till they reached his hotel room, then pulled his gun and shot them both. Farrid then hid the bodies, trying to buy enough time to get out of the country. Unfortunate for him, a maid on her routine rounds saw the blood in the room and called the police. When the police arrived, they found the bodies in the dumpster. They found notes in Fallon's pockets detailing Farrid's moves and even listed his tag number for the rental car. An all-points bulletin had gone out for Farrid. The bulletin warned that Farrid was armed and dangerous but if possible to take him alive. Unfortunately, he was shot and killed in a shootout with the airport police at O'Hare Airport.

Farrid, in his trip to the airport, had attempted to contact Saeed at the number Saeed had given him. When dialed, the number rolled into a text that simply said leave a message. The message he had left was that he was burned (cover blown) and leaving for Islamabad, Pakistan. By the time Saeed received the text, he had received a call that Farrid had been shot. Saeed smiled to himself knowing that the police had saved him from having Farrid, who had served his purpose, eliminated by other means. Saeed knew Farrid would not give himself up to the police. Saeed had no fear that his own identity and location could be compromised by the police. NSA ran into a brick wall when attempting to determine who Farrid was trying to contact. The text went to a throwaway cell that had been purchased along with many more from various outlets around the world. Saeed had received the text from Farrid just prior to the cell phone going dead.

Brady saw the concern, almost panic, in the eyes of this professional intelligence agent who had served his country for more than thirty years. Bradford expressed how sad he was at Fallon's death and how meaningless it seemed. Bradford then looked at Brady and said the two of them had to make Fallon's death not be in vain. They had to complete his work and uncover what evil actions had been planned by Farrid and whoever was involved with him. Most of all, he stated, they had to save America from whatever was about to take place.

Bradford confided in Brady that NSA had intercepted communications from persons of interest in the long list of terrorists and potential terrorists, that the big event that had dominated the chatter would take place that Saturday, and everyone in the US intelligence field, as well as around the world, was working 24-7 to pin down exactly what was about to occur. One important lead was the discovery of a call from a cell phone from the US to a cell phone in Dubai. The call originated from a cell tower in the Annapolis, Maryland, area, bounced off a satellite, and connected with a tower near Dubai, but from there was untraceable. By triangulating the call, it was determined that the originating cell phone was presently located in Annapolis, near the Naval Academy. Agents were currently running down the possibilities to see if they could identify the caller. Unfortunately, the number called was to a relay station which in turn dead-ended at the relay. Somehow, or some person, had created an automated self-disconnect of the call immediately when the communication was intercepted.

*****

Bradford explained that NSA had limited their search in Dubai to any location with frequent daily communications being transmitted in and out of Dubai. This brought the possibilities down considerably, and they expected to zero in shortly on the destination of Kareem's call. In the meantime, NSA was experiencing difficulty attempting to pinpoint the location of the originating cell phone before it had been destroyed. Kareem had done as his dad had directed. When they had finished their previous conversation, Kareem crushed the cell phone and threw it into the sewer in front of Ahmed's home.

Brady asked if Bradford had any leads on who Farrid was working with, but Bradford simply shrugged his shoulders and responded no. So far, the NSA only knew that Farrid had been communicating by disposable cell phones to numerous unknown persons around the country. However, at each of the areas Farrid had placed these calls, there were major installations. These installations included dams, refineries, major electric grids, and even several overseas calls to locations in the Caribbean and Middle East. These calls were made with disposable cell phones, and the conversations appeared to be in some kind of code—a code that NSA had yet to decipher.

Kareem had not been in touch with his dad since they had met at the restaurant. Kareem felt bad that he had not told his dad about his going with Ahmed and his family to attend the big football game. Saeed, because he had not heard from Kareem for a few days, was getting concerned, especially with what Saeed knew he had on his schedule for the coming weekend. He left an encrypted text for Kareem Thursday evening asking him to call.

Saeed, for the past week, had been very busy. Saeed was staying around the clock in his offices located in an abandoned two-story office building in Dubai, United Arab Emirates. Saeed had purchased the building three years ago. He had it remodeled and fully wired for the massive computers that he would be installing. In fact, the computer system had been in place for the past six months, and this is how Saeed kept in touch with his small band of fanatical Islamists who were strategically placed around the world. Saeed had each of his soldiers assigned to a small but integral part of his master plan—a plan that was about to be divulged to the world in a series of catastrophes that Saeed hoped would not only shock the Western world but would bring all nations closer to Islam. Although Saeed did not share the fanaticism of his underlings, he had no problem using them to further the word of Allah and to strike down the American infidels. He thought of these men as disposable commodities or collateral damage.

Saeed entered the room in his offices where his computer system was based. There were wall-to-wall computer banks, connectors, relay stations, and large-screen monitors, perhaps twenty in all. It was midnight Thursday in Dubai and 2:00 p.m. Thursday in Chicago. Saeed surveyed his equipment, made certain checks to make sure all were running properly, and then sat down at his desk. The desk was surrounded by 36-inch monitors, each with its own keyboard and hard drive computers. These computers were all connected through routers so that Saeed could interface as necessary.

First, Saeed pulled up his various bank accounts around the world. The money he had accumulated over the past five years was enormous. This included the large money transfers to Malcomb, who Brady had met at his bank's annual dinner/dance. Those transfers to Malcomb were used to purchase a substantial number of the approximately 2,500 oil tankers in the world. This gave Saeed control over the majority of the world's oil tankers. However, he had distributed and redistributed sums to maintain balances that would not cause suspicion. Now he would soon be putting those funds to use for carrying out what Saeed considered fulfilling Allah's will (and satisfying his vengeance). Saeed had bank account numbers for each of his soldiers, soldiers who were about to put his master plan into effect. Each of these associates knew only that Enius would wire into their designated accounts enormous sums for their completion of the clear and concise plans that Saeed had prepared and distributed by text to each. None of them knew how or where Saeed could be located. Their only connection was through their computers to websites that had to navigate numerous and baffling firewalls that Saeed had installed. Each had been previously put on a standby alert, according to Saeed's plans, and given thirty minutes to put each of their tasks into action.

Saeed had his checklist and website lists for each of his accomplices. He had already prerecorded directives to each so that he need only push the forward button to distribute the execute signal to each of them. By 3:00 a.m. Friday, Dubai time, Saeed had completed his checklist for his operational tasks as well as notification to each of his associates to prepare to execute immediately upon his command and to expect a communication from him around 4:00 p.m. (Eastern Standard Time) on Saturday.

*****

It was 9:00 p.m. Thursday, and Kareem was in the middle of playing baloot, a card game that Ahmed's family enjoyed, when his cell phone alerted him that his father had called. It was 5:00 p.m. Friday, Dubai time. Kareem figured he better return the call in case there was an emergency. Kareem had never been to his father's offices in Dubai, mainly because his dad never invited him. But he knew his dad worked there because Saeed had once let him use his gas credit card when he was away at college, and the pump required him to insert the zip code. Since the United Arab Emirates, of which Dubai is a member, does not use zip codes, Kareem had to type in 00000. Then, when the pump prompted, Kareem entered a post office box number his dad had given him. Kareem had been curious and checked out the location of the PO box, which listed Dubai.

When his cell phone vibrated, Saeed noted the call was from Kareem and immediately answered. Saeed was relieved when he heard Kareem's voice. Saeed first inquired if everything was okay, and after Kareem responded yes, Saeed wanted to know why he was not back in school. Saeed had checked at school, only to find that Kareem had taken a few additional days off. Kareem hesitated, realizing his dad had probably forgotten what he had told him when they last met at the restaurant. Kareem reminded his dad where he was and reminded him that he had told him he would be staying with the Jabar family for the next two days. Kareem knew that his dad would not take kindly to him attending an American football game on Saturday. Thus, he decided to bend the truth just a little and informed Saeed that he would be spending the next two days going on a boat ride with the Jabar family on Friday and a tour around Annapolis on Saturday. Saeed became alarmed and tried to hide his concern. He asked Kareem where Ahmed and the Jabar family actually lived. When Kareem mentioned West Port, across the river from the Naval Academy, Saeed calmed down somewhat. This seemed to satisfy Saeed, and after a few more innocuous questions and answers, they said their goodbyes.

Saeed then sent circuitous texts to each of his minions. He alerted the contact he had in the Spokane, Washington, area, a contact Farrid had known for years and one who shared Saeed's hatred for the American infidels. This contact had all the information Farrid had obtained on the major dams in the US. The two Arab brothers, Saul Ankar, who had conducted surveillance of the major US refineries, and Sou Ankar, who had computed and tracked the satellites of the US, including military, Global Positioning Systems, and communications, were waiting for further instructions. He had instructed Malcomb, now in Bermuda, where numerous oil tankers were berthed for maintenance, to stand by for further instructions. Saeed sent each of them an encrypted text message that they would be notified within twenty-four hours to execute their plans of action.

Saeed was well aware that once any or all of the actions took place, the US Armed Forces would immediately be on high alert, and the National Security and Intelligence Agencies for the US would increase security for all installations vital to the security of the US. These agencies would screen all intelligence sources for information, advance defense operations, and direct all military personnel and agencies to go to Defcon One. The President and Cabinet would all be secured, American embassies around the world would be in lockdown, and known persons considered risks would be rounded up. All countries that were anti-American, or even possible adversaries, would be scrutinized for any evidence of their involvement.

Saeed hoped for total confusion among American intelligence agencies, military, and politicians, who would compete for power to diffuse whatever strike might be occurring. Recent mistrust in the American President and his party would cause dissent, pejorative accusations, and chaos would erupt in many major US cities.

*****

It was getting late, almost midnight, and both men were tired and stressed from a difficult day. Bradford said goodbye to Brady and headed home. Brady knew he needed to get some rest and a good night's sleep since he would be driving all day Friday to Philadelphia for the big game. Brady let Bradford know he could reach him at any time over the next three days if anything developed. Brady silently prayed that nothing would develop and that this weekend would be simply a fantastic family outing.

Lois had packed their bags for the overnight stay in Philly. Brady headed home from the Hyatt and arrived just as Lois was heading up to bed. She saw his headlights as he pulled into the driveway. She had laid out some cake and milk, knowing he might be hungry before retiring.

Brady was up before Lois and put on a pot of coffee. It was 6:00 a.m. Lois came down followed by Sarah. All three were excited to begin the day, notwithstanding the long drive ahead. They were looking forward to the Army-Navy game and hopefully to seeing Michael play. Brady carried their overnight bags to the car, and by 8:00 a.m., they were on the road. The trip would take about eleven hours, and they would arrive at the hotel around 6:00 p.m.

Sarah slept most of the way while Lois took advantage of having Brady as a rare captivated audience. Lois brought him up to date with all the latest neighborhood gossip, including which houses had sold on their block and where the neighbors' kids were going to college. She adeptly slipped into areas she hoped would elicit responses from Brady. She asked how he was taking the death of Fallon, what was new at the bank, and why he had to meet so late Thursday night with Bradford. There she hit pay dirt. Brady seemed to have suddenly started paying attention to the substance of her conversation, and his furrowed brow reminded her of the way the ears of a dog or horse seem to indicate you have their attention.

Brady knew there was little he could divulge to Lois about the actions of Farrid and his surreptitious movements. He avoided discussing any conversations he had with Bradford, but Brady did feel the need to at least let Lois know why he had been somewhat reticent lately. He explained by referring to articles that had appeared in their newspaper recently. He discussed the problems with fake news concerning shortages of cash at the banks. He talked about the hacking into customers' bank accounts, not only with his banks but nationwide. He mentioned Farrid, but only to point out the occasions when he had seen him at the football games when Michael had played in high school, and how Farrid had encouraged his son to wrongfully hit a player after the player had crossed the goal line.

Brady was just getting warmed up, and Lois was excited. She had not enjoyed this much conversation with her husband in many years. She could sense that Brady had some pent-up feelings that needed to be expressed. She also knew not to press in areas she knew were taboo. When Brady appeared to catch himself from revealing more than he should, Lois diverted the conversation to Sarah. She knew Brady loved his daughter as much as his son Michael. She asked Brady if he had thought about which college he thought she might attend. Lois reminded him that Sarah had been an honor roll student with almost a four-point grade average. This, she said, would most likely earn Sarah a partial if not a full scholarship to the University of Chicago. Brady, seemingly relaxing now that the subject matter of their discussions had changed, smiled and told Lois how proud he was of both their children. Brady expressed to Lois how much he appreciated her providing the day-to-day rearing of both of them and how Lois had embedded a strong moral compass in each of them.

Lois smiled, a smile that let Brady know he had told her something that meant more than anything else he could have said. Slowly, the time went by as they continued their trip to Philly. Lois drifted off to take a short nap. When she awoke and looked out the window, she was amazed to see they had passed through Indiana and Ohio and were now bypassing Pittsburgh, Pennsylvania. Brady laughed at Lois, who had drool in the corner of her lips. Before she asked, Brady volunteered that they should arrive in Philly in approximately four and a half hours. It was now 1:30 p.m. (EST), and Brady suggested they stop at the next truck stop to use the facilities and get something to eat. Lois and Sarah agreed.

*****

In Dubai, it was 9:30 p.m. (EST), Friday, and Saeed was at his office. Saeed had just awakened from four hours of sleep, and he knew the next twenty-four hours would be hectic. Saeed inspected the rows of monitors and computers that covered nearly half his office space. The office area was a little more than five thousand square feet. He had on various monitors pictures of the United States, bouncing off the many global satellites, and more particularly, pictures of various dams in the Tennessee Valley and the northwest. He had some monitors set on various major cities, zoomed in on the electric grid locations. A couple of monitors projected oil refinery sites. And finally, one monitor, a jumbo screen, had inset pictures being emitted from various satellites orbiting the Earth. Saeed had mastered the art of intercepting the signals from each satellite without being detected and capturing zoomed-in pictures of his selected sites.

Bradford sat at his desk at NSA. Since meeting with Brady the night before, he had only slept six hours, and that was done on his small sofa in one corner of his office. Bradford was more concerned than he had been at any other time since he had been with the NSA. In the past thirteen and a half hours, since he left Brady at the Hyatt, he and others assigned to monitor the chatter and intelligence surrounding the buzz about the big event that was being bantered about had gathered in the NSA crisis room to coordinate their efforts and effect instantaneous sharing of intel. Bradford's team had intercepted communications in the last hour that indicated whatever was about to take place would do so shortly. The term "shortly" was what caused organized chaos in the crisis room. Did this mean in the next few minutes, hours, or days? There were now about fifty analysts in the room, some of the best military, scientific, and intelligence minds in the country. Each had a certain area of expertise, and each of their computers was routed to the others. Bradford was the team leader and answered directly to the director, Admiral Chesney, a thirty-year veteran who had served in several wars on several continents.

The Central Intelligence Agency, NSA, and fifteen other US Intelligence agencies were on alert, DEFCON 3. In addition, there was fierce coordination with allied intelligence forces around the world. Particularly Mossad and Saudi intelligence operatives and assets were requested to assist in trying to identify the substance, source, and location of the "event" that evolved from idle chatter to a full-grown threat to national survival. The Saudis frantically screened their contacts for any information. Mossad also sent out top-secret requests for the latest intel on the rumored "event." Even Russia and their GRU (intelligence successor of the KGB) were brought in to solicit whatever knowledge they might contribute. All of the major countries were well aware that any devastating attack on the US would place the world in a state of paranoia, not knowing from where the next attack might originate or break out.

*****

Kareem, after spending Thursday evening with his friend and Ahmed's family, had slept late Friday and did not wake up until noon. His friend Ahmed teased him about imitating the Americans, whom he and many Arabs considered lazy. Kareem laughed and threw a pillow at Ahmed. Still, Kareem felt guilty knowing his father Saeed would disapprove of his son's desire to enjoy a couple of carefree days. The Ahtari family was already packing food for the boat ride around Annapolis that Ahmed's father had planned. Kareem barely had enough time to shower and brush his teeth when Ahmed announced they were ready to leave.

The family and Kareem jumped into Ahmed's father's car and drove to Westport, where they boarded a twenty-seven-foot O'Day sailboat. Ahmed chuckled when Kareem's facial expression indicated he was surprised they would be sailing instead of motor boating. Ahmed's dad manned the mainsail while Ahmed and his brother handled the jib. After a few instructions on how to maneuver and stay out of the way of the mainstay and the swinging jib, Kareem settled in. They sailed out of the inlet into the Chesapeake Bay. It was a sunny day, somewhat chilly. Kareem had been alerted to dress warmly. He wore a nice cashmere sweater over a cotton turtleneck. Over the sweater, he had a three-fourth length topcoat, with gloves. Once out into the bay, he was treated to a beautiful view of the Naval Academy, as well as the Bay Bridge and surrounding scenery of expensive homes, yachts, and many sailboats.

Ahmed's father commented on how beautiful this part of America was and how different it was compared to the harsh landscapes of Iraq and Afghanistan. Mr. Jabar was obviously an accomplished sailor, and Kareem could see the peace and calm reflected in his subtle smile while steering the sailboat to catch the wind in its sails, keeping the shoreline in sight. They sailed down to Bloody Point and then circled back. Kareem chatted with Ahmed for the several hours while they were sailing, discussing their college experiences and dreams for when they would graduate. Mr. Jabar participated in some of their dialogue, often in a religious manner, wishing that the world Ahmed and Kareem would inherit might be safer and more pleasant than the current state of affairs. Kareem thought of his dad and silently wished he could've shared in this special occasion.

The wind had picked up, and it was looking like rain, so Mr. Jabar steered the boat back to the inlet and up to the slip where the boat was berthed. He mentioned that this would be the last occasion for sailing and he would soon place the boat in dry dock. Kareem and Ahmed helped with furling the sails and securing the ropes and bumper protectors between the boat and the dock. It was now 6:00 p.m. (EST), and they headed back to the Ahtari residence. Mrs. Jabar had prepared a fine dinner, and Kareem, Ahmed, his brother, and Mr. Jabar enjoyed the enticing aromas that filled the house.

*****

Bradford telephoned Brady just as Brady and his family were stopping at a service station to visit the restroom. Lois had offered to share the driving and was behind the wheel when the call came through from Bradford. Bradford requested Brady not put him on speaker so they could discuss information he had just received. Bradford explained to Brady that NSA was intercepting more and more chatter on various throwaway cell phones. These were suspicious communications—some texted, some telephone conversations, even emails, though obviously encrypted—that kept referring to activities across the nation that were about to occur.

Brady listened intently but wondered to himself why Bradford was sharing this apparently top-secret information with him. Brady was appreciative of the trust in him that Bradford was displaying, but nonetheless concerned that Bradford was sharing this information. Bradford, sensing Brady's curiosity about the phone call, stated that many of the intercepted communications used the name "Enius," often in context with the mention of payments, bank accounts, directions, and time deadlines.

Now Bradford had set off a light bulb in Brady's mind. Brady recalled the conversations he had with Bradford when Bradford had mentioned Enius in conjunction with the name of Saeed. Brady had wondered if there was any remote possibility that this could be the same Saeed that Brady had fought against in Afghanistan, and perhaps this was the real reason for the call. Bradford, recognizing Brady's escalating interest in their conversation, identified Saeed as Ahtari Saeed (a.k.a. Abdullah Saeed). Bradford explained that intel on Saeed revealed that he had served in the Desert Storm war against the United States, where he had lost his family in a miscue by an American pilot who had dropped bombs on the village where Saeed was raised. Saeed's family did not survive.

Brady asked how this Saeed was involved in the intelligence community's concern for the events that were taking place, or rather about to take place. Both Bradford and Brady were now feeding off each other for information concerning Saeed that might help to unravel the enigma surrounding the intercepted communications and the intel gathered by numerous intelligence agencies in the US and around the world. Brady was anxious to hear more about Saeed, especially his history since they had thrown stones at each other while trapped neck-high in dirt and rubbish in the cave in Iraq.

STOIC REVENGE

Bradford now believed that Saeed was deeply involved in the apparent terrorist activities that NSA believed were about to happen. He unveiled to Brady the bulk of the intel that NSA had on Saeed. They knew that Brady was acquainted with Saeed from the notes on file taken during Brady's debriefing before his leaving the Middle East to be discharged back in the United States. They knew that Saeed had attended school at Virginia Tech in Blacksburg, Virginia. They knew Saeed had majored in political science, physics, and computer science before leaving school in his senior year to return home after his family was killed by the American bombs.

NSA knew, according to Bradford, that after his service with the insurgents in Iraq and the incident involving Brady, Saeed returned home to what was left of the bombed-out village, now deserted. Saeed, it was believed, went back to school, finished his undergraduate work, and attended graduate school at Cambridge University. There, Saeed majored in computer science and physics. He excelled as a student, was generally regarded with an extremely high intellect, and was known to be a loner with very few friends. Once he obtained his graduate degrees in computer science and physics, Saeed returned to Iraq, and that is where the history ends. No one had seen Saeed thereafter, though rumors had him becoming an extremely successful businessman. Knowing Saeed's educational background, Bradford believed that Saeed might have connections to the attacks on the bank accounts and other activities related to Enius. Bradford could see the connection and silently prayed it wasn't true.

Brady was amazed at the information NSA had gathered on Saeed. Brady also wondered what kind of person Saeed had become—was he really a terrorist as assumed by the intel, or was he just a disillusioned, vengeful individual as Brady recalled from their brief contact? Brady wondered if he would be able to recognize Saeed if he met up with him.

Brady's reminiscing about Saeed was suddenly interrupted by Bradford bellowing to someone on another line, "Who was it? Do we know?" Bradford told Brady he would call him back, but not before he explained that someone had just destroyed one of our oil refineries in Tennessee. Brady sat back, aghast that the US had just experienced another terrorist attack. Brady tuned into the news station on the car radio to see if any of the media had more details on the attack.

Within fifteen minutes, all the stations were broadcasting the news of what was being described as a terrorist attack on a refinery in Memphis, Tennessee. Details of the attack or the amount of damage done were not yet available. Brady hoped that Bradford would call later with more information. Brady knew that Bradford would keep him in the loop if he thought Brady could assist with more information about Saeed. Apparently, NSA believed Saeed was a participant in the attack, but how and why were a mystery to Bradford and apparently to NSA.

Saeed was alone, as usual, in his office in Dubai. For the past week, he had confined himself to his surroundings, sleeping on the couch and ordering food from local eateries. He was surrounded by computers and monitors. He smiled to himself noting how easy, and yet successful, his computer hack into the intricate computer network at the refinery in Memphis, Tennessee had been. Saeed's man in the US had relayed back to Saeed's computers the nature and extent of the layers of anti-malware and system protections that had been employed by the operators of the refinery. That had been done weeks ago, the same time as the information Saeed had accumulated on the location of the oil tankers in the western hemisphere, the computers operating the major dams in the USA, and power grids, and substantial international banking transfers. After receiving each of his field personnel's reports, Saeed wired them the agreed funds for their services, and then these mercenaries had disappeared.

Saeed's computer setup resembled what one would expect to see at Amazon or Google headquarters. Saeed looked at the chart he had in front of him, one that he had prepared previously to assist him in keeping to the timeline he had projected for the disasters he had planned for the American infidels. Saeed also had several television sets tuned into local and global TV stations. This, he figured, would enable him to track the methods and procedures of the responses to each of his planned events. No one except Saeed, alone and fixated upon what he had planned for the next twenty-four hours, knew of the entangled web he had spun to spread fear and destruction upon the American infidels. It was now 11:00 p.m. (EST), and Saeed tuned in to the evening news from Washington, DC.

*****

Kareem was just going to bed, as was the rest of the Jabar family, when they heard the news come over the television networks. There was no celebration, only dismay at the destruction of the refinery, and everyone turned in for the night.

Michael had talked briefly with his mom. Lois told him that his sister and dad were in the car and they would arrive in Philly around 11:00 p.m. Michael had bifurcated feelings of joy that his family was coming to the big game, and anxiety that he may see action at quarterback during the game. Michael only briefly dwelt on the news about the terrorist attack earlier that day. Though concerned, he would not let this detract him from his big day Saturday.

Bradford was now fully occupied with the preliminary reports from NSA field operatives that had been flown into Memphis. The location of the oil refinery was now inundated with FBI, CIA, and National Security forces as well as Bradford's people. Early reports revealed that there had been a cyberattack on the plant computer system, including the backup system. It was reported that someone, or somehow, there had been a digital break-in of the highly classified protection programs employed at the scene, which in turn somehow spread through the computer system much like a virus, but much more complex and layered. Bradford, being well trained in cyberattacks, knew that there were several thousand different cyber break-ins discovered by NSA every day. Bradford stopped to rub his eyes while he cleaned his glasses, his facial expression belying from his colleagues, that he had worried this day would come. He was well aware of the potential and probability that this type of cyberattack would occur. Bradford was a master at masking his true feelings, and at this time, he knew he had to project confidence and calm as he struggled through each tranche of evidence he received from the scene.

*****

The explosion at the oil refinery occurred around 10:45 (EST). Saeed turned to a second computer, one of at least twenty positioned around his large office. Saeed had not only mastered the art of protecting trace backs on his computer, but he also utilized many different computers to complicate tracking his digital instructions to wherever he decided to seek his vengeance.

Saeed smiled arrogantly as he selected the next target listed in his schedule of destruction. He typed in an algorithm which transmitted particles on the backs of photons that were then bounced off global locations. Over the years, Saeed had equipped and installed receptors and echo chambers causing the photon carriers to bounce from receptor to receptor, finally having the piggybacked particles meet up at the appointed computers at locations designated for destruction.

Saeed's methods were not necessarily innovative; they had their conception during the life of Einstein, when he called this particular activity "spooky physics." This was a period when leading theoretical physicists were attempting to understand and delve into the world of quantum mechanics. Einstein and others were leery of the manner in which subatomic particles reacted, sometimes in opposition to known laws of physics. Saeed had explored this area of physics as it related to the cyber world and expanded on the theory of quantum entanglement. This was an area of physics that had captured Saeed's curiosity and one that fascinated him. How could two things such as particles or photons occupy the same space at the same time, contrary to basic laws of physics, and coexist as if residing in parallel universes?

Few of his peers had committed as much time and especially money to develop expertise in this field. Saeed was able to direct the subatomic particles that he piggybacked on the light photons traveling at the speed of light. These photons, when received at designated locations around the world, produced a coded message that invaded targeted computer programs. The piggybacked photons then deciphered and disabled any protective measures, and installed new instructions onto their hard drives. This allowed Saeed to control the computer operations at any particular location. The basic theory was based upon probabilities that only Saeed comprehended. Until now, Saeed had only used his expertise to intercept money transfers, funneling the funds back to his numerous bank accounts, thus accumulating vast sums which enabled him to amass his intricate and successfully hidden network of equipment.

Saeed quickly glanced at his list of sites and began his systematic entries into the second computer. He next selected one of the dams in the Tennessee Valley Authority network. He activated a particle collider he had hidden underground in a secluded area of the Sahara Desert in Africa, typed in the code that sent a message to the collider to transmit certain photons, laden with certain subatomic particles, to a receptor in the Andes Mountains of Peru. From there, the digital messengers would reverberate in the direction of the Chickamauga Dam in Chattanooga, Tennessee. By reversing the levy controls of water pouring through the dam and disrupting the turbines and dynamos, Saeed could unleash a torrent of water on the land, buildings, and houses downstream, causing mass destruction of property and lives.

The time was now 11:45 (EST). Brady, Lois, and Sarah had just pulled into the Hyatt in Philadelphia. Brady and Lois had been listening to the news of the oil refinery, and now they heard the initial reports from Chattanooga that the dam had given way and flooding of the valley below the dam was rampant and uncontrollable. Brady thought about Bradford and how he must be overwhelmed trying to coordinate information, evidence, and dissemination of what he had learned, to brief his superiors and then the public. Brady wanted to pick up his cell and call Bradford, but he knew he wouldn't get through. Lois searched Brady's facial expression to assess the degree of concern she should have. Brady assured her that US intelligence, the FBI, and hundreds if not thousands of highly trained specialists were using every means available to understand, control, and defuse the situation.

Brady checked in to their room, and he and Lois, after putting away their luggage, shared one double bed, while Sarah crawled into the other. All three were glued to the television, set on the latest news, for the next half hour before each drifted off to sleep. Brady, before falling asleep, wondered how Michael might be doing and if he was aware of what was going on with the news. He convinced himself that Michael was probably so engrossed with the big game the next day that he was not even aware of the events that had just taken place.

*****

Saeed selected certain algorithms from a reference book he had prepared from his in-depth studies over the years. These algorithms contained the formulas for evading and perplexing malware programs throughout the world. The formulas were designed to react to evidence that malware was activated and to disengage and divert the cyber obstacles such malware initiated. All this was accomplished within two or three seconds, not leaving enough time for the firewalls to become effective.

One set of algorithms dealt with piercing the firewalls protecting the electric grids in the USA. The more secure facilities had what was called a QKD ("quantum key distribution") system. The QKD sent out infrared photons in a particular set and ran them through a loop to see if the set of photons had changed, which would indicate something had interfered with the set. By utilizing a piggyback method of attaching certain particles to certain photons, he would be able to infiltrate and rewrite the software programs that had been installed in the computers that operated and controlled highly protected areas of national concern. Using this concept in physics of changing the polarization of photons, and by masking this change from the firewalls protecting the computer programs, he could take control of the grid computers and have his way with them without fear of detection. This is exactly what he had employed to effect the explosion at the oil refinery in Memphis, Tennessee.

It was now 11:15 (EST), and Saeed hit "Enter" on the keyboard of his computer, thus unleashing the irreversible cyber instructions that would immediately instruct the dam in Chattanooga, Tennessee, to open its intake gates in the fully open position, which in turn allowed the enormous supply of reservoir water to cascade down on the valley below. This all occurred within less than a minute.

Subsequently, houses, farm buildings, electric grids, humans, and animals were all immediately inundated with the torrent of water spreading throughout the lower basin.

Emergency services kicked into action. The National Guard was called out by the governor in Tennessee to assist in rescuing those persons who could be reached. The President, within hours of Saeed's dastardly act, declared a national emergency and directed FEMA personnel to Chattanooga, and the US Army to assist in whatever manner they deemed appropriate. The FBI had their top cyber warfare agents dispatched to the dam area. The NSA learned of the attack within minutes and diverted some of their assets already at work at the refinery destruction in Memphis, Tennessee, to Chattanooga. These NSA experts were scouring over internet transmissions, satellite disturbances (outsiders using without consent), and tracking digital records recorded by the on-site computers that were attacked.

Bradford sat back in his chair and pondered how someone or some entity could break through the several layers of protective firewalls employed to protect against the intrusion and breakthrough of an undetected malware. Even the most classified and leading-edge preventive measures had been employed at the major utilities, water sources, dams, electric grids, stock exchanges, and everywhere and everything that had been declared top priority. Quantum developments in the field of physics had been utilized, only recently, to protect our banking transfers, national and international, as well as our elite military weaponry, including the nuclear missiles. Were these also exposed, Bradford mused to himself.

Bradford paused and said a prayer that the Almighty would intervene and enlighten our intel personnel on how to intercept these dastardly attacks and to neutralize them.

The oil refinery destruction in Memphis not only created chaos at the site and with our response organizations but also caused concern that if other refineries were attacked, the US would have to release our oil reserves. This in turn would also require oil tankers to transport refined oil from other sources. Frantic calls by oil executives as well as applicable government personnel quickly revealed that there was a worldwide shortage of oil tankers. Saeed had anticipated this situation and knew his acquisition and restriction of available tankers, now based in Bermuda, would cause even more chaos and fear.

Top brass at the Pentagon, FBI, National Intelligence, and other agencies met at the NSA with the director and his top aides, especially Bradford. The meeting occurred in less than two hours. After a very brief summary of the explosion in Memphis and the dam release in Chattanooga, the director asked Bradford to provide a snapshot assessment of what the US knew to date and what else we could expect, if known.

General Hathaway, head of the Joint Chiefs of Staff, interrupted Bradford to recommend the President immediately declare a national emergency and that military personnel be deployed to protect all facilities that had been designated essential to our nation's survival. Bradford responded that he agreed, but that would not protect against what had been a cyberattack in both Memphis and Chattanooga. Most in the room agreed. Bradford briefed the assemblage on the intel NSA had to date concerning the chatter of a big event that was about to occur. Bradford went on to express his opinion that perhaps the attacks on the dams, grids, refineries, banks, etc., as a whole, were the big event. He went into the information they had on various figures identified as extremely dangerous, which led him to the intercepts of wire communications out of Dubai that might have some relation to the instant attacks.

*****

Next on Saeed's list of chaos and destruction was the electric grid for Chicago, Illinois. Saeed reached into his collection of algorithms for possible QKD destinations. He found the applicable formulas that would decipher the encrypted firewalls. He had studied how these QKD firewalls, once they were sent out as infrared photons in different directions in a loop, were examined to detect any change in the photons when they returned to their source. Such a change in the polarization of the photon is caused when an electric field disturbs the electrons in orbit about a positive atomic nucleus, causing the atom to have one side positive and one side negative, and in turn, causing the photon to have one side negative and the other positive. Saeed had learned that historically, physicists had determined that when scientists attempted to measure a photon, which is much smaller than an atom, it would in effect disappear or be lost. In addition, as a messenger, the photon itself could only be effective for about one hundred miles before the photon's quantum properties changed too much to be effective. This is why he coordinated the use of his echo receptors strategically placed around the United States. These receptors acted as relay stations to the quantum particles Saeed's equipment piggybacked on the intruder photons to intercept and replace those photons employed by the firewall.

Saeed knew from his attack on the firewalls protecting the electric grid for Chicago that intruders could be detected by any change to the photons being circulated by the firewall but could not identify the intruder. Thus, his identity was safe.

Saeed initiated the digital signals, utilizing the appropriate algorithms to start a domino effect upon the sub-grids comprising the power grid for Chicago. One by one, sections of Chicago and its suburbs went dark. Many citizens had followed the news recently of the floods caused by the failure of dams in various parts of the USA, the oil refinery in Memphis, and now the power grid in Chicago. Panic was beginning to spread. Bradford in his office at NSA and Brady in Philadelphia both wondered if these disasters were correlated, which they both believed to be true, and if Saeed could actually be the mastermind behind it all.

The ramifications of Saeed's work had caused panic, fear, and the intended chaos, and now permeated every city and state in the USA. State National Guards were called out, all emergency personnel and equipment were directed to affected areas, and our intelligence agencies were overloaded. All the while, there was a worldwide search for Saeed and his son Kareem. The NSA now knew the call from Kareem to Saeed had come from the Annapolis area to Dubai. But the trail ended with too broad an area of Dubai to pin down the exact location. Had Kareem taken just a few more minutes before destroying the cell phone as Saeed had directed, agents could have pinpointed Saeed's office. However, before it was destroyed, they were able to triangulate the cell used by Kareem to Eastport in Annapolis.

*****

It was now 3:30 a.m. (EST). Kareem had been tossing and turning in his bed. He had been dreaming that his father, Saeed, had been slain by unnamed men. Kareem tried to help, but could only witness his dad dying in the street. Kareem awoke with tears in his eyes. Realizing immediately it was just a dream, Kareem felt an urgent need to contact his father. Kareem loved his dad dearly even though he had not seen him regularly in the last ten years. In the past two years, Kareem and Saeed had become very close. Kareem attributed this to his father getting older and lamenting more and more the loss of his mother, Saeed's wife. Even when Saeed and Kareem had been somewhat estranged, Saeed always monitored Kareem's movements, his education, and his well-being.

Kareem, after flipping his pillow wet with his tears, softly shook Ahmed in the bed next to his. Kareem apologized for awakening him and then politely asked if he could use the telephone to call his dad. He mentioned the dream and explained his concern for his father. He promised to make it a collect call. Ahmed said of course and pointed to the telephone on the night table. Kareem picked up the phone and dialed a number that Saeed had explicitly told him to use only in a true emergency.

Saeed had just initiated his next act of devastation. This time he attacked both the Boulder Dam and the Hoover Dam. As in Chattanooga, the gates were opened, and flooding of the valleys below had begun. An already taxed national defense agency, the FBI, CIA, and NSA kicked into gear and the respective heads of the departments immediately convened again to assess and evaluate possible actions. The fact that the person or entity behind these attacks could evade the firewalls baffled computer specialists. The reversing of the closing of the dams proved difficult and backup measures had been thwarted.

Bradford had very little sleep in the last forty-eight hours. He opened his file on Saeed since this was the only real lead to what had transpired. The director demanded Bradford read every bit of data the agency had on this person Saeed. Bradford went through the debriefing report on Brady and specifically paid attention to Brady's description of Saeed.

Bradford reread the entry in the file where Brady assessed his enemy Saeed and his military and political leanings. Brady had stated his discussions with Saeed in the cave led him to the opinion that Saeed was a devout fundamentalist Muslim. That he was also a very intelligent individual who had his own moral compass and put family above all else. The hatred Saeed held for Americans was not merely as infidels in the eyes of the Koran but for the single act of misjudgment of an American fighter pilot, one who would carry that burden the rest of his life.

Brady's assessment of Saeed being family-oriented led Bradford to search for any immediate family for Saeed. Bradford shifted to NSA files for more updated information.

There Bradford found mention of a wife and son. Further investigations revealed the wife died and the son, named Kareem, was still alive. Bradford immediately sent out to all agents a BOLO request for the location of Kareem Saeed, male approximately twenty-two and most likely enrolled in a college or university in the Middle East. Almost instantaneously, a report came in from one of Bradford's agents in Pakistan, that he had come across a Kareem Saeed when investigating Farrid, a man associated with Saeed. It was believed that Kareem was the son of Saeed and was known to be a student at the University of Riyadh, in Saudi Arabia.

Bradford slammed the files down, picked up the phone, and called Brady. This time there were no amenities. He told Brady he needed his assistance in locating Saeed. He informed Brady of the existence and possible location of Kareem. Bradford's intel believed the Annapolis call was possibly initiated from Kareem, and if so, Kareem might be in the Annapolis area. Brady responded that he wasn't sure just what Bradford wanted him to do. Bradford said he hoped to have Kareem located and hopefully in custody very shortly.

If so, he wanted Brady to sit in on the initial interview, and perhaps assist in gaining Kareem's confidence by virtue of Brady's past experience with Kareem's father Saeed.

Brady was requested to keep his cell phone free and keep himself available for future discussions. Brady, after hanging up with Bradford, turned to Lois and tried to allay any concerns she had. But obviously, with all that was going on in the world, she was visibly shaken. He assured her that our top intel people were feverishly scrambling to stop the attacks and to identify the perpetrator. Brady then tried to convince himself that this was not Armageddon. Brady could not comprehend how Saeed could cause these horrific attacks unless he was allied with a country with powerful assets at its disposal. But Bradford had come across as believing Saeed was the creator of all the havoc that had been inflicted upon the nation. Bradford also made it perfectly clear that NSA was focusing all its resources on finding and stopping Saeed.

Bradford, in the midst of briefing the top brass and politicians, pondered over what and where the mastermind of these attacks might be planning next. Bradford likened himself as well as his immediate superiors to a boxer who had just been pummeled and was trying to maintain his bearings. His intimate knowledge of the effect and response to the latest attacks made him realize just how little the sharpest brains and intelligence officers understood the complexity of what Bradford considered to be an existential attack upon the USA. Not since Pearl Harbor had the American people endured a threat of this magnitude. The attack on the American naval base and even the 9/11 attack on the World Trade Center did not come close to what America was now experiencing.

Saeed, in the midst of his inflicting fear, panic, and mass destruction as his wanton vengeance upon the United States, was distracted by the alert on one of his throwaway cell phones. It was the one Saeed had marked with a bright red K. This throwaway cell phone he had designated only for Kareem's use and only for an emergency. Saeed hesitated but then answered hoping all was well with Kareem. Kareem blurted out the dream he had just awakened from and how much he was concerned for his father's well-being.

STOIC REVENGE

Saeed was in a state of euphoria with all the havoc he had recently unleashed upon the United States, but this call from Kareem unnerved him. His mindset immediately transformed from an evil-minded being seeking and taking revenge upon his adversary to a somewhat normal father concerned for his only child, Kareem.

While Kareem was relating the details of his dream to Saeed, Saeed was questioning why Kareem felt the call was such an emergency, especially at a time when Saeed was implementing a torrent of chaos and destruction upon a lifelong enemy, the USA.

Within minutes, Saeed calmed Kareem and assured him it was only a bad dream and Saeed was in no danger. However, Kareem did become concerned when his father truncated the call by admonishing Kareem for using the emergency line and counseling Kareem against such actions in the future. Saeed gave him a new number to use. Little did Kareem know that his father was responsible for the recent attacks on America. And little did Saeed know, because Kareem had decided not to tell him, that Kareem, instead of flying back to Riyadh, had planned to stay with Ahmed and his family to attend the Army-Navy game at Franklin Financial Field in Philadelphia that day.

*****

NSA and CIA agents were scouring the campus at Riyadh University for any documents or students or professors that had information on the whereabouts of Kareem. The agents, along with Saudi intel agents, visited the registrar's office. There they determined Kareem's courses and the days and times of his classes. Since it was now Saturday in Riyadh, Kareem had no classes scheduled. However, the agents discovered who his professor was for his computer science class and called him at home. The professor recalled Kareem but had no idea where he could be located. When pressed further, the professor did recall that Kareem was friendly with another student, Ahmed Jabar.

It wasn't long before the agents determined that both Ahmed and Kareem had requested permission to skip classes for a couple of days so they could travel to the USA to visit Ahmed's family. A little more investigation led to the address for Ahmed's family in Annapolis, Maryland. This news tied together the cell phone call to Dubai that NSA had determined originated in the Annapolis area. Putting this intel together with the knowledge that Ahmed and Kareem were staying at the Jabar's home cemented Bradford's belief that Kareem was indeed in Annapolis.

Now it was 9:00 a.m. (EST) on Saturday, and the agents had relayed the location of Ahmed's family address in Annapolis to Bradford's agents. They, in turn, briefed Bradford, and Bradford contacted Brady. Brady, Lois, and Sara were just having breakfast in the hotel restaurant when Brady got the call from Bradford. Bradford briefed Brady on what had transpired in the last few hours and stated the agency was closing in on locating Saeed's son Kareem. The local agents in Annapolis had found no one at home, but neighbors had seen them loading up the Cadillac SUV as if they were headed off on a trip. Where, they didn't know. A BOLO had been sent out for the Cadillac SUV with its tag number in hopes of intercepting the vehicle. What the agents had not discovered was that Ahmed's dad had rented a large recreational vehicle, like a trailer, but one outfitted as if it was a junket to Atlantic City. Ahmed's dad had parked the Cadillac in the public parking garage in downtown Annapolis, where the family boarded the RV along with the driver provided to do the driving.

Brady walked out of the restaurant to take Bradford's call. Brady had not slept well, with all the events that had taken place in the last twenty-four hours. Brady's mind was swirling like the rotor on a helicopter coming down in an LZ, a vision he had experienced many times when in combat. Brady asked Bradford what he expected Brady might be able to do if they did locate Kareem. Bradford quickly responded that he wanted Brady to try to win over Kareem's confidence by relating the short period Brady and Kareem's dad had been trapped in the cave and hopefully ascertain if Saeed could, in fact, be the one behind the recent attacks, and if so, what his intentions were, as well as figure out how to stop him. Brady told Bradford that he and Lois and his daughter were setting out around 11:00 a.m. (EST) for Franklin Financial Field to make sure they were seated by game time at 1:00 p.m. (EST).

When Brady walked back into the restaurant, Lois could see by his face that something was terribly wrong. When pressed, Brady decided it was okay to let her know he was working with Bradford and the NSA on matters related to the recent attacks. Lois knew not to push further. She felt comfortable that if there was immediate danger to their family, Brady would keep her in the loop.

Bradford laid down on the sofa in his office, and while gazing at the ceiling, he took inventory of the last twenty-four hours. A refinery had been destroyed, three dams had been unleashed, and the power grid for Chicago had been disabled. Whoever was behind these wanton acts was extremely astute in cyber warfare and had an enormous source of funds to carry out this monumental destruction and carnage. It must be Saeed.

While loading up the car to leave for the stadium, Brady received a call on his cell from Wayne at the bank. Brady was perplexed as to why Wayne would be calling him on a Saturday, let alone a Saturday Wayne knew Brady was with his family and about to attend the big Army-Navy game. Wayne sounded distraught and immediately asked Brady if he was up to date with these attacks nationwide. Brady assured him he was and informed him only that he had been in touch with a friend at NSA and had confidence that our military and intelligence forces were on high alert and putting in place the proper protections and responses.

It was then that Wayne explained the call. Wayne had received a call from one of his chief tellers that numerous withdrawals of millions of dollars had occurred on Friday. The reason Wayne felt this was important enough to call Brady was that the money withdrawn was from accounts in the name of Enius and was transferred to offshore banks in the name of Kareem Saeed. These withdrawals totaled hundreds of millions of dollars and were sent to trusts set up for Kareem Saeed at each of these offshore banks. Wayne remembered Brady asking to be informed of any transactions involving Farrid or Enius. Brady, after copying down the names of the offshore banks, thanked Wayne and assured him the information was valuable.

Upon hanging up with Wayne, Brady took some deep breaths and then tried to make sense out of what Wayne had told him. Brady kept going over in his head what Bradford had warned about this big event that NSA believed was about to take place. Bradford had explained to him that NSA did not believe any of the attacks that had already occurred were the big event the intel community had uncovered. Unless it was the totality of these attacks that made up the big event. Maybe, he thought, the attacks were over, and Kareem was somehow involved with his father Saeed. This would account for the large bank withdrawals placed into trust accounts for Kareem. Then again, perhaps Saeed was following a similar path to a suicide bomber and was about to kill himself. Brady knew he was merely guessing, and if in fact Saeed really was a genius, as seemed to be the consensus of the intel community, perhaps the worst was yet to come.

*****

Within the last hour, first responders had controlled the fire in Memphis at the refinery, used the turbines to reclose the three dams, reignited the Chicago power grid, and put into action FEMA and thousands of response teams. Many Americans had lost their lives in the flooding and the lack of power at hospitals and emergency facilities. The Department of Energy not only released the oil reserves but also secured some oil tankers to take up the slack for transportation and distribution where needed. The President called for all Americans to provide whatever assistance they could to those in need and to show whoever was responsible for these evil attacks that America would never succumb to such maniacal acts.

Bradford was summoned to the War Room at NSA for another briefing and strategy meeting. Bradford coordinated with his chief lieutenants and prepared to brief the Joint Chiefs of Staff as well as the President. So far, all that was known about who was behind these attacks was that the usual suspect terrorists on the agency's lists had all been cleared or discounted, given the enormity and complexity of each attack. More and more, it appeared that this one person called Saeed had somehow amassed a fortune and harbored a deep animosity towards the USA. This animosity evolved from a simple mistake by an American fighter pilot on an errant bombing mission that took place some twenty years ago.

Ahmed's father had driven the RV to Philadelphia for the big game between Navy and Army. It was noon (EST), and they had just arrived at the stadium parking lot. Ahmed, his family, and Kareem were excited about participating in their first tailgate party at an American college football game. Mrs. Jabar had brought hot dogs and hamburgers and a mini grill that Mr. Jabar set up on the pull-down tailgate of the RV. Game time was 1:00 p.m. (EST). Kareem was like a little kid, enjoying the excitement and amazing displays of taunting and good-natured insults from opposing fans.

At first, Kareem wondered how each side could hurl insults and what he had learned was trash talk at the other without either side taking umbrage. It was his first American hot dog. Kareem was ecstatic, as if he had an epiphany of what America might be like when participating in one of their national sports. Kareem had always been very respectful to his elders, and he lifted his hot dog to Mr. Jabar as if to toast the occasion and his thanks for being made a part of this event. Mr. Jabar and the rest of his family returned the gesture.

Michael had left his dorm and suited up for the game around 10:30 a.m. after leaving the film room located in the stadium. He had gone over the films for previous Army games and familiarized himself with their various defenses. This was just a rehash of what the quarterback coach had been hammering into their heads the past week. Michael felt confident he had absorbed the data provided by the scouts and was anxious to get in the game if needed.

Brady, Lois, and Sarah arrived at the stadium about 12:30 p.m. (EST) and proceeded to the will-call window. Brady asked Lois to stay at the will-call window for their tickets while he checked in with Bradford. Brady did not get through the first few times, but finally, he heard Bradford in a voice that sounded curt and slightly high-pitched. Brady immediately knew that Bradford was under tremendous strain and stress. He asked Bradford if there was any news on the whereabouts of Kareem or Saeed.

Bradford had just stepped out of the war room at NSA. He quickly brought Brady up to speed with respect to the latest intel on Saeed. Intel had pinned down the location of Saeed in the northwest section of Dubai. They had not discovered the local address, but they were sure he was in one of the high-rise office buildings in a four-block radius. Bradford was more concerned with passing on the latest information he had on locating Kareem. Agents had scoured the neighborhood where Mr. Jabar had parked his Cadillac and discovered where he had rented the RV as well as the make, model, and tag number. It was believed by the person renting the RV that the Jabar family was headed to Philadelphia for the Army/Navy game.

Brady immediately reminded Bradford that he and his family were in Philadelphia for the Army/Navy game. Bradford drew a long breath and then relaxed as he informed Brady that intel had concluded that the main event everyone was trying to uncover was believed to be the Army/Navy game. But this latest intel that Kareem was attending the game appeared to dismiss this theory. Brady at first was concerned, and his first impulse was to rush back to Lois and Sarah and leave the stadium. However, after listening to Bradford and reaching the same conclusion about the game being the possible target, Brady was somewhat reassured but still unsettled. He thought of Michael on the field and knew there was no way he could protect Michael without alerting the rest of the team, coaches, and the rest of the stadium.

Brady wanted the name of the family Kareem was visiting so he could check with the box office to determine whether there was a record of their seat location. Bradford agreed that if Brady did secure Kareem's location, it could well bring Saeed out in the open. At least, it might create a line of communication with Saeed.

Saeed had taken time to eat the dinner he had ordered delivered, and as he paused, he decided to make what might be his final communication to his son Kareem. Saeed dialed Kareem's dorm room, hoping to catch him just before or after his evening prayers. He let the phone ring seven or eight times, and just as he was about to hang up, a man's voice answered. Saeed asked for Kareem, and the voice of one of the resident students on the other end said Kareem was not in and, in fact, was not even in Riyadh. Saeed's intuition told him to hang up, but with the urgency of the situation, with all that was happening in the United States, Saeed felt the need to speak with Kareem immediately if possible. Saeed identified himself as Kareem's father and asked the student where Kareem might have gone. "To America," the voice responded, "I believe to Annapolis, Maryland, with his friend Ahmed Jabar." Saeed was stunned as he disconnected the line.

The last thing Saeed anticipated was that Kareem would be in America, let alone Annapolis, at the same time Saeed was unleashing his vengeance on the Americans. Saeed slumped in his chair and contemplated how suddenly his carefully formulated plans, as well as his grand finale, were now complicated by the presence of Kareem in America. The one thing of value to Saeed, the only thing that Saeed valued more than his revenge on America, was Kareem. Kareem was the first thing he thought of in the morning and his last thought at nighttime. Saeed's thoughts turned to locating Kareem and ensuring his safety from the final act of havoc that Saeed was about to wreak upon America.

Saeed's plans were on a tight timeline that, once activated, could not be disrupted or terminated except by his personal intervention. He had planned out the preliminary disruptions of the refinery, the unleashing of the dams, and the electric grid blackouts to distract US intelligence agencies from his grand finale. What Saeed had planned would bring the US to the realization it is not the most powerful nation on Earth. In fact, Saeed envisioned America being humbled, if not emasculated, before the rest of the world.

*****

Brady met back up with Lois and Sarah, and they found their way to their seats. Lois saw the concern on his face but knew better than to ask questions at that moment. Brady sat down with them, but his mind was racing. He wished he had more information on Kareem's whereabouts. He wondered if Bradford and the intel groups could locate Saeed and whether he could be helpful in any way to assist in avoiding what might well be a devastating attack upon America. He kissed Lois and told her he had to check on something for Bradford. Again, Lois knew better than to ask.

Brady arrived at the box office two minutes later after hustling through the crowd. There were ten or so people in line to pick up their tickets. After waiting for a few minutes, Brady decided to approach the next in line, inform him that it was an emergency and that he had to locate someone. The gentleman understood and stepped aside. Brady leaned into the window and stated a friend's house was on fire and he needed to locate him in the stadium. The man behind the window asked for the last name; and after Brady answered, "Jabar," the man pulled up the name on the computer. Jabar, he said, was in seats one through five, Section 201 in the upper deck. Brady tried to hide his anxiety as he ran to the first usher he found and inquired about the location of the seats.

Brady, for the first time in his life, could feel himself trembling. Even his combat experiences never caused him this much emotion. He pulled out his cell phone and redialed Bradford. This time Bradford did not answer, so Brady left him this message: "Found the Jabar family. Assume Kareem is with them. Await your instructions." About five minutes went by, which seemed like an eternity, before Bradford finally called him back. Bradford told Brady that his intel people had already located Kareem in the crowd and had eyes on him. Bradford repeated what he had said to Brady earlier: that the powers that be had previously decided that the Army/Navy game was the next site for Saeed's attacks. However, since Kareem was in the stands and intel had decided unquestionably that since Kareem was the most important thing in Saeed's life, it didn't make sense that Saeed would carry out a dastardly act which would most likely endanger or perhaps harm Kareem.

Brady's heart was thumping, and his voice was quivering. He took solace in the fact that Bradford's voice, though not quivering, was louder than usual and just as excited. Bradford informed Brady that Intel had reviewed Brady's debriefing when he had left the service, and the part that included Saeed led Intel to decide that Brady might be the only one who could contact Saeed and see if the anticipated attack could be avoided. Brady felt his heart skip a beat, and he asked how he was supposed to contact Kareem. Bradford said that he was to look over his shoulder and a man dressed as an usher would wave to him. He was to approach the usher and coordinate with the usher, who would contact Kareem with an emergency call from his father. The usher was to take Kareem back to a secure room in the main office of the stadium that had been acquired by Intel officers.

Brady responded that the game was about to start, and he was nervous as to when and how the attack would occur. Did anyone in intel know? Bradford shot back that Intel had surmised that any attack would not occur until the President arrived and took his seat at the stadium. Although the President and his security forces had been alerted, as well as the top military brass who normally would attend, there was a reluctance to cancel all their appearances when nothing concrete had been discovered. The stadium had previously been scoured and secured by secret service agents knowing the President and several military leaders would attend. Still, Brady wanted to shout how insane it was for America's President and highest-ranking military officers to take such a chance by attending the game. But instead, he knew this concern was already addressed by Bradford, and given the urgency of the situation, he proceeded as instructed.

Bradford and NSA had already made emergency plans for rapid change of plans if any iota of evidence indicated the game was Saeed's target. It was imperative in Bradford's mind that Brady execute his instructions and interrogate Kareem. He knew that Bradford was anticipating that Kareem would be nervous, and the last thing they all wanted was for Kareem to go silent, or even worse, become belligerent. Brady, in his mind, agreed with Bradford that Brady's familiarity with Kareem's father might have a settling effect upon him. Brady spoke with the usher, found the room Bradford had mentioned, and waited nervously for the appearance of Kareem.

*****

Saeed was becoming fearful for Kareem's safety after the information he had received about Kareem's whereabouts. Saeed knew he must adhere to the timetable he had previously set and did not want to abort the operation. Saeed had, in fact, prepared a backup plan in case any one of innumerable changes might occur, rendering the attack at the stadium undesirable. That event had not yet occurred.

Saeed took pride in the fact that he had disciplined himself to maintain his self-control regardless of the speed and intensity of various situations in which he found himself. However, he had never been faced with the specter of losing Kareem. Saeed had always expected that he would predecease Kareem. Now, he found himself frantically racking his brain to find a way to contact or at least communicate with his son.

Saeed had previously deciphered NSA's codes, both through his understanding and utilization of the mathematical probabilities contained in the theory of quantum entanglement and his own algorithms. Particularly, Saeed took great pride in the quantum computer he had developed in the last year. It not only gave him insight into tightly guarded encryptions but it also gave him the key to the secrets of nations. The exponential speed of the quantum computer, literally a thousand or more times faster than a conventional one, allowed him, if he desired, to inflict horrific destruction, misery, and fear in those he held in disdain. And now, he was in a position to inflict the same misery and pain that he had felt when learning of his parents and sister suffering and dying from the explosion and fire caused by an infidel American bomber. Saeed knew he only had about two hours before the American President, as well as his entourage of military leaders, would enter the stadium. He knew he had to locate Kareem to make sure he was not attending the game.

Bradford was in the war room with the top officials from the CIA, National Security Council, Joint Chiefs of Staff, as well as a slew of intelligence advisors, and the top names in computer science from Silicon Valley and across the nation. Bradford asked an open question, "Why, if this issue is the main event they had been hearing about repeatedly in their eavesdropping, would Saeed choose the Army/Navy game?" Bradford cited numerous alternative sites that made more sense for a terrorist like Saeed to choose. "We need to get into his mind, find out what motivates this person, what does he want to achieve by this heinous act?" Bradford shared the debriefing of Brady with the rest. He mentioned the unfortunate bombing of the small village where Saeed's parents resided. "Is this the seminal reason for such hatred and disdain he had for human life? Could revenge be the sole motive?" he asked rhetorically.

Brady was nervous and tried to control his anxiety so as to appear calm and decisive with Kareem. The usher brought Kareem into the room and locked the door behind them. The usher, a nice-looking African American in his mid-forties, introduced himself and Kareem to Brady. Fortunately, Kareem spoke excellent English as he shook hands with Brady. Brady asked him to please have a seat at the small table in the center of the room. Brady sat down across from Kareem. Brady began by asking Kareem if he knew why he was there. Kareem answered no, and the usher mentioned that he had not spoken with Kareem other than informing him he had an urgent call. The usher then left the room.

Kareem was obviously nervous. He immediately asked if this involved his father. Brady responded yes and that Kareem's father and Brady had met during the war in Iraq. Brady began by telling Kareem his background, his education, his family, and his service years. Then he expounded on his tours of duty, including Afghanistan and Iraq. And yes, even during the period when Kareem's mother, father, and aunt were killed by an American bomber pilot. Brady observed Kareem's sensitivity as he discussed the circumstances of how the American pilot had mistaken their small village for an alleged meeting place for top-level insurgents. Brady also asserted his own sadness for this human error but quickly acknowledged that this, unfortunately, was part of war. Brady could see disdain appear in Kareem's eyes, the same as he had seen in the eyes of Saeed, his father.

Brady quickly shifted the conversation from the unfortunate bombing to the situation in which Brady had met Kareem's father when they were trapped together in the cave. Brady began by describing Saeed as a handsome young man who was not quite the same as the other enemies that Brady had faced in battle. He described how he and Saeed had been trapped in a cave-in that plummeted them to the bottom of one of the many tunnels that ran beneath the hills and mountains of Iraq. He went on to relate how he and Kareem's father were buried in dirt and rocks up to their shoulders and how they had flung anything available at each other until their strength and available missiles ran out.

Brady continued that the two, then bleeding and too tired to fight anymore, settled into a dialogue in which they each hurled verbal insults at each other. When they tired of verbal onslaughts, each being aware that this accomplished nothing, Brady described how they retreated to philosophy and religion. Brady felt compelled not to demean Saeed in his conversation with Kareem, but to accurately describe what he saw and understood in the dialectic he shared with Saeed.

Kareem sat intent as he listened to Brady, almost as if he enjoyed hearing an American describe his father and some details of his beliefs and philosophy—things that Saeed had never shared with his son. Brady continued how they had discussed democracy versus dictatorship, how Saeed had pointed to the hypocrisy in Americans, especially as it related to racism, feminism, and America's interference in other nations' affairs. It was here that Kareem interrupted Brady. He stated how his father had been a kind and caring father, how his father had raised him to be a good Muslim and to abide by the Quran. Kareem stated that his father was extremely intelligent, and other than his father's disdain for Americans, he cared for all the people of the world. Kareem described how his father had donated funds all over the world for new vaccines for HIV, for research for new cures for cancer, heart disease, and many other humanitarian needs.

Brady was impressed with Kareem. He liked the fact that Kareem respected his father and yet expressed his own views garnered from his education and upbringing. Kareem appeared to be a very respectful, reasonable, intelligent, and sensitive young man. Brady sensed a similarity of sorts between Kareem and Michael. Brady inquired about Kareem's college experiences and why he was in America. He asked if Kareem had enjoyed his stay so far in this country. Brady then told Kareem about Michael and how he might play against Army this day and that he was in uniform and on the playing field. Kareem seemed excited to hear about Michael and the fact he was on the Navy football team. Brady also mentioned that his wife Lois and daughter Sarah were both at the game.

Kareem's thoughts turned to the Jabar family and what they must be thinking of his leaving his seat to meet with some stranger. It was now just a few minutes before kickoff, and he asked if he could return to his seat to watch the game. Brady knew it was time to let Kareem know exactly why he had been summoned from his seat.

Bradford had reviewed every bit of intel the agency had on Saeed. They had slowly pieced together some of the different phases in his life. They had tied Saeed to a substantial portion of the financial hacks that the world's banks and their customers had experienced in the last few years. NSA had been able to tie Saeed in with Farid and the many instances of sightings at important US monuments, crucial oil and electric grids, dams, etc.

What they had not been able to accomplish was understanding the nature of the big event they had heard mentioned in much of the intercepted communications, and what part Saeed had to play, if any. Over and over in his mind, Bradford had tried to think like Saeed. Saeed obviously did not need more money; he didn't appear to have disputes with other nations. There was nothing in the intel that indicated strong political or religious aspirations. What then, he asked. Bradford kept coming back to the experience Brady shared with Saeed, as well as the errant bombing of Saeed's family and their village.

Bradford knew time was of the essence. It was almost kickoff time at the Army/Navy game. But why would Saeed pick this game to unleash whatever dastardly deed he had in mind? Why would he do so with his son present? Did he have some way of protecting Kareem? Was there an exit strategy of which Kareem was aware? Many questions, few answers, less time.

While talking to Kareem, Brady had been contemplating the best approach to Kareem for the purpose of extracting any information that might indicate Saeed's location and intentions. Brady did not know how much Kareem knew of his father's activities, especially those activities that implied his involvement in the recent attacks on the US and its banks, dams, refineries, and electric grids. Brady decided to probe Kareem's moral character first so that he could better assess and analyze his responses.

Just as he was ready to continue his interrogation of Kareem, Bradford called. Hearing that Kareem was present, Bradford informed Brady that he was the last resort. Intel had no further information on the big event and the location of Saeed. Literally thousands of agents worldwide were attempting to intercept communications, using a variety of digital equipment to hone in on untold wavelengths, even satellites, to warn of any impending attacks. Yet with all the exotic, advanced, and extremely complex methods and procedures at their disposal, Bradford and the powerful NSA were not yet able to uncover the exact location and intentions of Saeed.

Bradford informed Brady that NSA had been working closely with the best minds in Silicon Valley. The agents had inquired as to what, if any, new concepts in the computer field the US should be exploring, given the fact Saeed was considered a genius in physics and computer sciences. The immediate response from many leading scientists was to concentrate on Saeed's ability to break and/or hack sensitive codes—codes that protected our secret passwords and procedures protecting our military weapons, defenses, etc. This meant delving into the quantum world and, more specifically, quantum computers. Brady interjected here with his admission of limited knowledge in the computer field, let alone physics, and the mention of the word "quantum," to him, might as well have been from a foreign language. Bradford assured Brady he would be able to navigate the waters without knowing the depth thereof.

After hanging up with Bradford, Brady sat back down with Kareem, apologized for the interruption, and continued with the interrogation. Brady covered religion by inquiring how often Kareem attended worship services at the mosque and how often he said prayers. He probed Kareem's moral concepts of right and wrong—whether Kareem valued the life of one of a different faith as much as a Muslim. Would Kareem recognize or simply condemn automatically a country with nonreligious leaders? Would he harm someone solely because he was non-Muslim? And finally, did he believe in "an eye for an eye, a tooth for a tooth"? Brady was well aware his background was not psychiatry but he hoped to be able to extract from Kareem a feeling of concern if not love for his fellow man.

Kareem's answers indicated his deep feelings for his fellow man. Ironically, Kareem firmly believed his father, Saeed, shared the same feelings. When asked why, Kareem again cited the many humanitarian actions Saeed had taken to better mankind and improve the world. Brady paused and let Kareem's responses settle in so he could reconcile them with the knowledge he and the NSA had acquired on Saeed. Then, Brady decided that Kareem deserved, and the exigencies of the situation demanded, that Brady put all the cards face up on the table.

Brady explained that America had recently experienced catastrophic events, interference with dam operations, electric grid shutdowns, as well as intelligence reports of a coming existential event in America that could be the onset of a nuclear war from which no country would survive. The intelligence reports, detected by other nations, had borne out these concerns. Brady became more specific by relating to Kareem the intel reports connecting Saeed to Farrid and the recent attacks upon America that Kareem must have read in recent news reports.

Brady closely observed Kareem's demeanor as he detailed the many communications between Saeed and Farrid, as well as communications between Farrid and his legion of paid mercenaries. What he observed was astonishment, disbelief, and total bewilderment that Kareem's father could be the person Brady had just described. Kareem responded that his father, as he had stated, was just the opposite. He described Saeed as a gentle, loving father devoted to his family and his religious beliefs. Kareem stated his father was incapable of the actions Brady had just described.

Brady now felt it was time to discuss what Brady and the entire intel community considered the seminal event that may well have been the catalyst for the havoc directed at America. Brady began with Saeed's explanation in the cave about how his family—his father, mother, and sister—had been blown to smithereens by the senseless bombing of their village by an American bomber during the Iraq war.

Brady attempted to convey to Kareem the hatred that Saeed exhibited as he excitedly shouted epithets at the United States and all it stood for. Saeed had stated how he would exact his revenge one day and destroy America.

Brady decided to alter his approach by referring to the good aspects of his dialogue with Saeed in the cave. Brady began describing his own impression of Saeed as sincere in his beliefs, rational, logical in his repartee with Brady, and yet completely emotional on the issue of the bombing. Brady felt it necessary to admit the error of the bomber pilot and how this whole situation never would have occurred but for one inadvertent error—the slight misdirection of the latitude and longitude numbers given to the pilot for his target. The village had never been the target. The pilot's target was a small group of houses a mile away where American intel believed an enemy tribal chief and his lieutenants were expected to be meeting.

Kareem now listened intently. Kareem had never heard from his father the exact details of the deaths of his grandfather, grandmother, and aunt. He had been told by Saeed that they were killed in a bombing during the Iraq war. To hear these details from a stranger somehow made the deaths even more senseless than his father had expressed. Brady could sense the emotion building in Kareem and feared it was causing him to reach a similar emotional state as had Saeed in the cave.

Brady again changed his approach when he decided to draw upon the humanity involved in this incident by the pilot and navigator involved. Brady related how, once the navigator was informed of the error, he immediately resigned from the US Air Force. He spent the rest of his days, according to reports, trying to rectify and atone for his mistake. The pilot was cited for failing to double-check the destination and has lived his life in mental flagellation for his error. Brady was suddenly taken back. Kareem had been listening intently and Brady could see Kareem's eyes watering. Had he reached Kareem's moral side? Had he projected a situation where both sides had suffered losses, where each side grieved for their losses?

Kareem spoke next, responding how much of what Brady had related about his father coincided with discussions, though limited, that Kareem had had with his father. Kareem recalled his father mentioning that he had rushed back to Iraq from college when he heard of the bombing, only to find his family had been wiped out by the Americans. Saeed had told Kareem that one day he would respond by taking his revenge. Kareem had done so by joining the insurgents' cause and taking up arms against American forces. He did, as he explained to Brady, believe that his father still harbored such animosity.

Brady realized that indeed Kareem did exhibit a moral compass, and indeed he had feelings not only for his father Saeed but for others as well. Brady knew that twenty minutes had passed and time was running out if, in fact, Saeed intended to wreak havoc upon the crowded stadium. Brady wanted to get back to Bradford as soon as possible, for he knew Bradford and the whole defense department would be implementing preventive measures to minimize as much as possible whatever havoc Saeed had planned for the stadium.

Brady paused to consider his next approach with Kareem. Time was now top priority. How could he condense all the background data on Saeed, Farrid, the incidents at the dams, electric grids, refineries, bank hacks, and the intel, all pointing to Saeed, into just a few moments? Brady decided to risk losing Kareem's cooperation by zeroing in on what, if anything, Kareem knew of Saeed's intentions.

Ever since the NSA had learned of the possibility that the Army/Navy game might be the site for the big event they had been hearing about from intel and various sources, the emphasis had been on intense security surrounding the stadium. However, with the knowledge they now had of Saeed's son Kareem attending the game, Bradford now discounted that view. Bradford, knowing Brady was with Kareem, texted Brady to glean from Kareem anything that might give some indication of what Saeed was planning.

Brady had until now assumed, like Bradford, that Saeed's interest was not the stadium and the appearance of the President and many military leaders, but elsewhere. But what he heard next caused Brady's heart to beat faster. When asked by Brady when Kareem last spoke to his father, Kareem responded about a week ago. Kareem added that he had not told Saeed that he was attending the game. This was not something Saeed would have approved.

Brady's first thought was to have Lois and Sarah removed from the stadium. This Brady knew was not practical, given the crowd and time factors. Brady knew that suddenly it was even more imperative he find a way to identify Saeed's plans, or, in the alternative, let Saeed know his son was at the game.

Bradford had texted Brady to see if Kareem could contact Saeed to let him know he was attending the game. This, everyone, including Brady, believed, would cause Saeed to terminate any action he might have planned. Now, Brady tried to control his fear for his family as well as the disaster that seemed ominous. Brady then turned to Kareem and, in a voice that reflected his fear and concern, asked Kareem if he had any means of contacting Saeed. He related the concern that the stadium was Saeed's next target. Brady, with a sincere tone in his voice and grief written on his face, pleaded with Kareem for his answer.

Not only was Brady visibly shaken, Kareem's face suddenly changed to an ashy color, and tears were forming in the corner of his eyes. Kareem could not fathom the idea that his father was a well-known international terrorist—not the father that had raised him, taught him his faith, and taught him to care for others, to love, honor, and respect people of all nationalities and walks of life. The optics Brady now observed were familiar to Brady; they were the same as many an enemy that had just learned their leader was not what they thought he was.

But Brady quickly reminded himself that Kareem was not an enemy, at least not as far as Brady was concerned, but Kareem was a person from whom Brady must extract extremely valuable information, and right away. Brady's next move was important, and he knew it. He had to make Kareem believe in him and that Brady was being honest and straightforward. He reminded Kareem that his son Michael was on the playing field where the assumed attack might take place. His voice quivered as he reminded Kareem that Lois and Sarah were in the stands, as well as the Jabars, all of whom would be vulnerable to any attack.

Kareem took a long breath, wiped the sweat that had been forming on his brow, and slowly looked up at Brady, who was now standing and pacing back and forth. Then Brady snapped at Kareem that they had little time left to avoid this potential disaster. Brady stated that if Kareem needed absolute confirmation that what Brady had been saying was true, he need only call his father and mention that he was at the stadium where the Army/Navy game was being played, along with the Jabars he was visiting.

The mention of the Jabars immediately brought another reality to Kareem—the fact that his close friend from college, and that friend's immediate family, were also at risk if he believed this stranger. Kareem's mind was swirling, thoughts of love and loyalty to his father, love and concern for his friend and family, coupled with suspicion and disbelief about what he had just heard about his father from this American stranger. Yet Kareem was intelligent. He pondered the pros and cons of giving his father a call on the private cell phone that Saeed had given him. Kareem did consider that this call could simply be for the purpose of locating his father. But then, Kareem reasoned, if his father had not done the dastardly acts that Brady had described, then there would be no obvious harm in the call, and if he did, was something Kareem did not want to consider.

*****

Suddenly, Brady's cell phone rang. It was Sarah. She was concerned; the game was about to start and wanted to know if Brady was on his way back to his seat. Brady felt as if he was back in combat, only there was no target to attack, no enemy to fight, only a battle for words—words that could save thousands of lives or perhaps infuriate Saeed and lead to the destruction of all that Brady cherished.

He tried to be calm as he quickly dismissed Sarah by lying that he was on his way. He knew he had no time to explain. Kareem had moved to the corner of the room to gain a slight measure of privacy. He dialed in the coded number that Saeed had given him in their last communication. He heard several rings before Saeed answered in an excited voice. "Are you okay?" Saeed shouted.

Kareem responded immediately that he was fine, but that he was sorry he had failed to tell Saeed that he was attending an American football game, the Army/Navy game, with the Jabars. Kareem heard the phone drop from Saeed's hand. Quickly, Saeed recovered it and yelled into the phone that Kareem must exit the stadium immediately as Saeed had heard over the television that there had been a bomb threat at the stadium. Kareem responded that he was at the stadium and there had been no such announcement. Kareem now began wondering if, in fact, his father was involved with the matters Brady had described. Saeed instantly surmised that Kareem had been detained and that the scheme Saeed had planned in great detail may be compromised.

Saeed had, over the last few weeks, intercepted and deciphered the complicated and exceedingly extensive algorithms belonging to the American nuclear submarines and aircraft carriers with his quantum computer. He had been able to ascertain the keys or passwords by identifying the entangled particles that formed the means of protecting the system from an outsider and breaking through the quantum key distribution system. The system Saeed had to master to break through all the obstacles involved was one that Saeed had helped design in his last year at Cambridge. This same system was being used by the United States for all of its secret codes necessary to protect the unintended unleashing of naval and continental nuclear weapons. Saeed was well aware of the need not to share this information with anyone lest Armageddon become a reality. Saeed had purchased some of the most sophisticated quantum equipment in the world, which he located in his office in Dubai. Each piece was brought in at different times, and the more complicated pieces were brought in and assembled. This equipment formed the means for his excursions into the world of quantum mechanics. Not only had Saeed mastered the use of his quantum computer, but he had also been able to employ immediately his directions to computer sites about the world in a nanosecond by using entangled particles that he could separate and dispatch to opposite ends of the Earth and have instantaneous contact with when needed. What Saeed liked to say to himself was one of the secrets of the universe.

Brady got Bradford on his cell while Kareem spoke with his father. Brady quickly briefed Bradford on his conversation so far and that Kareem was now on the cell with Saeed. Bradford almost choked at hearing Kareem was on the phone with Saeed. Bradford paused and yelled to an aide that he wanted satellite coverage immediately over the stadium, especially on whatever cell phone Kareem was using. Saeed, knowing NSA would soon be listening in on the conversation and realizing he had only a few seconds before terminating the call, picked his words carefully. "Son," he said in a calm, controlled voice, "I am going to hang up, but I want you to know I love you and what I am about to do is for your grandfather, grandmother, and your aunt, and mostly for Allah. I will get back to you once all is accomplished." Kareem tried to ask questions, of which he had many, but he next heard the dial tone indicating the connection was discontinued.

Brady awaited Bradford's response as to whether NSA had located where Saeed had answered Kareem's call. Bradford came back on the line, and the sound of his voice indicated there was not enough time to pinpoint Saeed's location. Bradford then asked Brady to continue his conversation with Kareem. Specifically, Bradford wanted to know if Kareem could or even would furnish information on Saeed's whereabouts. Bradford further requested Brady see if Kareem would divulge any information he had with regard to what immediate plans Saeed may have shared with Kareem.

The immediate alarm for NSA was to neutralize any immediate danger that Saeed may have already unleashed. Brady, still on the phone with Bradford, indicated that he did not believe there was any danger of Saeed causing harm to the fans in attendance at the stadium—not with Saeed having knowledge that his only son was in attendance also. Bradford, who had first considered canceling the game based on the intel of a big event about to occur, then considering emptying the stadium when NSA had picked up an increase in such chatter that morning, now breathed a sigh of relief. But that sigh was short-lived because Bradford knew he and the best minds at NSA, CIA, and around the world would be demanding the capture and defusing of any disaster or disasters Saeed might have planned.

Brady was not a psychologist or psychiatrist, but he prided himself on being a good judge of character. Right then, Brady surmised that Kareem was frustrated as well as concerned about what actions his father might be planning, where, when, and how. Brady knew not to press too hard for fear he would cause Kareem to go silent. Brady read Kareem's eyes. He saw the anxiety and fear Kareem obviously felt for his father. Brady also detected a deeply sensitive side of Kareem. Kareem immediately posed questions to Brady about what his father might do and to whom. Brady knew in his own mind that Saeed had not shared his plans with Kareem. Brady believed the best approach with Kareem would be to continue to explore the relationship between him and his father. Brady kept reminding himself that time was a luxury he didn't have and he must find a communication link to Saeed.

*****

Saeed settled down in his high-back leather chair. He pondered his alternatives. He could proceed with his initial plan to attack the stadium and destroy a substantial number of the elite US military, but that could result in harm, if not the death, of Kareem. Or he could reconfigure the algorithms, disconnect the timer, and select another target.

Saeed knew his time was running out. He knew that the intelligence branches all over the world would be anxiously searching for his location. One of the thousands of satellites orbiting the Earth would soon pick up the power source for all the heavy-duty equipment he had so carefully installed to facilitate his mission.

Kareem had wandered over to a corner of the room he now shared with Brady. Kareem felt like his mind had suddenly been accelerated to Mach speed, and the possible scenarios were flashing by. Kareem said to himself to slow down, try to think like his father, try to imagine the pain that Saeed still harbored from that fatal day over twenty years ago. What, he asked himself, assuming that Brady had spoken the truth about his father, would Saeed be planning as a retaliatory event?

Brady wondered if this might be a nightmare he was having, but the situation was too real, too horrifying for him to imagine. Bradford had his people at NSA scrambling for information on Saeed's location. Bradford surmised that even if they located Saeed, there was not enough time to ward off whatever action Saeed may have set in motion.

Saeed knew that whatever he was to do, it would have to be his final act. He knew he could not again set in place the profound network of intrinsically complicated equipment that would be able to confuse, bypass, and dismantle the firewalls and digital communications he had assembled. Saeed decided he would go for broke. He would unleash his most powerful neural network of forces—forces that none of the scientific minds of this generation could counteract. Saeed decided he would deploy his arrangement of quantum-entangled photons, which he had previously created in his strategically assembled and positioned quantum light sensors, separate and emit the disentangled particles into the atmosphere. Once the disentangled particles had arrived at their designated positions around the world, at a speed faster than the speed of light, Saeed would enter his password and the elongated algorithms that would unlock the most secretive malware known to mankind. This, in turn, would provide Saeed access and control over the most sensitive nuclear weapons, the world banking systems, stock exchanges, and most of all, the internet itself. Saeed rolled up his sleeves and began his psychotic scheme.

Brady phoned Bradford to let him know that Kareem had lost contact with his father. Brady told Bradford he did not believe Kareem had any idea what Saeed had planned, but he was sure that it was not an action to destroy the stadium—not now, with Kareem present. Brady did inform Bradford that the body language of Kareem while talking to his father indicated that Kareem was uninformed of Saeed's plans. What was clear was the close relationship between Saeed and Kareem. The latter, Brady thought, might be the most powerful leverage they had against Saeed.

Brady hung up with Bradford and turned his attention to Kareem. Kareem was silent, and confusion was dominating his consciousness. Brady could see that Kareem was fearful for his dad and what he might be planning, as well as concerned for his father's welfare. Kareem wanted no harm to come to his father, and yet, he wanted no harm to come to anyone else as a result of his father's actions.

Brady sat back down and asked Kareem to do the same. Sitting across the table, Brady asked Kareem to relate some more of his background, his younger years, his college experiences, and the relationship he shared with his father Saeed. Kareem began with his teen years when his mother was still alive. He spoke of the warm relationship between his mother, Saeed, and himself. He explained how once or twice a year, Saeed would take them to some faraway place in Western Europe to allow Kareem and his mother to experience and study how other parts of the world live and thrive. Kareem related how his father very seldom mentioned politics, and although Saeed was extremely religious, he did not overly press Kareem or his mother to abide by the strict rules of the Quran.

Kareem spoke of the times when he was alone with his father and how Saeed taught him how to play chess and checkers, and how to speed read by concentrating on the center of the page he read while forcing his eyes to swiftly move down the pages. Kareem told of times when he knew his father dearly missed his own father, mother, and sister after the bombing. Kareem, glassy-eyed, interjected his own remorse for not enjoying his grandparents and his aunt. He digressed from the familial relationships to the years when his father attended graduate school at Cambridge. Saeed had few friends, and those that did associate with him were colleagues from school. Kareem described the many times his father would spend an "all-nighter" staying up for his exams, only to hear his father the following day declare he had stymied his professors with his obvious intelligence and ability to see far beyond the exigent sciences, including the world of mathematics, astrophysics, and of course quantum mechanics. Kareem had often heard from those who came in contact with Saeed his profound comprehension of the universe, his love for the philosophies from the early Greeks, and of course his ability to decipher the complex theories of leading scientists, i.e., Einstein and those that followed. But most of all, Kareem had marveled at the intense study his father undertook to comprehend and even expand upon the latest forays into the world of artificial intelligence. Kareem, his respect and admiration for his father spilling out, described the enjoyment he derived from having his father educate him as to the latest discoveries and theoretical studies in the world of quantum mechanics as it relates to computer science, especially quantum computers.

*****

For now, Brady concluded there was little peril for those in the stands, including Lois, Sarah, and of course Michael. As much as Brady wanted to see Michael and the Navy football team play, he knew he had to assist Bradford in any way he and the country needed. Brady dialed Lois on his cell and explained to her that there was no need for concern and that he had been contacted by Bradford to discuss an urgent problem the NSA felt he could assist with from his military experiences during his time served in the Iraq war. Brady never outright lied to Lois, but a little bending of the truth he felt was now in order. He told Lois he would join her and Sarah shortly.

Brady then turned to Kareem and continued their conversation. Brady did not want Kareem to feel he was being interrogated, so he decided to add to his discourse some of his personal experiences with Kareem's father, Saeed. Brady related to Kareem the battle with his father and how they both were swallowed up when the ground beneath them disappeared and they were both engulfed in dirt and debris up to their shoulders. Brady described how he was fearful this was the end for him and perhaps for Saeed.

Brady tried to inject some light humor into his narrative by describing how he and Saeed, with each having an exposed arm, slung small missiles, mainly small stones, at each other. Some landed, but most bounced off the edges of what was then a vacant, unlighted space of unknown size and shape. Saeed and Brady were near enough to make out the other's head and shoulders, but little else. Brady recalled yelling at Saeed that his comrades were not only poorly trained and schooled in modern warfare, but couldn't even build adequate, functional tunnels.

Saeed had countered by calling Brady a pawn of a regime that couldn't solve its own problems, so it had to create diversions by invading the countries of others. Brady related how Saeed admonished Brady and the United States for attempting to impose democracy on the Arab states when America could not make it work in their own country. Kareem smiled, acknowledging this scenario was one he could indeed picture of his father. Brady sensed he was gaining a certain rapport with Kareem and so he continued with his narrative.

Aside from the ridiculous thrusting of missiles at each other, hurling insults and expletives, and insulting each other's political inclinations, Brady expanded into the religious aspects of their discourse. A discourse that lasted for several hours before there was any indication they may be discovered in the makeshift cave. Kareem was now drawn into Brady's narrative as one reading a novel and hanging on each page. Kareem was excited to hear his father described from his younger years, the years when he was an insurgent defending against American invaders of his country. Kareem also enjoyed the humorous manner in which Brady was relating the time in the cave, knowing neither of the two combatants had been seriously injured.

Brady continued how Saeed expounded upon the teachings of Allah and the Quran. How Saeed pointed out the hypocrisy of Americans espousing equality among men while at the same time treating blacks and people of color as if they were second-class citizens. Kareem listened intently, occasionally nodding his head in agreement with the words Brady would attribute to Kareem's dad. Brady continued how he and Saeed discussed the existence of God and how each pondered the concept of God. Slowly, Brady had melded the outbursts between him and Saeed into the areas of agreement they had in common.

Brady told Kareem how he had confessed to Saeed his own doubts of the books of the New Testament, and the many instances where miraculous events were recorded that Brady just couldn't find believable and therefore questioned. Saeed, in turn, had confessed that the whole concept of an omniscient, omnipotent god had its shortcomings, and he too shared some of the doubts expressed by Brady. Brady pointed out to Kareem how he had told Saeed that he did not believe the story of Muhammad receiving from God and memorizing the Quran in a cave. The same as Moses receiving the Ten Commandments atop Mount Sinai. But he and Saeed, Brady emphasized, maintained and defended vehemently their own belief in God and the goodness and grace of God. Brady emphasized to Kareem that Saeed in no manner forsook or committed sacrilege against his god Allah.

Brady continued his conversation with Kareem with the goal of determining whether Kareem could be a conduit for Brady to speak with his father, Saeed. Attempting to lessen the anxiety Kareem obviously was feeling, Brady asked if he knew anything about American football. Kareem acknowledged a rudimentary understanding of the rules and strategy of the game, but little else. Brady saw an opening and took advantage of the opportunity. Brady explained briefly that his son Michael was playing for the Navy team and might well get in the game in the second half. Kareem was excited and promised to root for Navy. Brady verified where Kareem and the Jabar family were seated and promised that he would try to drop by their seats before the end of the game. Kareem seemed genuinely interested and said he would enjoy meeting Michael one day.

Brady looked at his watch. It was 2:00 p.m., and it was almost halftime for the game. Brady interrupted his conversation with Kareem in order to phone Lois to let her and Sarah know everything for now seemed alright and there was no need to worry. Brady was now convinced Saeed would not initiate any action that would endanger the life of his son.

A brief call to Bradford confirmed that the NSA was in agreement with the level of danger from some dastardly act by Saeed, but warned Brady they needed to know Saeed's whereabouts as soon as possible. Brady agreed and told Bradford he was on the way to his seat to enjoy the second half of the game. What Bradford did not tell Brady was that he had already assigned a team of agents to follow Kareem wherever he might go with the hope of discovering Saeed's location and possibly Saeed's intentions. Bradford had considered placing Kareem under protective care but decided this would only add entropy to an already volatile situation.

Brady said goodbye to Kareem. He gave him his business card with his cell number. He let him know he could contact Brady at any time, night or day, if Kareem needed to get in touch with him. As Brady left to return to his seat to watch the second half, he had a good feeling about Kareem and surmised that there was definitely a close familial bond between Saeed and his son Kareem, and further, that he could perhaps unravel the confusing, frustrating, and convoluted signals Saeed was emitting to the world by ingratiating himself with Kareem. Brady reached his seat just in time for the second-half kickoff.

*****

Saeed sat silently in his swivel chair, his array of computers in front of him. Slowly and sequentially, he reviewed in his mind the various statements that had just been uttered by Kareem. First, Saeed became frustrated that his son had not alerted him in advance of his travel to the United States. Secondly, he was angered that his plans to utilize drones to strike the stadium had been thwarted. Finally, he smiled, knowing that Kareem was safe. Saeed knew now the American intelligence agencies would all be on high alert. He knew that all of the US would be aware that their safety and welfare were in danger—the fear that Saeed believed his family had felt when they heard the American pilot's low-flying fighter jet just before unloading his bombs on their village.

Saeed realized that his plans for Plan B had to be expedited in what little time was left before intelligence agents located his whereabouts and zeroed in with their drones. Saeed guessed he had no more than a few hours before his location was compromised.

While Saeed began mapping out and initiating action under Plan B, Kareem was enjoying the second half of the Army/Navy football game. He had identified the number 11 jersey and assumed that was Brady's son Michael. Brady returned to his seat with Sarah and Lois and immediately became enrapt with the game. Brady ignored the multitude of questions Lois directed towards him and insisted he would brief her later. During lulls in the action on the field, Brady's thoughts were split between his son Michael's possible entrance into the game and what Bradford and the agency were now planning for the capture or neutralizing of Saeed.

Kareem returned to his seat and explained to the Jabars it was a case of mistaken identity. Kareem balanced his interest in the game with his concern for what he had just heard concerning his father. Kareem could not accept the notion that his father might be a terrorist, or worse yet, that he might be planning some horrific action against the United States. Kareem decided whatever his father may or may not be planning could wait until the game was over. He settled in and focused his attention on the game at hand.

Bradford, on the other hand, was engulfed with frantic inquiries from intelligence agencies, the Pentagon, and military leaders who envisioned the worst scenarios and voiced their concerns. Bradford had already put into place DEFCON One, the US defense level indicating an attack from unknown sources. NSA, FBI, and the CIA were all on standby as well as furiously searching for the whereabouts of Saeed.

Back in the stadium, it was now the fourth quarter. Navy was down 21 to 14. The Navy quarterback had just completed a thirty-yard pass to the Army 49-yard line. However, there was a penalty on the play. Kareem turned to his friend Ahmed and asked about the penalty. Ahmed explained it was "roughing the passer," a fifteen-yard penalty and first down for Navy at the 34-yard line of Army. However, the Navy quarterback was still down, and it seemed he was favoring his right shoulder. After a fifteen-minute delay, Michael was sent into the game to replace the injured quarterback for Navy. Kareem, as well as Brady, Lois, and Sarah, became excited that Michael was now in the game. Kareem took great joy in knowing he now knew an American college football player, now in the game and about to play his first down for the Naval Academy in a classic Army/Navy football game.

No one, however, was more excited than Brady. To see his son in the Navy uniform and leading the Navy team in this game was one of the things Brady had dreamed of but never thought would happen.

*****

Meanwhile, Saeed sat alone in his office, an office about the size of a school cafeteria, surrounded by sensitive lasers, crystals, interferometers, and special receptors and transmitters for executing QKD transfers of quantum particles, including photons. All of which he had utilized to hack into bank and financial institution accounts to steal money and demand ransom, as well as to invade and disrupt highly classified and advanced protective measures of the US defensive armaments, including nuclear weapons and the equipment for delivering the payloads.

Saeed mused to himself how he had built his financial empire through his grasp of reality that few men (or women) could even imagine. Saeed indeed was one of a very few who could visualize a world where knowledge had no limits and where he could distinguish between theory and reality without confusing the two. Saeed, though harboring a deep-rooted hatred for the Americans, also realized that the knowledge he had acquired from his education and experience in the quantum world was far beyond the prevailing concepts in the field of physics and metaphysics. He reveled in the arrogance of most modern-day scientists who, as Saeed envisioned, expounded their theories of the meaning and existence of the macrocosm world versus the microcosm world and how differently the laws of physics applied to both. Saeed knew well, as do most theoretical physicists, how atomic and subatomic rules do not agree with the standard view of the conventional laws of physics, which often collide with the reality of the quantum world. What separated Saeed from the others was the extent to which his knowledge extended into this surreal world of physics called quantum mechanics.

Saeed was perhaps exhibiting his own arrogance by these musings. Saeed, though a devout Muslim, tried hard to reconcile his belief in Allah and His teachings with his knowledge of how the universe, including the Earth, must have evolved over billions of years, with the tenets of Muslim teachings. Saeed had imposed upon himself the duty of discerning some meaningful unified theory that would include a practical explanation of how the universe exists and how man fits into the equation. Saeed had set a monumental goal for himself to reconcile religion and science. Once the curtain of reality is pulled back, he believed, we will unravel the mystery of God, man, and the mysteries of existence.

STOIC REVENGE

Nonetheless, Saeed knew that recent events, including the present experience with his son Kareem visiting America and being detained by US intelligence, required him to fast forward his plans for the punishment of Americans and inflict what he knew would be a crippling blow to the United States of America. Time was of the essence, and he knew for him it was about to run out.

Saeed smiled to himself with the knowledge that his threat of an attack on the stadium where the Army/Navy game was being played was only a prelude to distract from his true intention of striking a blow upon the American military that would not only cause shock waves throughout the US military and its politicians but would also be a harbinger for all to see that the mighty Americans were not invincible. Americans would live in fear of what might be the imminent destruction of their way of life, in fact, their life itself.

*****

Brady had regained his composure, calmed himself, and focused entirely on the game at hand. He had Michael in his field glasses that Lois had brought. It was first down, and Navy was still down 21 to 14. The ball was on the Army 34-yard line. Michael led the huddle and was calling the play the coach had communicated in Michael's headgear. The play was a screen to the right side. Michael received the snap from center and faked a throw downfield. At the same time, the halfback slid out to the right flank, feigned a block on the defensive end, and then looked back at Michael just as Michael threw a perfect spiral to him. Army had chosen to blitz on the play, which allowed the halfback to penetrate the defensive backfield all the way to the goal line—touchdown, Navy.

Brady was excited as he yelled his approval, knowing Michael couldn't hear him. Navy lined up for the extra point, and Brady pondered whether they would try for a one- or two-point conversion. Michael called the play, and the teams got down in their stances. Michael knelt in the position of the ball holder. As the ball was snapped, Michael suddenly rose to his feet, grabbed the ball, and sped up the middle as the defense ran to block the kick in a pincer movement. The pincer movement was simply running as if the quarterback was back to pass, a tactic often used in football to block a punt. But this left them vulnerable up the middle, and Michael jubilantly crossed the goal line for a two-point conversion. Navy went on to win the game 22 to 21.

*****

Saeed had studied the Americans' propensity for utilizing quantum entanglement by separating entangled photons, then digitally sending half of the entangled pair to the complex quantum computers aboard the nuclear subs. The person setting the operating sequence for firing a nuclear missile would check the key of the QKD procedure and, if it matches what has previously been determined, would allow the firing sequence to continue. It was something similar to having a lockbox; you open to find your lockbox key, match that with the photon wave received on the ship's receiver and, if matched, fire away at the accompanying target designation. What made this feasible was Saeed's ability, from his array of quantum computers, to intercept the missile en route, change the destination by hacking into the missile's onboard guidance computer, and force it to recognize Saeed's new algorithm (i.e., target destination). Saeed knew the commander aboard the nuclear sub would have to contact NORAD, but by the time the commander and his computer expert thrashed their way through the quagmire of obstacles Saeed would have initiated, it would be too late—the missile would have landed and exploded.

By sending a separated pair of entangled photons, one of the pair to the submarine and the other to the New York Stock Exchange, Saeed could implement a shared secret key (meaning one shared characteristic of the entangled pair) between the sub and NYSE, which he would insert digitally from the highly complex equipment in his office laboratory. Saeed had learned how to infiltrate the sub's computer without detection by distracting the operators aboard the sub by crashing its navigational programs.

*****

But back at the NSA, Bradford had his team diligently searching through the background data they had on Saeed. There wasn't an awful lot—mostly just some military transmissions from the Iraq War describing the errant bombing of Saeed's village and the reprimands that followed for those involved. The only personal data on Saeed, of course, was the information that Brady had related in his debriefing upon his discharge from the Navy. Bradford and the rest of the intelligence participants around the world knew that Saeed would not be discouraged by his failure to successfully execute the explosion at the stadium. Bradford sensed that Saeed would not be disillusioned by his failure, nor would he abandon his quest for revenge against the USA. The only actions that Bradford believed had to be pursued were locating Saeed's whereabouts, determining his objectives, and defusing the immediate crisis.

The NSA was not sure of the extent of Saeed's influence in the Arab world, his access to US intelligence, and most of all, his intentions going forward. Bradford wiped the sweat from his brow, peered at the ubiquitous array of televisions in the war room at the NSA, and summoned his top intelligence officers. He knew the director of the NSA would be calling soon for an update. Time was passing quickly, especially since so much was at risk. Bradford called Brady and asked him to reengage Kareem to see if there was anything—any way Kareem could facilitate locating of Saeed or even if he would be willing to help.

*****

Michael had celebrated with his teammates the victory over Army, especially his own contribution thereto. Brady, Lois, and Sarah had waited till he had showered and dressed, and were now heading out to have an early dinner with just the family. That's when Bradford's call came through, and Brady pulled the car over to the side of the road so he could speak with him.

In short, Bradford wanted to know Brady's impression of Kareem. Was he intelligent, did he seem to have basic humanitarian values, was he simply a faithful Muslim, or was he a religious fanatic like the ones who took down the Twin Towers? The gist of which was to determine whether Kareem could be trusted, how close he was to his father, and whether he would assist in preventing his father from any terrorist-type actions against the USA.

Brady was cautious in his response to Bradford's inquiries. He had only known Kareem for a few hours, but then he had known his father a lot longer, especially during the time they shared in the cave-in during the war. Brady shared as much as he knew about Kareem with Bradford. His summary of his experience with Kareem was that he was an intelligent young man, devoted to his religion but not apparently fanatically devoted. He added that his gut feeling told him Kareem was a sensitive individual who would shun the idea of destroying his fellow man, no matter his nationality. Brady knew there was always the possibility that he could be misjudging Kareem, but again his gut feeling told him otherwise. Bradford then unloaded on Brady the toughest burden he had ever faced: he had to gain Kareem's confidence and convince him to acknowledge Saeed's misguided thirst for revenge against the USA, and most of all, to convince his dad to abort any plans Saeed may still have in mind for the USA. Brady suddenly stiffened, exhaled, and inhaled a deep, long breath—something he had taught himself in combat whenever he knew he was about to engage with the enemy.

After he hung up with Bradford, Lois immediately pelted him with questions, questions Brady knew he couldn't answer. Not yet.

*****

Saeed was now busy setting up an interferometer using a high-voltage transformer to shoot lasers laden with photons through a crystal, allowing the photons to become entangled and then separated for transmission. Since the missiles aboard the American subs traveled at Mach 6 (about 4,500 mph), Saeed figured he had about one and a half hours since the closest US nuclear submarine was in the mid-Atlantic. Saeed also was aware that the NSA would locate him by tracing back his signals in just about the same time. He had to hurry.

Brady knew what he must do. He had to double back, try to locate Kareem, and see if they could meet somewhere. Brady knew Bradford was keeping up on Kareem's whereabouts. Brady told Lois they should stop for dinner somewhere, hoping that would coincide with wherever Kareem and the Jabar family would be stopping also. Bradford answered his call, and within minutes told Brady that Kareem was in the Philadelphia area at a restaurant known as "Taeam Ladhidh," and gave Brady the address. Brady headed to the restaurant, praying Kareem would be there.

Bradford had relegated himself to the fact he now would have to rely upon Brady and his connection with Kareem. With all the super intelligence the NSA had acquired over the years, Bradford knew in the end that it would come down to the human element—the ability of one human communicating, not entangling ironically with one another, so that each shared something in common with the other. Bradford said a silent prayer that Brady could be the one and Saeed the other. Bradford informed Brady that Kareem was indeed still in the restaurant, and Bradford's agents were in and outside the restaurant incognito.

Saeed figured he was now down to an hour and a half. He tuned his quantum computer to an algorithm he had previously determined was one of many used by the personnel aboard the USS *Lincoln* nuclear submarine. The quantum computer then tuned into the sub's airwaves to start delving through the myriad of wavelengths that it would have to decipher in less than an hour. This, of course, Saeed would have to accomplish without alerting those aboard the sub that someone was tinkering with their radio signals. Saeed's computer whisked through the onboard computer to establish the proper position to insert the Zero Day. Once his computer showed a green light, Saeed knew he had mastered the sub's radio signals and was ready to send a disentangled photon along with the key (or password) the sub's computers would recognize and erroneously think was theirs. All this was accomplished in less than fifteen minutes. Next would be deciphering the algorithm for unleashing the nuclear missile. Another ten minutes and this too was completed. All that remained was for Saeed to substitute the target destination (i.e., the New York Stock Exchange, New York City) and insert it into the onboard missile computers. The flight of the missile from the Lincoln to New York City would be about twenty minutes. All of this being done without the knowledge of those on board the submarine, but in another twenty minutes, the missile would be airborne and the arming of the missile would take place thirty seconds prior to landfall. Manhattan would be obliterated, and the radiation would spread throughout New York City. It would be Nagasaki and Hiroshima all over again.

Saeed had one more surprise for the hated Americans. He knew the stock exchange backed up its data daily, coded it, and shipped it to Iron Mountain, in Butler, Pennsylvania, for storage. Saeed had already hacked into the armed drones (that he had initially intended for the stadium) at Andrews Joint Air Force Base. These armed drones were programmed to detonate into Iron Mountain. After activating the hypersonic nuclear missile aboard the *Lincoln* nuclear submarine, Saeed would set off a previously planted program monitor glitch in its computer system. The destruction of the exchange and the backup data would cause America's credit rating to sink, and all over the world, America's currency would tank. Saeed had planned well; revenge was near.

*****

Brady, Lois, Sarah, and Michael exited the car at the entrance to the restaurant, and Brady gave the keys to the valet. As Brady held the door for his family, he noticed a couple of nondescript men hovering to the side of the restaurant. Brady rightfully surmised these were Bradford's agents. Kareem was seated with the Jabar family and was just about to order dinner when he noticed Brady. Kareem had explained to Mr. Jabar and his sons that the cause of his absence at the stadium was due to a misinformation of someone that matched Kareem's appearance with that of a suspected terrorist.

Kareem immediately stood up and acknowledged to Mr. Jabar that the same man from the stadium had just entered the restaurant. Kareem felt it necessary to see if there was anything else the agent, or whoever he was, needed from him. It was then that Kareem realized the man had what appeared to be his wife and daughter with him. Brady saw Kareem rise from the table and met him halfway between the tables. There was a small bar off the dining room, and Brady whispered to Kareem that he had just a few more questions that shouldn't take more than a few minutes. Kareem nodded his agreement and told Mr. Jabar to please excuse him for a few minutes and followed Brady to the bar.

Brady noticed a small table in the corner and motioned for Kareem to follow. As they sat down, Brady immediately asked Kareem if he knew the whereabouts of Saeed. Kareem tersely answered no. Brady then asked if Kareem had any inkling of what Saeed intended to do next. Again, Kareem said no. Brady, drawing upon his intelligence training and experience, aware of the importance of exacting any information pertaining to Saeed, persisted in his attempts to appeal to Kareem's inner feelings while at the same time emphasizing how important it was to the US as well as the world that Kareem reveal whatever tidbit of information he might have concerning Saeed and Saeed's intentions.

After several minutes and numerous questions with no answers, Brady accepted the fact that Kareem would be of no help. Brady thanked Kareem and pleaded with him to contact Brady if he heard from Saeed again. As they walked back to their respective tables in the dining room, Brady said goodbye and proceeded to the table where Lois, Sarah, and Michael were seated. The two agents inconspicuously rose and exited the restaurant.

Brady leaned down to Lois, asked her to order him an iced tea, and excused himself to go to the men's room. Brady immediately called Bradford and related his conversation with Kareem. Brady added that he felt Kareem was cooperative and honest in his answers. Bradford had hoped for more from Kareem and now knew the agency was traveling in uncharted waters. Not one of the worldwide intelligence agencies had located Saeed, and not one person had furnished an iota of information that would reveal Saeed's intentions. What Bradford was sure of was that Saeed intended something disastrous for the USA, but what and where was unknown. Bradford slammed his fist down upon his desk. On another line, Bradford informed the two agents seated in the restaurant to follow Kareem and the Jabar family as they left the restaurant. The agents had waited in the parking lot and had attached a GPS locator mechanism under Mr. Jabar's SUV.

Brady came back to the table, dismissed questions from each of his family, and ordered his dinner. Thirty minutes later, Brady and his family, after paying their check, left the restaurant. The Jabars and Kareem left shortly thereafter. Brady headed back to the motel in Annapolis, expecting a call from Bradford if he was needed. Mr. Jabar drove Kareem and the others back to Annapolis in the SUV. Neither Brady nor Kareem was aware of the vengeful actions Saeed had already put into action.

Little did they know that Saeed had already calibrated the algorithm for arming one of the drones at Andrews Joint Air Base, as well as inserting of another cyber directive that would indicate a system malfunction for the drones to the airman on duty at the base. By the time the airman discovered the subterfuge and notified his superior officer, the drone would be airborne. The fail-safe safety switch that the airman would have to initiate also would be overridden by Saeed's digital instructions to the program controllers of the drones.

*****

Back at the NSA, the director was being briefed by his top generals, admirals, and regional analysts about unusual activities around the world. The whole world was now aware that something bad was about to occur. China was maneuvering ships and submarines off the coast of Taiwan. Iran was threatening Israel with invasion. Russia was rattling its sabers with military buildups in the Baltic and Black Sea areas and pointing hypersonic missiles at the East Coast of North America. North Korea was aiming missiles towards Japan and boasting of its war powers. Bradford decided to immediately contact Brady. He had an idea working in his head that might be a long shot, but then again it just might work. He called Brady.

This alarming news had American intelligence, military, and politicians pointing fingers, and the war rooms at the Pentagon, NSA, and the White House were obviously hard at work attempting to put together a game plan for retaliatory actions by the USA.

There was universal agreement among these agencies and politicians that the actions being taken by Iran, Russia, China, and North Korea were the result of America's vulnerability caused by Saeed's cyberattacks in the banking industry, the power and energy grids, and dams.

Bradford decided to concentrate his department on locating Saeed and determining what he intended to do next. Bradford believed that much of the sudden increase in actions by these recalcitrant countries could be countered or abated by US forces and its allies. He also believed if Saeed could be neutralized, the damage suffered thus far by America could be contained and future destruction minimized or avoided entirely.

Bradford silently acknowledged this was a big IF.

Brady had just pulled up to the motel in Annapolis when his cell rang. He knew it would be Bradford. He listened while Bradford related to him his idea. Bradford told Brady that he believed if Brady could somehow ingratiate himself with Kareem and convince Kareem to ride back with Brady to NSA in Greenbelt, Maryland, Bradford would allow Kareem access to the information in the files on Saeed, as well as show him the situation room where the big television screens would show all the activities in play by Saeed around the world. Especially, the results of the grid shutdowns, dam releases, cyberattacks on the banks, and the warlike activities put into play by Russia, China, and North Korea. Bradford reasoned that the possibility of neutralizing Saeed and preventing the big event, or accumulation of events, certainly outweighed any risk of exposing Kareem to the inside of the NSA.

*****

Brady knew from Bradford that Mr. Jabar was driving the family and Kareem back to Annapolis. Brady pulled over to the side of the road while he tried to figure out how he would coax Kareem into accompanying him back to NSA. What about Lois and Sarah? Bradford interjected that Brady could let Lois and Sarah go on alone, and Bradford would have a helicopter pick him up in the motel parking lot in ten minutes. Brady calmed down Lois, gave her the keys, and kissed and hugged them goodbye.

The Black Hawk picked Brady up precisely at ten minutes. Brady and Bradford had already planned that the copter would locate Jabar's SUV, the agents trailing the SUV would stop it, and hold them for Brady. Brady had no idea how Kareem would react to this intrusion, but considering the importance of his mission, Brady really didn't care.

The SUV was stopped by the agents who explained there was an emergency and for them to await Brady, the man that Kareem had met with at the stadium and later at the restaurant. The copter sat down in the parking lot, Brady jumped out, and approached Kareem. Quickly, Brady said that the situation with his father Saeed had worsened and it was no longer just the USA that was in danger, but now the whole world may be on the brink of a nuclear war.

*****

Saeed was now faced with his greatest challenge: Does he unleash the pain and destruction as retribution for the murder and destruction of his family at a time when his son may be caught up in his thirst for revenge? Or does he unravel the well-thought-out plans to strike at the heart of America and wait to fight another day?

Saeed knew he might never have another opportunity as he did this day. Now that Kareem was under the eyes and spotlight of US Intelligence, he knew it was only a matter of hours before he and his elaborate complex of quantum computers and monitoring equipment would be located and destroyed. Saeed cared not for his own safety, but the only thing in this world he cared dearly for was his son, Kareem.

Saeed made his decision and began destroying and dismantling most of his computer technology, leaving only one quantum computer, a laptop with a router, which could be operated while mobile. In less than an hour, Saeed had disconnected and destroyed the remaining and most advanced computer technology and equipment that the world would never see, understand, and benefit from.

Until now, Saeed, in addition to the action taken against the USS *Lincoln* nuclear submarine and the drone strike, had entertained and prepared for multiple actions he had been planning for months. He was prepared to unleash computer malfunctions leading to shutdowns and even explosions that would create a shortage of active refineries in the world, a shortage of oil tankers to deliver what oil was produced, the opening of major dams causing extensive damage to crops and property, hacking into the US minting system to cause an enormous amount of various denominations of US currency to be produced and unleashed into circulation, malfunctions in plants to cause overloaded dynamos and generators leading to shutdowns of vast industries relying on electric power, and finally an attack upon American, Chinese, and Russian nuclear weapons aboard nuclear subs, battleships, and carriers causing a cascade of antiballistic nuclear warhead missiles to be fired at each country, causing worldwide panic.

Saeed had spent months, even years, putting into place the far-advanced and extremely intricate network of zero days or glitches in the manufactured computer chips that went into the enormous amount of products and services that control our everyday environment. But now, Saeed had to streamline his intentions. He had to concentrate on those actions that would satisfy his need for retribution against the United States and, at the same time, ensure the safety of his son, Kareem. The wheels were speeding up in the mind of this genius, and the world was about to go for a wild ride.

*****

Brady, after offering to no avail Kareem refreshments and the use of the men's room, asked Kareem if he knew where he had been brought as well as the significance of NSA headquarters in the world of espionage. Further, Brady enlightened Kareem on the extent and depth of the intelligence collection equipment and activities he saw before him in the vast collection of screens, monitors, and communications, including contact and control of the literally hundreds of airborne satellites. Brady could see the amazement and awe with which Kareem took in all that he could see. Kareem immediately asked how all this related to his father, Saeed, and for what specific purpose he had been brought to this apparently hallowed place in the US.

Now Brady felt the full weight of his responsibility to evince and convince Kareem of the importance, not only to the US but to the whole world, of determining and neutralizing any nefarious vengeful activities planned by Saeed to punish the US for the honest mistake of one fighter pilot's erroneously bombing his family and their village. Kareem listened intently, and his education and worldly upbringing wove into his subconscious and settled into his common sense. Kareem acknowledged to Brady that he understood the significance of what was at stake, that he still maintained his father was a good and caring person, if not obsessed with something that happened many years in the past.

Now Brady felt confident that he and Kareem were on the same wavelength, and he proceeded to implore Kareem to contact his father for the purpose of dissuading him as to what he intended to accomplish. Kareem agreed reluctantly but with the understanding that he was not being asked to harm Saeed, only to extract his agreement, if not his acquiescence, to discontinue any activities driven by his hunger for revenge.

Kareem again dialed the numbers Saeed had provided him and awaited Saeed's answer. Saeed heard the call and recognized the numbers he had only given to Kareem. Saeed assumed Kareem was now in the custody of US Intelligence, and whatever Kareem wanted from him would be inspired by the US Intelligence. However, his love for Kareem outweighed any thoughts of preservation for himself, and he answered the phone. Kareem first asked if his dad was okay and then immediately stated where he was and why they asked him to call. Kareem explained the people at NSA were aware of his identity, his compulsion for revenge for the inadvertent attack on their family and the village. Kareem went on to state he too lamented the horrific killing of their family, but that Kareem had been informed of the nature of the attack on the village and that the fighter pilot was erroneously directed to fire his missiles at the wrong target.

Saeed, at first, screamed at Kareem, noting his naivety as well as his ignorance as to the extremes the US would go to avoid retribution for the harm that had been done to their family. Kareem, now with tears running down his cheeks, pleaded with his father not to commit whatever dastardly acts he was about to unleash. Saeed, notwithstanding the pain he felt in his heart, nor the flashback memories that now pervaded his mind of his lost mother, father, and sister, started to hang up the phone. Saeed, in his mind, had reconciled himself to the fact that his only child, his only son, was now begging him to erase and forget the horrible images in his mind and the lifelong suffering he had endured, including raising Kareem without his mother, aunt, grandmother, and grandfather. Now, Saeed was so shaken he felt himself trembling, almost as he felt when learning of the news of the devastation and murdering of his family many years ago.

Brady whispered to Kareem that he would like to speak with Saeed. Kareem spoke into the phone with Saeed, asking if he would please allow Mr. Brady, who said he knew him from back in the days of the Iraqi war, to speak. Saeed at first started to hang up, but knowing that US Intelligence, especially NSA, had probably already zeroed in on his location, he decided to listen to what this stranger had to say.

Brady nervously accepted the phone from Kareem. Brady knew that whatever he said now might have an existential effect upon the whole world. He began by mentioning two words: "the cave." "Do you recall the cave in which you were buried up to your neck along with an American soldier?" Brady admitted he was that American soldier. Saeed concentrated on his years as an insurgent in Iraq and the many battles he had fought against the Iraqi army and the American intruders. Saeed scanned his memories for the incident Brady was mentioning, and slowly the experience he and Brady had shared came into focus. "Yes," he answered. "I recall you and your arrogant attitude and weak excuses why your hypocritical nation felt compelled to exert its political influence upon Iraq."

Brady knew now that he and Saeed had some common ground on which to communicate. Brady began conciliatory by conceding that America may have acted prematurely but that history since then had shown that both sides were at fault. However, Brady continued, the years that have intervened in our histories have shown that dictatorships never win out against the freedoms of democracy. Brady winced, hoping the Saeed that he recalled would enter into a discourse on what was and what is now. Saeed immediately responded that America still practices racism, heretical religions, and a propensity for wanting to intervene in other countries' domestic policies.

Brady, realizing the discussions of these subjects could take more time than was available, and if he was to dissuade Saeed from whatever he was contemplating, he would have to do so quickly. Brady conceded to Saeed that America was still learning, that our racial policies and attitudes towards females as well as our international policies, all are in a state of flux. That no matter how either of them felt about each other's country, politics, or religion, one thing they could agree upon was the importance of family and friends. Brady told Saeed that his own memories of their experience and discussion in the cave was that they had become somewhat close, and their hopes and fears were of a similar nature. Brady asked Saeed if whatever action he might be planning took into consideration these fundamental feelings.

Now, Saeed was forced to fall back upon questions he often had asked himself. Yes, he thought, my family is the most important thing in my life, and that family is Kareem. However, Saeed concluded he had no real friends. It was he and Kareem.

Saeed, while speaking to Kareem and Brady, had already released the zero-day glitch to activate the nuclear missile aboard the *Lincoln* sub. It was less than an hour before the missile would arm itself and complete its mission. This is why Saeed allowed himself to languish with Brady in what he considered foolish dialogue. Yes, indeed, Saeed did recall the incident in the cave, and he did recall the informative discussions he had shared with Brady. Saeed still considered Brady naïve and misguided, but he also respected him for his concerns for humanity and the well-being of others. Brady then decided to reveal a takeaway from the incident in the cave that he often had pondered and couldn't resist the opportunity to broach the subject with Saeed. Brady wanted to know if Saeed realized that Brady had only escaped from the cave by digging himself out with a stick he found close by in the dark.

Saeed's mind swirled as he began running that time through his mind. Yes, he did recall being saved by Micah, who had found a piece of wood apparently left from when the cave was first dug. Micah used the stick to unearth Saeed, and as they left Brady behind supposedly to die, Micah had pressed Saeed as to whether he should kill Brady.

Saeed now recalled he had told Micah no, let him die slowly. "Was this what you intended, or in fact, did you know I would find the stick and extricate myself after you two had left?" Saeed, on the other end, smiled to himself, knowing this was his contribution to humanity from which Brady had benefited. Saeed's silence was enough for Brady; his instincts were correct—Saeed was not as stoic as he led Brady to believe.

*****

The nuclear missile aboard the Lincoln was now in the air. The CO and executive officer aboard the sub were on the phone with the Pentagon and the White House. There was no way to terminate the missile by aborting or interception because of the computer glitches inserted by Saeed into the onboard computer system. The same thing with the drone headed for Iron Mountain, which was flying too low for radar detection. Saeed now disclosed this information to Brady. Both men were silent for a few seconds, then Brady, supported by Kareem who had been privy to the whispered conversations flying about the room, implored Saeed to call off the attack. Saeed, at first, dismissed their pleas, but the way in which Kareem now implored him to call off this existential threat was arousing feelings Saeed had not felt in many years.

Brady wiped his brow from the sweat streaming down his face and turned to Bradford, who had been monitoring all that had just transpired. Bradford looked tired and bewildered by what was unfolding. He turned to Brady and asked, "Why would someone of rational mind like Saeed want to destroy America, which may well be the last bastion of hope for the free world?" Brady, ever the believer in God and His infinite wisdom, prayed silently, then turned to Bradford and replied that unless God intervened, there were only minutes left before annihilation of their country and perhaps the world.

Saeed came back on the phone asking to speak with Kareem. Brady handed Kareem the phone, and Kareem again pleaded with Saeed to do something to at least mitigate the damage he was about to inflict. Saeed asked Kareem if he was free to go, and Brady answered that none of the personnel at NSA or elsewhere would prevent Kareem from leaving of his own accord. Brady, in one last attempt to convince Saeed to undo what he had unleashed, appealed to Saeed's intellect. He asked Saeed if he had considered the fallout of his actions—not only the radiation, but the ripple effect a crippled America would have upon the rest of the world. He asked if Saeed had considered that his son would soon be involved, if not severely injured, from the fallout that was about to occur.

Saeed quickly reviewed what he had done and why. He did think about the billions of people that would be affected by his revengeful actions, and he thought of the most important thing in his life, his son Kareem. He thought about the legacy he would be leaving for his son. Now was the time to reveal his real intention: to make Americans search their souls for their real values in life beyond their greed for wealth and power, to cause Americans to reassess their family values, their consideration and respect for their fellow man regardless of race, color, religion, or politics. And most importantly, what Americans could lose by failing to consider and have concern for all those countries and their people who do not have the advantages of living in a land of freedom and opportunities.

Brady was visibly shaken. Bradford slumped into the nearest chair, and both turned to Kareem. Brady asked if he had ever seen this side of his father and, most importantly, what was his next move, what would happen now. All over the military command were orders to protect against attacks from all belligerent nations, from an influx of terrorist activities. The prevailing mood was sullen and fearful. Fear for the unknown, fear for what was about to happen, and fear for the ripple effect throughout the world.

Saeed began the destruction procedure for his office space. He knew a missile directed there was probably already initiated by NSA now that they had his location from intercepting the phone call with Brady. Saeed had an eerie smile as he pushed the buttons and switches that launched the sequential destruction of his computers, monitors, etc. In his own way, he had taken his revenge for the loss of his family, but he had accomplished it by hopefully causing most of the leaders and people of the world to take more seriously the adages to love, honor, and respect your neighbors, whomever they are, and to understand that life, because it is fleeting, because our station in life is accidental by birth, because helping those who may be less fortunate is in effect helping ourselves, and finally, to realize that mistakes can and will happen, but the lessons we can learn from those mistakes and put them to use can and will benefit us all in the future.

Saeed then, with Brady still on the phone and all the others present listening in, related to Brady that the nuclear missile from the *Lincoln* would fall harmlessly into the Atlantic, the drone headed to Iron Mountain would crash without an explosion, and there would be no more retaliation against America from Saeed. Only his warning, before his imminent death, that although he was destroying his own collection of quantum computers along with his own advanced knowledge of how to manipulate the computers of the world, especially in the realm of quantum mechanics, it will only be a matter of time (a short time) before his knowledge will be commonplace among the computer hackers of the world, able to do what he had accomplished, but with more serious consequences.

With that, the phone line went dead. Brady felt emotionally exhausted, and Kareem sobbed uncontrollably. Bradford slumped into the nearest chair, feeling both relief and fear for what the future might hold.

THE END

ABOUT THE AUTHOR

Mr. Thomas is a retired attorney. He has over thirty years in private practice, specializing in criminal and civil litigation. He served three years in US Army intelligence, which forms the basis for this story. He has a doctorate of jurisprudence from the University of Maryland Law School.